Made to Break Your Heart
A Novel

6/11/17

Richard Fellinger

Mike,
Thanks for being
part of my launch!

Ril Fllj

Published by Open Books

Copyright © 2017 by Richard Fellinger

Cover image "pitch batter catch throw catch out" by André Pester

Learn more about the artist at www.flickr.com/photos/andrepester/

ISBN-10: 0998427438/ISBN-13: 978-0998427430

For Casey

"It is designed to break your heart. The game begins in the spring, when everything else begins again, and it blossoms in the summer, filling the afternoons and evenings, and then as soon as the chill rains come, it stops and leaves you to face the fall alone."
—A. Bartlett Giamatti

1
OUR LITTLE CORNER
OF THE WORLD

On a spring-like Saturday in early March, Marcy and I decided it was time for our only child to explore his little corner of the world. Time to befriend the boys on the block. Wesley was seven, and two boys his age lived down the street. One was nicknamed Moose, a stocky, round-faced kid with two older brothers who were standout ballplayers and wrestlers. The other was Cameron, a skinny, discombobulated boy whose chief interest seemed to be Cub Scouts. He wore his rumpled blue scout shirt whenever we drove by and saw him playing outside. Wesley hadn't interacted with these boys much because he wasn't yet allowed to roam free on the block, and he'd obeyed our orders not to leave our yard or driveway. Since he'd been a toddler, Marcy had been determined to socialize him by taking him to a weekly play group in the basement of the Misty Hill Methodist Church, centered on Main Street with a pristine white steeple, then scheduling follow-up play dates with kids from the group. But now that the kids were getting older, play dates were passé.

Marcy and I convinced Wesley to grab his baseball glove, and we nudged him down the sidewalk, underneath the bare arms of old oak and maple trees which, oddly, lined Chestnut Street. The block was humming with activity. Kids whizzed around on scooters and skateboards. Moms scrubbed windows or raked dead leaves out of their flower beds. Dads washed cars or scooped up doggie droppings that had piled in their yards over the winter. A light breeze carried the smell of Windex, Armor All and thawed-out poop. Someone's car stereo pumped the faint sound of The Doobie Brothers into the air: *I ain't blind and I don't like what I think I see...Takin' it to the streets.*

Moose was in his front yard playing a one-boy game of catch—he tossed a baseball in the air with a sweeping underhand motion then trapped it in his own glove. Directly across the street, Cameron the Cub Scout was scootering in circles in his driveway.

Wesley walked just ahead of us, slowing a couple times to glance back and make sure we were still there. His big hazel eyes revealed a hint of the willies. "Go ahead, buddy," I said encouragingly. "It will be fun."

I was supposed to say something along those lines, right? Something helpful and upbeat? I was still feeling my way through this whole dad thing. I'd never had much of a fatherly role model myself. I was an only child, too, a chubby kid who grew up in Johnstown, a beaten-down steel town in Western Pennsylvania. But my own dad was a bum. Not a real bum, because Mick Marhoffer had a decent job. He was an accountant at Bethlehem Steel before it shut down in the 1970s, and then he landed a job as a number cruncher at Johnstown Hospital. But he drank too much—way too much. I have ample memories of him sitting at the kitchen table downing green bottles of Rolling Rock, his shoes kicked off and starchy white shirt untucked, but none of him throwing a ball in the backyard or urging me to make friends. He died when I was fourteen, when the booze and his high blood pressure finally took its toll on a weak heart.

First stop for Wesley—Moose's house. "Go ahead," Marcy said. "Ask him if he wants to play."

As Wesley approached cautiously, Moose didn't acknowledge him. Moose seemed oblivious to his surroundings as he played his own little game of toss-and-catch. Marcy and I crept up to the edge of Moose's yard, just within earshot.

"Wanna play?" Wesley asked meekly.

Moose shot him a who-the-hell-are-you look.

"No," Moose said flatly. "My big brother's coming out soon. I'm playing with him."

Wesley whipped himself around, face sagging. He ran into Marcy's arms and my heart sank.

"Let's go across the street and see if the other boy wants to play," Marcy suggested.

"No," Wesley said, shaking his head, tears welling in his eyes. "I don't wanna play."

"C'mon," I said. "We'll go get your scooter. It looks like fun."

"No," Wesley insisted as tears slid down both of his soft cheeks, which still had a little baby fat in them. "I don't wanna play."

Marcy and I walked him home, exchanging painful looks and releasing deep sighs of parental anguish as Chestnut Street buzzed around us. Wesley spent the rest of the day stacking Legos in his basement play room as Marcy and I took turns playing with him. That evening, just after I'd opened a lager and poured Marcy a glass of merlot, I got a call from Sam DiNardo, president of the Misty Hill Little League, who wanted to confirm my intentions to manage a team that spring.

A few weeks earlier, when I'd signed Wesley up for baseball, I'd also signed up to coach his team. Not being much of a baseball guy, I knew I wouldn't be able to coach when Wesley grew older. So I wanted to take advantage of the opportunity now, even if it was only for a year or two. I'd assisted on Wesley's T-ball team the previous year— which meant I was responsible for little more than directing runners around the base paths—but I still found myself surprisingly drawn to this sport of baseball, with its sense of permanence and constancy, a soothing thing for a guy who found himself fretting about the future of his only son. And I earnestly wanted to help cut a path for a strong and confident adult, not be forced to accept the blame for raising a loser who, in a worst-case scenario, would eat meals of bread and water in a rat-infested cell, or if things went somewhat better, would make a living by barking into a drive-up speaker with questions such as, *Wanna make that a value meal?* And what about dying in the desert? I felt like I should be worried about that, too, considering American boys were coming home in flag-draped coffins from a pair of wars in the Middle East, both launched by our dim-witted president from Texas. Then there was the nagging image of my son as an old man, a lonely coot who'd spend his days cooped up in his boxer shorts, relying on benevolent neighbors to bring him his prune juice, stopping the mailman for his most meaningful conversation of the day: *If it's another bill, ol' pal, just mark her 'return to sender.'*

After watching Wesley's snubbing by the boy down the block, there was no doubt in my mind that I wanted to coach his next team, no doubt that I wanted to be at my son's side and in charge of his surroundings—whatever they might be.

"I definitely want to coach," I told Sam DiNardo.

A week later, League Orientation Night. This was an annual get-together in mid-March when players and parents of the Misty Hill Little League crammed into a smelly school gym with the heat cranked up too high. We listened to Sam and the other league leaders speechify about things like what size bat to buy and how to play catch with your youngster—*Step into your throws; don't just stand there like you're waiting for a bus*—and then we were ordered to break into small groups to meet our teams.

My team was the Rockies, and the first person in our circle was Diet Coke Mom. Her son Carter had played T-ball with Wesley the previous year, and she was impossible to miss on the sidelines. She was in her mid-thirties, with sleek brown hair and full lips, and she always toted around a half-full bottle of Diet Coke. On this night, her lips were smacked with smoky crimson lipstick, and her gold hoop earrings were the size of golf balls. She wore a cashmere V-neck and tight jeans with a low-cut waist, the kind teenagers wear, with just a sliver of belly peeking out.

"I'm so glad you're coaching this year," she said to me, striking a pose with the bottle raised shoulder-high, wrapped in a feminine curl of her wrist. "You were so positive with the boys last year, and Carter really needs that."

"Thanks, I'm excited about it myself."

Never mind that Carter was a weak little ballplayer. I found myself excited about the fact that his mom would be at our games. I was, after all, a red-blooded male of a particular age—creeping toward forty, with young adulthood dead and gone and middle age lurking ahead. And as the years whooshed along, I was learning that the male ego never tires of the attention of a tantalizing woman, even if she's just watching a guy point a boy toward second base.

I began my speech to the Rockies parents—practice times, rainout protocols, equipment needs. All the while, I felt like Diet Coke Mom was my only audience. She stood in the middle of the circle, one hand perched on Carter's shoulder. She seemed to be hanging on my every word.

Her brown hair and gold earrings sparkled in the light of the gym, and her whole face, with those full red lips, glowed. Yet I was also acutely aware of Marcy, with her strawberry blonde hair and those big hazel eyes that Wesley had inherited, standing beside me, practically rubbing elbows with me, one of her hands resting on Wesley's shoulder. My head was a jumble as I tried addressing my new team while my eyes clung to one woman and some part of my brain flashed warnings that my wife's finely tuned radar was on high alert. After laying out the expectations for concession-stand duty, I lost my train of thought and began stammering.

"The Rockies suck," one of the Rockies said, interrupting me.

I didn't know who said it, though the remark seemed to have come from the right side of our circle. So I looked right, glancing from one little face to another.

"The Rockies suck," the boy said again, and this time I saw him. "I wanna be a Ranger."

It seemed like the jaws of other parents in the circle dropped all at once.

He was a little rug rat—not your typical Misty Hill kid. His mom, a heavy woman in tight pants and baggy sweater, yanked his arm and scolded him. "Lance, don't!"

"Now, now," I said.

"I'm sorry," the boy's mom said. "Really sorry."

I didn't know what else to say. Should I get tough with the little punk? Discipline someone else's kid? After all, I was the manager, and the other parents had already shown concern, with their jaws hanging down by their belts. But I also had to remember that these kids were so young, only seven or eight years old. So should I try something diplomatic, maybe tell the kid he and I would talk one-on-one afterward? Or just try to dismiss it with humor?

I froze. All I said was, "Okay."

I stammered some more, then remembered I'd been discussing concession-stand duty. Rather than try to recall exactly where I'd left off, I told the group I'd send out an email with a schedule. When it was all over, and the Rockies and their parents began scattering, I asked Marcy how it went.

"Fine," she said curtly, as Wesley left her side to run circles in the gym with other kids.

Marcy had a habit of scrunching her face when she was withholding the truth, and sure enough, she was scrunching now.

"Tell me the truth," I said.

"Okay. It was a disaster."

"Disaster?"

"Yeah, a disaster. Think about it. That one kid kept saying 'sucks.' He's going to be a handful. And you should have said something more to him tonight, shown the parents you know how to discipline a kid like that. They want that."

"Oh."

"And what's up between you and that skinny mom with the big earrings and the Diet Coke? Huh?"

"What do you mean?"

"You were looking right at her the whole time, like she was the only person in the room, and she looked back at you the same way."

"You're reading into that," I said. "I think it's just because she was standing in the middle."

"Yeah, right," she snorted.

Afterward, we filed out of the gym with the rest of the crowd but couldn't go anywhere—we were parked in. And I knew exactly who'd blocked us in. My neighbor, Rocco Spinelli, with his sleek black Audi.

Rocco was a South Philly guy who'd grown up on a little row-house street where creative parking was a tradition as old as the automobile itself, and he'd never broken himself of the habit. Besides, he was the kind of person who could get away with things that other people couldn't. He was trim and good-looking, with bronze skin and a perfectly manicured black goatee, and was chief of staff to a state senator—not just any state senator, but the chairman of the Appropriations Committee. Rocco and his boss knew how to get their hands on things, namely money. Though technically just an aide, Rocco was largely responsible for state grants that had built, among other things, new dugouts and a snazzy new scoreboard at Misty Hill's aging baseball field, and a whole extra field, complete with home-and-away bleachers, for the town's growing soccer league. And not only did he enjoy the admiration of the entire town, he also had two beautiful children, a twelve-year-old ballplayer and a teenage daughter, though his daughter never seemed to interact with anyone outside of her household who wasn't between the ages of fifteen and eighteen.

After we leaned against my two-door Honda Civic for several minutes waiting for Rocco to emerge from the gym, Marcy lost patience and decided to walk home. It was a four-block walk and relatively warm for mid-March, and she took Wesley with her while I waited. I could tell from the way she marched off that she was also still mad at me for my accidental bout of gawking, but I also knew she'd get over that soon enough. I didn't think she was too ticked off at Rocco, though, because we were friends with the Spinellis and we'd grown used to those little inconveniences that came with the territory.

He was the last one out of the gym, wearing a shiny navy blue warm-up suit, carrying his clipboard comfortably under one arm. I figured he was coaching one of the twelve-year-old teams, because he always managed his son's team. He saw me leaning against my car with my arms folded and cracked a guilty smile.

"Sorry about that, Nick," Rocco said, digging into his pockets for his car keys. "I got here late, then had some extra details to attend to. This is Justin's last year in Little League, so I want to make sure it's a good one."

"I see," I said, in a tone that indicated I was accustomed to his antics.

"Where's Wesley?" He clicked on his key ring and his car doors unlocked and the lights turned on.

"Marcy walked him home. They were tired of waiting for the asshole who parked us in."

Rocco let out an unashamed little chuckle: "Sorry about that."

"Where's Justin?" I asked.

"Rode his skateboard home with a group of buddies. Heed my advice, my friend, and enjoy this whole experience while it lasts, because before you know it your son will be trying his best to get the hell away from you."

Halfway across the parking lot, which was now nearly empty, a car horn honked. We both turned to see where it came from, and Rocco seemed to recognize the vehicle, a white Range Rover. I could see the silhouette of the one person inside, and it looked like a woman. Rocco held a finger in the air, a sign he'd be over in one minute.

"Everyone's waiting on you tonight," I said mockingly.

"I'll move my car for you, and then I have to go see her. It's one of the moms from my team. Nothing too important. Have a good one, old buddy."

He moved his car, hopped out and jogged over to the Range Rover. I pulled out of my space and headed toward the quiet street. When I stopped at the street to check traffic, I glanced in my rearview mirror and saw Rocco lean into the open driver's side window. I swear to God, I saw him kiss the woman inside.

2
THE COMMISH

*W*esley needed a cup. So that was Equipment Priority One, because our team was now in the "coach pitch" division, in which coaches knelt down and pitched the ball from about thirty feet away, with a seven- or eight-year-old catcher as backstop. Jake's Sporting Goods, our local sports mega-store, stocked an entire wall of cups. Big cups, small cups, white cups, yellow cups, expensive cups, and cheap cups. On the bottom row was the cheapest and the smallest, the only one I thought would fit a seven-year-old boy. I bent down and plucked it off the rack, telling Wesley, "Here's a good one."

"No," Wesley said. "I want a bigger one."

He surveyed the vast array of cups, as if they were chocolate bars in the world's biggest candy store. His big eyes grew even bigger.

"I want that one," he said, pointing to a gold cup with thick rubber lining. The cheap one I'd proposed was plain white with a thin lining.

I pulled the gold cup off the rack and looked it over.

The package said it was for boys age ten and over—and to boot, it was twice as expensive as the white cup.

"No," I said. "It's too big for you."

"I want it."

"Listen to me. No. It's for boys ten and older. It's too big."

"It will fit."

"No, it won't."

"Yes, it will."

"Besides, it's expensive. I'm not spending a lot of money on a cup. So the answer is no."

"Yes."

"No."

"I want a big one."

I felt myself getting riled. Scenes like this were rare with Wesley, who was generally a well-behaved kid, but he was still only seven, and any seven-year-old is prone to fits in a store. I grabbed his arm firmly and bent down to look him eye-to-eye.

"You're not listening, and you're being naughty," I said sternly. "You need to listen to me."

"I want a big one," he repeated, and became teary-eyed.

"All right, listen," I said, switching to a diplomatic approach. "Let's take them both into the changing booth. Try them both on, and you'll see that the one you want is too big. Will you try them both on for me?"

"Okay," he said, wiping his eyes.

Sure enough, when he tried on the expensive cup, his attitude changed. He shuffled out of the changing booth in stocking feet and ran down the aisle, then wobbled back, one arm jammed down his pants in an attempt to adjust the oversized cup.

"It's jiggling around," he said.

"Yes, and that's because it's too big. Now, can we buy the other one?"

"Okay."

Not only was I a first-time manager, I was the new commissioner of the entire coach-pitch division, even though I wasn't completely sure of what being the commissioner entailed. I landed the post because in Little League these volunteer jobs often go to the only person willing to do it.

The week before orientation night, we'd held a managers meeting in the school gym, and Sam DiNardo gave the seven of us in attendance an impassioned speech about the importance of "stepping up" to volunteer. Sam was a lifelong Misty Hill resident, a gung-ho guy with bushy eyebrows, thick shoulders and four kids in the league, all between six and twelve.

"Without volunteers," Sam pleaded as his eyebrows fattened and his shoulders broadened, "the league simply wouldn't exist. And so without volunteers, this remarkable experience of Little League baseball wouldn't be available to our children anymore, and just having to mention that possibility makes me cringe."

While most of Sam's rhetoric seemed overblown, the general thrust of his speech made sense to me. Someone must do the work—recruit the coaches, draw up the schedules, buy the equipment. Even so, when he got to the part of his speech where he sought someone to step up to be commissioner, I didn't want to do it.

I'd been a lousy Little Leaguer. I was a chunky kid who played in the 1970s, back when Walter Matthau and his Bad News Bears were in the theaters. I remember feeling only one proud moment during my T-ball days—scoring from second on a defensive mishap in the infield. And in the following seasons of real baseball I'd mostly been stuck in left field. The only chance I had to pitch was in a preseason scrimmage at age twelve. I didn't pitch well, and that was that. I played teener ball at age thirteen, but I rarely got in the games, and I quit baseball after that.

Looking around the table at the coach-pitch meeting, I could tell that no one else wanted to step up to be commissioner. After Sam's speech, the other guys shrank into their seats like schoolboys who forgot to do their homework. At first I wondered if I had time to do whatever work a commissioner did, because my job at the newspaper had not been going well. Pinched by advertising losses as readers flocked to the Internet, the *Harrisburg Telegraph* had just offered buyouts to employees, and some of our most experienced reporters and editors had cashed in, leaving the rest of us with a bigger workload. At the same time, rumors about layoffs were swirling. But then I figured extra Little League duty would be a pleasant distraction, something to help take my mind off of editing newspaper stories about car crashes and school taxes and the threat of unemployment. I raised my hand and said, "I'll do it."

And I must admit this: I kind of liked the title, and the way it sounded next to my name—Nick Marhoffer, the Commish. Much cooler than Nick Marhoffer, Assistant Metro Editor.

My first assignment as the Commish had been to recruit one more coach-pitch manager. There were seven volunteers for eight teams, and I had one week to find someone before League Orientation Night. I spent that Tuesday night on the phone, calling the fathers of young ballplayers, but I had no luck. Guys gave a range of excuses, some of which struck me as lame. *I have two boys in the league now. I take a class one night a week. I have too much to do at work.* By the end of the night I was frustrated and wanted to tell some of them off—*Yeah, knucklehead, I have too much to do at work, too, but I'm spending my whole fucking night calling you lazy assholes so your kids can play ball.* But I didn't say anything like that. I simply said "Okay, thanks," and moved on to the next name on the list.

On Thursday morning I began to get nervous, because I'd dialed up half the list of coach-pitch parents with little success, so I stuffed the list in my pocket and took it to work with me. When the other editors were busy, I pulled out the list and made a couple of calls from my desk. Mostly I reached voice mailboxes or stay-at-home moms who said their husbands were too busy, but at around four o'clock I reached an older guy who sounded nice. It turned out he was a boy's grandfather, and managing a coach-pitch team seemed to me to be a good fit for a grandfather, so I went ahead and asked him. He didn't hesitate. "Sure," he said.

I sat at my desk and beamed, having resolved my first dilemma as the Commish.

A week before the season opened, Sam called me and said he'd heard from some concerned parents on the grandfather's team, the Devil Rays. At practices, it seemed like Grandpa was drunk.

"You're kidding," I said. "In Misty Hill?"

"Not kidding," Sam said. "Not everyone in this town is a doctor or lawyer."

Misty Hill is not a town for day drinking. A tidy suburb of Harrisburg, the state capital, it's a small and affluent town full of smart and successful people. Many of the boys are the sons of orthodontists and podiatrists, financial planners, lobbyists and high-ranking state officials. There are salesmen, but they are the top-notch salesmen who win trips to exotic locals and have access to the best seats at professional games. At a typical game, the sidelines are a tableau of stay-at-home moms in canvas chairs wearing something from the At-Ease collection at Talbots, their bright Vera Bradley purses plopped beside them. Siblings of the players are usually dressed in Gap Kids and Hollister wear. On weekdays, dads often show up late in dark suits from Jones New York or Pronto, ties loosened, and there's chit-chat about dinner parties, buzzings at the state Capitol, or the beach-house market at the Jersey Shore. The gleaming white steeple of the Methodist Church is visible from the field—and from almost every backyard. Folks always say it's a great place to raise a kid.

"What makes them think he's drunk?" I asked.

"They say he smells like booze," Sam said. "They say he yells a lot. They say he even cursed once."

"Oh, shit," I said.

"Excuse me?"

"Sorry," I said, realizing how bad a curse word sounded in this particular conversation.

"That's okay. How did this guy get into the league?"

"I called him and asked him," I said. "I called a lot of guys. This guy was the only one willing to step up."

"We can't let him manage. Our bylaws are clear—no alcohol. Zero tolerance."

"But how can we be sure he's drinking?"

"I'll need you to look into this. They practice tomorrow at six."

I didn't want this chore, but I didn't know what else to say. So I said what newspaper types often say when they get a loathsome assignment. "I'll check into it."

"Oh, and Nick," Sam said. "If he's drinking, he has to be discharged as manager. Our bylaws are clear. Call me if you need my help."

I went to the Devil Rays practice the next day, just as I promised. The grandfather didn't look much like a grandfather—he was definitely in his fifties, probably early fifties. He was short and stout with hair that wasn't yet gray—more of a salt-and-pepper color, long in the back, where it curled out of his green Devil Rays hat. His name was Tom, and he lived on the edge of town with his daughter and grandson. Nobody seemed to know what had happened to his son-in-law.

I watched practice from a tree line beside the field, and I sensed trouble. Tom seemed irritated, hollering frequently at the boys. He also didn't notice some things he should have. One little Devil Ray sat down in the middle of a drill and dawdled for a good five minutes before Tom saw him, and two Devil Rays started wrestling and went at it for two or three minutes before Tom finally separated them.

After practice, I approached him, close enough to smell his breath. The alcohol smell was unmistakable. A raunchy, hard-liquor smell. I bit my lip and backed away, just a step. What, exactly, to say? I'd never faced a task like this before, and I wasn't comfortable confronting him, but then I remembered that I'd signed up for this responsibility, and I was a newspaper guy who didn't usually back down from an assignment. Besides, this son of a bitch was in charge of a bunch of seven- and eight-year-old boys, and I was the one who'd recruited him.

"We need to talk," I said.

"What's up?"

"Listen," I said. "Some of the parents on your team complained to the league, to the president. They say you've been acting strange. They think you've been drinking before practices."

His face tightened into a scowl, and he looked away.

"Who complained?" he said. "Who said that about me?"

"I honestly don't know. I was only told it was some parents, more than one."

"Nope, not me," he said, finally looking me in the eye.

"And I gotta tell you something else. You smell like alcohol right now."

"You don't know what the hell you're talking about."

"I wasn't born yesterday, Tom."

In fact, as the son of a drinker, I had bad memories. Tom's boozy breath and the glassy look in his eyes and the tone of our confrontation made the blood pound behind my own eyes. My dad never once coached any of my teams. Instead, he often showed up late for my Little League games in his rumpled shirt and tie, and sometimes he'd get loud and testy, and once he even started an argument with the ump and got thrown out. No longer was I uncomfortable dealing with Tom. Now I was ticked.

Tom turned away from me, a defiant look on his face, and started packing balls and helmets in his equipment bag.

"Leave the gear for me, Tom."

"Why would I do that?"

"Leave it," I said. "The league considers this a serious thing."

He kept packing.

"Fine," I said. "But you can expect a call from Sam tonight."

I walked away, so disgusted with him that I didn't even want to be around him. I'd done my job. From here, I'd turn the matter over to Sam. After all, Sam was the league president, and he'd surely had some experience dealing with these types of problems.

As I left the field, Tom yelled my name. I didn't want to hear anything he had to say.

"Hey, Nick!" he said. "Nick!"

I just kept walking.

———

That night, as I switched off the bedside light, my mind whirled with anxious thoughts of the drunk granddad, the threat of cutbacks at the paper, and Lance the foul-mouthed Little Leaguer. Though I'd been counting on baseball to take my mind off of life's troubles, my career as coach and Commish was off to a crummy start. It wasn't supposed to be like this. Wesley's previous season, T-ball, was different. Every game was a mishmash of high energy and fumbling cuteness: You might spot a boy picking dandelions in the outfield, or you might see a runner sprint to the pitcher's mound rather than first or second base. Yet nobody was ever ruled out and every runner scored, and it was never obvious when one team outplayed another. And after each game came the crowning jewel, the moment every player would come to savor: the Player's Snack. This cost parents an extra twenty dollars at the beginning of the season, but it was so worth the money. The players dashed to a designated window at the side of the concession stand to choose from a menu that included nachos, soft pretzel, hot dog or pizza, plus a soda or juice drink. They sat together at picnic tables and scarfed down their Player's Snack—and most splattered juice or nacho sauce on their uniforms in the process—while coaches and parents circled and congratulated everyone on a game well-played. The occasion felt like more than just a friendly little post-game gathering: It was almost familial. While they slurped and munched and giggled, those other boys warmed my heart—happy, surrogate siblings for my only son.

Marcy must have sensed that I wasn't tired. She nestled beside me, slipped her hand under my shirt and massaged my chest with her fingertips. She popped her head up for a kiss, then slid her hand into my boxer shorts. But nothing was happening. This was new territory, because we had a good sex life—usually a few times a week, and at thirty-nine years old, I'd never had trouble rising to the occasion. So Marcy seemed surprised when I remained limp after several minutes of kissing and rubbing. Eventually she just started tugging, with little success.

"What's wrong?" she asked.

"Nothing," I said. "Just tired."

Her eyes drooped and she let out a sad little sigh, as if she was offended and that my failure to get it up was a sign she was no longer attractive. She tugged a little harder, and I shut my eyes and tried to block out all of my problems. Eventually, and incomprehensibly, my mind shifted to the Diet Coke Mom. Her sleek brown hair and full lips, her tight jeans and slim waist. Before long, I was hard.

"Finally," Marcy said.

3
THE ROCKIES

*F*irst game: the Braves. The April sun rose early and warmed the town—perfect weather for Opening Day—but the day roused mixed emotions for me. Relief, for one, because the Devil Rays' manager situation had been settled: Sam had canned Tom, and one of the dads who'd complained about the drinking agreed to coach. I needed that piece of good news, because I'd been feeling strained about life's bigger problems. The previous week, on April 1st, the beginning of the new financial quarter, layoffs were finally announced at the *Telegraph*, and while I had enough seniority to spare my job, I was demoted to beat reporter. It was part of a massive reorganization to cut 15 percent from the newsroom budget, which left my assistant metro editor's job officially eliminated. I was forced to take a 10-percent cut in salary, too, but at least I still had a job. A dozen newsroom employees were handed pink slips.

I was also looking forward to spending a Saturday mingling with baseball families, especially Diet Coke Mom, whose name was Tess Sugarmeier. But I didn't want to be tempted to gawk at her on the sidelines or picture her naked or anything like that, and of course I didn't want our team to get embarrassed while she looked on. So I was apprehensive, too. And the Braves were big—just looking at them in warm-ups made me nervous. They were stacked with eight-year-olds, plus they had seven-year-old Moose, and they looked even more imposing in their dark, all-navy duds. Navy jersey with red letters, navy pants, navy hats, navy socks.

My Rockies didn't look so tough. The staff at the jersey store had misread our order and printed us light purple jerseys, just a tone darker than pink. I tried to darken up our look by ordering gray pants, but they didn't help much. Making matters worse, our sponsor, which was apparently assigned randomly, was the Misty Hill Beauty Salon and Boutique, and its name was emblazoned on our backs. That meant I was forced to lead a bunch of little seven-year-olds, with only a couple eight-year-olds mixed in, wearing near-pink jerseys with a beauty salon as a sponsor.

"Hey, Nick," said the other coach, a gigantic guy named Ed Simmons, while our teams warmed up. "Shouldn't you be looking for the softball field?"

"Very funny," I said. "I'm sure we'll play better than we look."

Ed Simmons was already a legend in Misty Hill. He'd been a star lineman on the high school football team in the 1980s before playing at Rutgers University, and though he was a backup for the pathetic Scarlet Knights, it was an achievement for anyone from tiny Misty Hill to play Division I football. He may have been the largest man I'd ever seen—six-foot-seven with a barrel chest, and his belly had grown just as big as his chest in the past twenty years. He also had the biggest and shiniest forehead I'd ever seen, bulging at the top in a Frankenstein way that forced him to wear his Braves cap loose and tilted upward. He was a high-ranking beer salesman for a large distributorship in

Harrisburg, and despite his imposing frame and scary forehead, I knew him to be outgoing and chummy, which is why I didn't let the softball crack bother me. Understandably, everyone in town knew him simply as Big Ed.

"I hope you have your boys ready," Big Ed said with a cocky grin. "I've got mine ready."

"We're ready."

"I've been working them hard. I coached my oldest son at this level a few years ago, but I'm working them harder this time. You should see one of the new things I've been doing: I put the catcher's gear on them in practice, and I throw the ball at them hard—really hard. It *forces* them to learn to catch."

"Yeah?"

"You should see us catch. Wait here a second." He yelled for his own son, Raymond, to come over, and told Raymond to bring a ball. Raymond was the biggest of all the Braves. Big Ed motioned for him to hand over the ball.

As Ed accepted the ball, his attention was diverted. Tess Sugarmeier strode by in tight khaki shorts and a form-fitting white V-neck, her brown hair shimmering in the late-morning sun, her well-toned legs already tinged with a light spring tan, a full bottle of Diet Coke in one hand. She gave us a tickly little wave with her free hand as she passed. We both smiled, like schoolboys harboring a crush on their teacher, and waved back.

"At least," Ed acknowledged, "you have some hot moms on your team."

"Yup."

As Tess settled in on the sideline, making pleasantries with other moms, Big Ed turned his attention back to his beefy son Raymond and his catching prowess.

"Back up, and let's show Coach Nick how well you catch," Ed said.

Raymond nodded confidently and backed up several

paces, then punched his glove and held it chest high. Big Ed backed up a few steps himself, reached his arm back and whaled the ball at his son. It was a laser. It nipped the top of Raymond's glove and smacked him in the nose. Blood came pouring out. Raymond bent down, his glove over his bloodied nose, and bawled.

"Oh, my God!" Big Ed said. He ran to his son and shouted to one of his assistants, "Get some ice! And a towel! Hurry!"

The assistant ran over with the ice and towel, and Big Ed wiped his son's face and sat him down with the ice pack over his nose. I waited with them in case they needed an extra hand, but Raymond didn't appear to have a serious injury. Just a messy one.

"I can't believe that happened," Big Ed told me, wiping his sweaty forehead with the back of his hand. "You must think I'm the worst father in the world."

"Nah," I lied.

Big Ed's son was able to play, albeit with a swollen nose, and his team promptly began handing our squad a beating. On the game's first pitch, the Braves' leadoff man hit an easy grounder to second, but my second baseman threw it wide and the Braves bench erupted with shouts of "Go! Go!" My young first baseman chased after the ball as it ricocheted off the fence, and when he finally cornered the ball, he fumbled it. By the time he picked it up cleanly the Braves runner was rounding third and heading for home. My first baseman turned toward home and reached back to throw, and the ball slipped out of his hand. It was an inside-the-infield home run, of sorts. Indeed, we were in deep trouble.

Why did I think I could do this? I wasn't a "real baseball guy"—the term bandied about our league to describe the most desirable coaches, the former college or high school players who knew the game inside-out—but I figured I knew enough to coach seven-year-old boys. And for what it's worth, I'd played baseball all the way to the teener level.

And I was an athlete. After quitting baseball, I'd become a self-conscious teenager, and I set out to put my pudgy youth behind me. While a growth spurt in junior high helped me drop some weight, I also began running. As a tenth grader at Johnstown High, I joined the cross country team—far from a glory sport, no doubt, but still a sport of grit. While poking around the mall one weekend I came across a book titled *The Race of Life* by Angelo Tannabaugh, a Yale English professor and running philosopher, a true guru. His book became my bible. I stuffed it in my gym bag so I could read passages before every race. Passages such as this: *If you find yourself obsessed with it, whatever it is, embrace it. Chances are it's what you were meant to do.*

By college, I was lean and lanky and six-foot-two, and a serious distance runner. And when I really want to do something, I tend to go all out. I ran my first marathon at age nineteen, and nine more after that. I felt like that chubby Little Leaguer who'd been sentenced to the outfield was a completely different person. But as Big Ed's Braves put a licking on my Rockies, it seemed naïve to think that Angelo Tannabaugh's wisdom could translate so easily to Little League, and I was struck by the thought that this was not what I was meant to do.

So naturally, without really thinking about it, my eyes wandered over to the sidelines and landed on Tess Sugarmeier, who was always a sight, not just for sore eyes, but also wounded egos. Her cozy skin, her thick lips, her sleek hips. *No, stop it*, I told myself after one prolonged glance. I forced my eyes back on the field, where my Rockies were already looking slumped and defeated in their defensive positions. An instant later, as the next Brave strode to the plate, waving his bat like an ax, my eyes were back on the dazzling mom with the Diet Coke tucked lovingly against her breast. *Stop it!* But I couldn't. My eyes shifted back to the field, back to her. *Shit, where's my wife? Can she tell what I'm doing here?* The next Brave singled to left, where the outfielder swatted at the ball but couldn't field it, allowing the runner a free pass to second. I spotted Marcy along the far edge of our own sideline, legs stretched out from her folding chair, as if sunbathing, eyes hidden behind her sunglasses. Another Brave at the plate, another single and error, another run. And then Moose smashed one deep over my center fielder's head and jogged around the bases, like a conquering hero, for a two-run dinger.

Because most seven- and eight-year-old boys still couldn't throw or catch well, and mercy rules weren't in effect at the younger levels, high-scoring games were normal. Yet Big Ed's Braves threw and caught *much* better than my Rockies and jumped out to a 15-3 lead after four innings. Big Ed had even kept his bigger and stronger kids in the infield for the first four innings, while I rotated all of my players into the infield to give them all a chance at different positions. That's how everyone had managed their teams in T-ball, and I figured the coach-pitch division was little more than glorified T-ball. The results were clearly disastrous, and my kids were dejected after four innings. Wesley had grounded out in each of his first at-bats, and he returned to the bench the second time with his chin buried deep in his chest. I tried consoling him at the end of the inning with a pat on the back and a few words of encouragement: "You took good swings, so just keep swinging that bat."

I flashed back to the previous year, to T-ball, when Wesley had stepped into the left-handed batter's box to swing the bat in his very first game. It started as a moment of parental angst. I'd been worried about the sound that reverberated across the field at practice when boys would miss the ball and smack the rubber tee—*fwud*. I was afraid

Wesley would hit a fwud. And the fact that Wesley was left-handed caused me added anxiety because, even though it increased his chances of landing a million-dollar contract if he could someday throw a baseball ninety miles per hour, it also increased his odds of going through life with an inferiority complex if his arm strength was closer to the other 99 percent of the population. Or so I'd heard. But the look on Wesley's face as he'd approached the tee gave me hope, because he was all business, eyes fixated on the ball. A game face. He took one measuring swing, stopping inches from the ball, then wound up like a golfer and popped it. The ball scooted straight up the middle and into the outfield, where a small gang of defenders pounced on it. Wesley reached first base and stood on his tip-toes like a soldier returning home from war, beaming and waving to Marcy, who sat in the grass behind the first-base line and waved back like a giddy Army mom. It developed into a snapshot of our life that I wanted to file in my mind forever.

But now, halfway through our dismal opener with the Braves, I already wanted to forget about baseball. Then finally, in the fifth, Big Ed began rotating his weaker players into the infield, and we staged a little rally. As a result, most of the Rockies reached base and scored, and the mood on my team improved. My eyes were no longer peeping over at Tess, though I did take a couple of scans at Marcy, trying to gauge her mood and how much of my leering she'd discerned over the course of the game. But I couldn't—she was a stone-cold blank behind those sunglasses. Except when Wesley scored. He scored in each of the last two innings—reaching first base on clean singles, not errors, although he made it home each time on a Braves miscue—then returned to the bench with a bounce in his step, and I noticed a hoot and head-high claps from Marcy. Still, our rally wasn't enough to make the game close, though it was enough to make my kids feel like they'd played a decent game. We lost, 21-12.

"Great game," Big Ed said, beaming. "Aren't you glad I let you score some runs there in the end?"

"Yeah, thanks," I said, trying not to sound too sarcastic.

"It's my way of showing folks I'm not as big and bad as I look."

I felt conflicted about the big galoot at that moment, because he'd managed ruthlessly for four innings, and there'd been a point in the game when I wanted to walk over and bloody *his* nose. But at least he changed tactics at the end, allowing all of the kids to finish the game on a high note, and especially Wesley. When I'd huddled with my team at the end of the game, they seemed upbeat and eager to run to the concession stand for their Player's Snack. So I couldn't stay too mad at him.

"That's how I like to manage," Big Ed said, as if I should be grateful for the gift he'd just given me. "We all want to win, but I don't want the other team to go home feeling bad. Let them score at least some runs. That's what I figure."

Marcy waited for me at the end of the dugout, with her folded chair hanging off her shoulder. Uh oh, I thought. Could I be in trouble for my shifty eyes? After Ed and I shook hands and parted, I did my best to control the topic of conversation.

"Ugh," I said, rolling my eyes toward the field. "Not exactly how I envisioned it."

"It's just the first game," she said in a common-sense tone, and I could tell I was not under suspicion.

And I was so glad, and so attracted to her at that moment: After sitting in the open sun for a couple hours, her skin was coated with a light glaze of sweet and sexy sweat, reminding me of the summer nights when we'd started dating and were often rolling in sweaty sheets together—that is, when we weren't doing it in the kitchen or shower.

We were both twenty-nine, living in Center City Philadelphia. I'd spotted her at an Irish pub on Walnut

Street, a real meat market and regular hangout for urban twenty-somethings. I downed a beer and ordered another before mustering the courage to flirt with her, a trim strawberry-blonde with light freckles, those big hazel eyes and a killer smile. My pickup line: "I love your smile." She immediately seemed flattered—her head cocked sideways as her smile broadened. The next six months were a blur of happy hours at side-street bars, late-night stops at pizza shops, and sex-filled sleepovers at each other's apartment, and I could feel things getting serious. So for her thirtieth birthday, I maxed out my Visa card and bought a five thousand-dollar engagement ring, then took her to the art museum and proposed at the top of the front steps, the famous spot where Rocky had trained before his triumphs. She didn't hesitate.

It's just the first game. Marcy's five words and her down-to-earth delivery helped lend some perspective to my ghastly start as a baseball manager, and it reminded me that I was loved. Still, I was embarrassed. I gathered my gear and hoisted the equipment bag over my shoulder, and as we strolled off the field together I forced my eyes straight forward, ignored everything and everyone in my peripheral vision—until we reached the concession stand, where the Braves were gleefully downing their pizza and nachos.

Moose was seated in the middle of a picnic table full of Braves, nacho sauce dripping down the front of his jersey. He must have sensed my eyes bearing down on him, because he looked up and we locked eyes. But neither of us said a word or did anything to acknowledge that we'd been acquainted. Not even a little nod. I thought to myself, *That little thug.*

4
BAD COACHING MOMENT

I faced a dilemma for our second game. Should I stick with a lineup that gave every kid equal playing time, or switch to Big Ed's tactics? I didn't have many strong players, but I had enough talent to field a decent infield for several innings and maybe keep the game close. I had two eight-year-olds, plus Wesley and two other fairly solid seven-year-olds. The rest of my team was a mix of kids who'd never played before, had hyperactivity issues, or, like Carter Sugarmeier, wouldn't be able to throw a ball into water if they were sitting in a rowboat.

My decision was complicated by our next opponent: the Rangers, whose manager was Reggie Knox, a renowned cutthroat who also served as our league treasurer. Reggie was a real tight-ass, a deputy secretary for the state Department of Corrections, and he had twin eight-year-old boys who were among our league's best ballplayers.

Two nights before the game, I was up half the night, wrestling with my decision of how to craft my lineup, and trying to determine if it was even possible to have a fighting chance against Reggie Knox and his Rangers. I could already imagine the Knox twins patrolling the infield, throwing out my Rockies with ease. One, two, three. Inning over.

So the next morning, over coffee and a bagel, I drew up my lineup, and it was the toughest lineup I could imagine. Hunched over the kitchen counter with pencil in hand, I was largely oblivious to Marcy and Wesley as they got ready for work and school, though I glanced up once and saw Marcy rolling her eyes at me. I would assign my five best players to the infield for the first five innings, and I'd keep Wesley at second, where he'd be in a position to make some plays without leaving other parents with the impression I was handing my own kid the key assignments, like shortstop. In the sixth, I'd finally rotate my weaker players into the infield. And I went off to work, carrying a second cup of coffee and at least some hope that my Rockies would be able to compete the next day.

Still unsure about whether I was doing the right thing, I decided to seek counsel—from Rocco, who'd been through these ranks with his own son several years earlier. The day before the Rangers game, I knocked on his door and his uppity teenage daughter told me he was at a game. Our field complex was just a couple blocks from our house, so I decided to walk over, hoping an evening of baseball would help me clear my head, then I'd be able to chat with Rocco afterward for some advice.

The game proved to be soothing for my psyche. It resembled real baseball, with fastballs and stolen bases, capable fielders and few errors. After Rocco's Yankees scratched out a 4-3 win over a pesky Pirates team, I sauntered over to the dugout and caught Rocco's attention.

"Yo, buddy," I said, leaning over the back end of the dugout fence. "Can I bug you for a few minutes?"

"Hey, skipper. Of course. Did you catch our game?"

"Most of it," I said. "Big difference between this and

coach pitch."

"No doubt."

A dishy brunette in a velvet-pink sweatsuit nudged up beside me and interrupted us. "Hey coach," she said teasingly. "Great game."

"Thanks, honey," Rocco said with a wink.

"Catch up with you later?" the brunette asked.

"You know it. Let me finish up here, first. Okay?"

"Okay," she said with a shimmy of her hips, as Rocco's eyes followed her tight pink ass over to the concession stand.

When he finally looked back to me, I raised my eyebrows suspiciously at him.

"What was that about?" I asked.

"Shhh," he said, holding a finger to his lips.

"Where's Felicia? Doesn't she come to these games?"

"Never," Rocco said, a little distracted. "She hates baseball. She wants Justin to be an artist or something."

"So are you double dipping?" I asked.

"Shhh," he said again, even though no one was standing close enough to overhear us. "I'm just enjoying the fringe benefits of coaching."

"Does she happen to own a white Range Rover?" I asked, recalling the vehicle I saw Rocco dipping into on League Orientation Night.

"No, that's another mom," he admitted. "That's my catcher's mom—one hot little blonde."

I shook my head in disbelief.

"Anyway," I said. "I came over to ask how you used to handle your lineups when Justin was younger. The last guy we played really stuck it to us."

"How so?"

"He kept his best kids in key positions as long as possible, but I hate to do that, too. These kids on my team are so young."

"Yeah, they're young," Rocco conceded. "But they have to learn to win. Teach them how to win, and they'll figure out how to play baseball along the way."

"I don't know about that philosophy."

"Trust me," he said. "I managed Justin's teams every year since T-ball, and we never had a losing season. Did you see him tonight? Doubled in the winning run."

"I actually made out a really tough lineup for our next game, but I'm still not sure about it."

"Stick with it," he said. "The kids want to win. I have to run now, so let me know how you make out."

I knew he didn't *have* to run, because I knew who he was chasing after, but I left it at that and thanked him for his insights.

I was bothered by the knowledge that Rocco was enjoying certain fringe benefits as a coach. His wife Felicia was probably Marcy's best friend in Misty Hill, though I found her hard to relate to. Felicia was a tiny woman with straight black hair, dark complexion and a pretty but pouty face. She was a stay-at-home mom and artist. I often saw her on my morning jogs through Oak Park, with a small easel set up in the grass, painting watercolors of the old oak trees beside the stream and trail that ran along the northern edge of Misty Hill. I rarely waved to her, though, because she seemed the type who lived inside her head and didn't take well to interruptions. She spent most weekends in the spring and summer, while her son and husband were busy with baseball, among other things, selling her work at art fairs across Pennsylvania. The Spinellis' home, which we'd been invited to for dinner on occasion, looked like an Ethan Allen showroom, and her paintings covered the walls: Oak Park, the little main streets of central Pennsylvania, and the green-and-gold state Capitol dome. Judging from the quality, she didn't sell many at the art fairs.

Marcy and Felicia belonged to a neighborhood book

club, power-walked together regularly, and often shared a glass of chardonnay on weekend afternoons. And in a town full of the wives of lawyers, doctors and high-ranking state officials, there didn't seem to be many down-to-earth women with whom Marcy could connect. And while I was troubled by Rocco's dalliances, I didn't know what to do with the information. After all, he was my friend, too, and so finally I did what guys are expected to do when they stumble across such incriminating information: I convinced myself that it wasn't any of my business, and didn't say a word.

But that night, on the eve of the Rangers game, I couldn't sleep. And once again, I had baseball on the brain. What about those kids whom I'd sentenced to the outfield and the bench for most of the game? Like Carter Sugarmeier. Hell, they were only seven years old. If they didn't get a chance to play now, when would they? And how would they ever improve or learn all the positions? And did I want to risk angering any of their parents? Like Tess Sugarmeier? I also wondered why I should take any advice from Rocco Spinelli, who, despite being my friendly neighbor, also seemed to be a chronic womanizer. I remembered my own experience in Little League, standing in the outfield, such a lonely place for a young boy. I remembered walking off the mound in that one preseason scrimmage that I'd been allowed to pitch, and the horrible feeling of knowing that I'd blown my only chance, and was headed back to the outfield. I remembered the day at age thirteen when I told my parents, "I don't want to play baseball anymore." I remembered the scene six years later, after I'd finished my first marathon. I'd collapsed on a park bench after finishing a respectable forty-first, and was sipping grape juice and trying to rub the soreness out of my legs as the race director paced the finish area, bullhorn in hand, blaring to each runner who hobbled across the finish line, "Everyone's a winner here!"

So the morning of the Rangers game, dog-tired from a

dire lack of sleep, I brewed a big pot of coffee and tore up my first lineup. I sat back down at the kitchen counter and started over again, rotating all of my Rockies in and out of the infield. Each kid would get into the infield by the third inning, and each would enjoy at least two innings in the infield by the sixth. No one would sit on the bench more than two innings. I made sure to start Wesley in the infield, though, as originally planned at second base, and I finagled it so that he'd only have to spend one inning on the bench. I assigned Carter three innings at third base, hoping the Rangers wouldn't pull the ball his way. When Marcy walked into the kitchen and saw me revising my lineup, she shook her head at me, her signal that I was taking this baseball thing way too seriously. I trudged off to work, convinced it was going to be a long day, and an even longer game with the Rangers, but that was my choice. I'd decided it was better than cheating half of my kids out of a chance to play baseball.

As I toted my bags to the field, Carter Sugarmeier sprinted by me, and I turned to look for his mom. She was just a few paces behind, grinning like a schoolgirl and holding a chilled, unopened bottle of Diet Coke.

"I'm glad I bumped into you," Tess said. "Tough first game, huh?"

I didn't want to complain or come across as a whiner, so I just said, "We'll keep plugging along."

"Carter had fun, though," she said.

"Yeah?"

I was eager to hear more, but I didn't want to seem overeager, so I dropped my equipment bag and acted as if there was a problem with the strap. She reached into her rosy, posy-covered Vera Bradley purse, pulled out a tube of lipstick and touched up her lips with the deep crimson shade.

"Yeah," she said. "I know he's not the greatest player in the world, but it's nice to see him get a chance. If he didn't play until the end of the game, he'd lose interest. Maybe he'd even fall asleep out there. So I really like the way you handle the boys."

I gave the strap a good tug, as if testing it, then hoisted the bag again, and we started walking toward the field together. Deep down, I was beaming. Someone agreed with me! Someone recognized the value of treating all these young kids fairly and saw that I was doing things the right way. And it wasn't just anyone—it was this attractive and friendly woman with whom I clearly had a nice rapport.

"I'm glad to have him," I said, still trying to play it cool. "He's a nice kid."

"Well, I better let you go," she said. "Have a good game."

"Yeah, thanks, and I hope Carter has a good game, too. And listen, thanks for the kind words. You have no idea how badly I needed to hear that."

"Ah, really?" she said, with genuine sympathy in her voice.

Reggie Knox was tall and sinewy, and he came to the games dressed sharply, with well-pressed khaki shorts and his Rangers cap square on his head like a drill sergeant, shading a set of BB-pellet eyes. His team looked just as sharp—hats level on their heads and shirts tucked in neatly. I plopped my equipment bag in front of our bench, and my stomach plunged as I watched Reggie's team warm up. My kids were running around the bench playing some made-up variation of tag.

Just as I'd feared, the Rangers pounced on us, racking up nine runs in the first two innings while holding us to only one. When we batted in the third, the Knox twins shut us down completely—three up, three down. As the Rockies straggled out of the dugout to play defense, one boy asked me if he could go to the bathroom. Yes, I said, but hurry up. Then another boy asked to go to the bathroom. Yes, I said again, but hurry up. It dawned on me that some of these kids were losing their attention span and wanted to go to the bathroom for something to do. A minute later, as the inning's first Ranger batter strode to the plate, a third boy asked to go to the bathroom. It was Lance, the boy who'd said the Rockies suck on orientation night, and he was holding his crotch.

"You're kidding me," I said.

He shook his head no, an innocent look on his face.

"Can you hold it?"

He shrugged his shoulders. I took that as a yes.

"I think you can hold it," I said, and pointed to third. "You're the third baseman this inning, so go play that position."

And we took the field. Two batters later, Lance's mom started yelling at me from the sidelines.

"Coach Nick, Coach Nick," she said, stabbing a finger in the air in the direction of third base. "I think we had an accident."

I looked over at third base and saw Lance holding his glove over his crotch. I called timeout and jogged over to third base. Around the spot where he held the glove were wet spots on his pants.

"Lift your glove, buddy," I said.

He shook his head no, this time with a frightened look on his face.

"Oh, boy," I said. "Go see your mom."

He waddled off the field and met his mom on the sidelines, and the two of them skirted toward the bathroom.

I walked back to the dugout, joining Wesley and two other Rockies who'd been assigned an inning on the bench, but they weren't behaving. They were pounding each other in the crotch with baseballs. Each whack to the crotch was followed by the sound of the ball hitting the hard plastic cup, then giggles from all three boys.

"What are you doing?" I demanded to know.

They froze.

"Tell me," I said, my voice growing louder. "Tell me what you're doing!"

"Making sure the cups work," Wesley said, a completely innocent look on his face.

In a blink, I felt all of the frustration from the first few innings and all the stress from the past several days rise to a boil. I felt my voice coming to a crescendo, and I knew I was about to lose it, but I couldn't stop myself.

"You can't do that!" I screamed. "You never, ever touch a teammate! On any part of his body! Especially there!"

Immediately, I knew I'd just made a scene. Silence fell over the entire field, and I sensed that every parent on the sidelines was watching me. I caught a glimpse of Tess, who held her Diet Coke protectively against her chest, gaping at me along with everyone else. I turned my back to the three boys I'd just scolded, took off my hat and wiped my brow. I took a deep breath, but it didn't help.

"Grab your glove, Wes, and run out to third," I said, waving toward the field.

I leaned against the backstop fence to watch the Rangers hit, and soon I felt Marcy's fingers lightly rubbing my back.

"Bad coaching moment," she said. "Relax. It's just a game."

"I know."

"Do you?"

"Yes," I said, irritated at the question. "Just a game. Got it."

She must have sensed my annoyance, because she dropped her fingers and walked back to the sidelines with the other parents. Clearly, I'd gone over the top when the boys were testing out their cups, but it was hard to completely relax as the Rangers piled up the runs. They scored another five in the third, making it 14-1. I figured we had to endure only one more lopsided inning before Reggie called off the dogs and rotated his weaker kids in the infield.

But when the Rangers took the field in the fifth, the Knox twins were still at shortstop and first base, and two of their better players were at second and third base. What the hell was Reggie doing? Wasn't he supposed to lighten up now, give us a chance to score a few runs and go home on a high note? Wasn't that an unwritten rule here? Apparently not for every manager. The Rangers held us scoreless in the fifth, with Wesley grounding to first for the last out of the inning, and as he turned back toward the bench one of the Knox twins sneered at him, "We're killing you guys."

Wesley came to the bench fighting back tears. "Try to ignore him," I said. "Kids can be jerks sometimes, but let me know if it happens again."

At last, Reggie rotated his weaker kids into the infield in the sixth. But by then, losing 19-1, my Rockies were beaten-down and dejected. "When do we get our Players Snack?" two kids asked me, and it was clear they just wanted the game to end. We managed just two runs against Reggie's weaker fielders in the sixth, and the final score was 22-3.

I gathered the Rockies in the dugout and tried to think of something to say to lift their spirits, something hopeful and full of coaching wisdom. But I too was worn down from a lack of sleep and the heinous game that had just ended, and the only thing that popped into my head was the message I'd replayed in my head the night before from my first marathon.

"Listen kids," I said. "I know this was a tough game, but everyone's a winner here."

"We stink," one kid said.

"No," I said, waving a finger at them. "We don't stink. Don't ever say that again."

"I just want my nachos," another kid interrupted. "When do we get our nachos?"

As much as I wanted to recite something inspiring, along the lines of Angelo Tannabaugh for Little Leaguers, I also did not want to press my luck and risk another Bad Coaching Moment. So I waved toward the concession stand. "Just go ahead. Go get your nachos." I wanted an extra moment with Wesley, to make sure he wasn't too down in the dumps, but he was gone in a flash along with his teammates, sprinting toward his date with his Player's Snack.

Still, I was pissed. Not at the kids, but at Reggie. Unlike Big Ed, he'd kept the heat on as long as he could, made a bad game worse than it had to be for a dozen seven- and eight-year-old boys. While he gathered his gear on his bench, I marched over there.

"Hey, Nick," he said, smiling. "Great game."

"Really?" I said. "Great game, huh? You guys slaughtered us."

"Well, I have a strong team. Your guys will come along."

"You're pretty tough yourself," I said. "Did you have to keep your best kids in the infield for five innings?"

"What are you saying?"

"I'm saying you didn't have to keep your best kids in the game until we were completely annihilated. I'm saying you didn't have to send my kids home feeling so bad. They were just begging for their snack at the end. That's what I'm saying."

As a deputy secretary, Reggie must not have been used to being challenged. His head rocked, eyes floating, and I could tell that I'd flustered him.

"I can't believe you're saying that," he said, gaining control of his head once again. "Nobody's ever talked to me like this after a game. Nobody's ever accused me of running up the score."

"I only know what I saw today, and it was ugly."

"You're a hothead," Reggie said. "I can tell you're a hothead. I saw that scene with your kids on the bench today. Everyone saw it. So I'm not going to worry about what you have to say."

I wanted to strangle him, make those BB-pellet eyes pop out of that skinny, drill-sergeant head.

"Okay," I said in my own dismissive tone. "You can spin it anyway you want, but a 22-3 blowout just isn't right, and I hope you think about that. You should think long and hard about it."

I turned and stomped away, and I heard Reggie say, "See you later, hothead."

I stopped in my tracks, but then immediately thought, *Let it go. Keep walking and let it go.* It wasn't easy, but I did.

5
I WANT TO TRY AGAIN

I needed a beer. It was midseason, a Saturday afternoon in early May, and my Rockies hadn't won a single game. Wesley had been invited to a birthday party, so Marcy and I dropped him off and went out for drinks. The party was for Cameron the Cub Scout, with whom Wesley had recently forged a friendship. A few weeks after that painful snubbing by Moose, we'd walked Wesley back down the block again, but this time to Cameron's house, and the two spent half the afternoon scootering together, and since then they'd hooked up at least once a week, sometimes in our driveway, sometimes in Cam's, for a low-key session of scootering or skateboarding. Moose never even bothered walking over to say peep to them.

We chose a new brew pub called Sudzies, a bright strip-mall place with trendy yellow pendant lights hanging above the bar—the kind of pub designed to attract men and women. No sports memorabilia. Instead, the walls were covered with dark-framed, black-and-white photos that looked like they came from a local historical society: State

Street in Harrisburg in the early twentieth century, with the Capitol rotunda in the background; Teddy Roosevelt surrounded by a mob of people on the Capitol steps; a cart and buggy lumbering down Misty Hill's Main Street before it was paved, circa 1880. A faux sense of history, and therefore faux homeyness. I ordered a pint of the Lavish Lager while Marcy ordered the Luscious Lite.

"I'm a little depressed about baseball," I admitted to Marcy as I sipped my lager. "I thought I'd be better at this."

At the midseason mark, we were 0-7-1, with our only tie coming that morning against the Padres, who were managed by Terry Hipple, Wesley's first T-ball manager. A gangly man with mussy hair, Terry had been a good T-ball manager—gentle, but also distracted and spacey. He owned the Misty Hill Diner, which had been in his family for three generations, so he worked ungodly hours, and he even found time to volunteer as our league secretary, all of which probably explained his spacey demeanor. Because Terry was so passive and preoccupied all the time, I'd woken up that morning hopeful that we'd finally get a win, but I rotated my kids evenly, as always, and the game turned out to be a comedy of errors on both sides, ending in a score of 17-17.

"What did you expect?" Marcy said. "You're not a real baseball guy." Her tone was matter-of-fact, and the expression on her face was flat. No compassion whatsoever.

"I know, but I'm still a sports guy, and I know a little about baseball. I thought I could teach these kids something."

"They're young, and it's just a game."

I hated it when she said *it's just a game.*

She took a taste of Luscious Lite, smacked her lips and said, "Maybe you shouldn't manage next year."

"Huh?"

"You shouldn't manage if it causes you this much

stress. Wesley will be fine without you. And besides, you could always be an assistant."

"I couldn't be an assistant if Wesley wound up on Reggie Knox's team. That guy hates me."

"What are the chances he'd end up on Reggie's team?" That flat expression on her face again.

"I don't know," I said with a light sigh. I took another sip of lager.

"Let's talk about something else," Marcy said with a little shake of her head.

"Okay."

"Do you ever think about having another baby?"

I took my time answering. I rocked my head back and forth thoughtfully, as if I might be able to offer a constructive response, but I didn't have one yet. For us, there was no easy answer to this question. So I took a gulp of lager and hoped for the best—hoped we weren't headed down a road where heartstrings wreak havoc.

The very first time Marcy became pregnant, we were both thirty-two years old and living in Center City Philly. I was writing for a fairly popular tabloid called the *Philly Reader*, and she was working for a big public relations firm, and the economy was humming along, so we felt secure enough to start a family. But she miscarried. It happened just before we left for one of my cousins' weddings in Ohio. Marcy's doctor had warned us that she faced a higher-than-usual chance of miscarriage, but we hadn't taken it too seriously—or at least I hadn't. Marcy's uterus wasn't the usual pear shape; it was shaped more like a horn. We'd figured her doctor was issuing her a stock-and-trade warning that he gave a lot of his patients. Besides, a horn didn't sound so bad.

Marcy cried off and on after losing the baby, while I moped over the possibility of a life that would never include sandcastles on the beach or backyard Frisbee tosses with my child. I was also haunted by an image of Marcy and me, old and toothless, my pants pulled up to my rib cage, her legs smothered in varicose veins, consigned to a bench at a nursing home, nothing to say to each other, no one to visit. Grudgingly, Marcy agreed to travel to the wedding in Ohio, but she remained uncomfortable talking about the miscarriage until we arrived at the reception and had some drinks. In a dark corner of the banquet room, she began chatting with my Aunt Donna, my Uncle Wesley's widow. Uncle Wesley was my dad's brother, and he was the closest thing we had to a family hero. Back in the 1950s, he played football at Ohio State, and in 1960 he spent half a season with the New York Jets of the old American Football League before blowing his knee out. Aunt Donna was a Buckeye majorette, a gentle woman who'd once been a beautiful redhead and always maintained her kind, Midwestern personality, and in that dark corner of the banquet room, Marcy opened up to her about how terrible the miscarriage felt. Marcy hadn't known Aunt Donna very well, but it didn't matter. She was Uncle Wes' widow, and she was the right person in our lives at the right moment.

On the way home, while driving through a light rain in Columbus, I reached over and took Marcy's left hand, squeezing gently.

"Do you want to try again?" I asked delicately.

She didn't move her head, just kept her gaze on the sprinkles of rain being brushed aside by the windshield wipers, and paused for only an instant.

"Yes."

When Marcy became pregnant again, her doctor scheduled extra appointments to keep a close eye on her, yet Marcy never seemed convinced that she'd carry the baby to term. She developed a sudden and mysterious aversion to red sauce, even pizza sauce, claiming it gave her indigestion. But I thought anxiety was giving her the indigestion. She became especially uptight before every doctor's visit, but all of the ultrasounds were encouraging and the doctor reassured her there were no signs of any serious problem. There was only one hitch, which the doctor said was to be expected without a pear-shaped uterus: The baby was not settling into the usual head-down position. So a cesarean was scheduled, and I drove Marcy to the hospital on a splendid June morning with a bright sun high in the sky.

At 7:05 p.m., our son was born. Marcy's upper body was screened off from her bloody belly, and I had to stand off to the side, dressed in disposable, pale-blue surgical garb—gown, cap and shoe wrappers. The doctor held the baby up for Marcy to see, and then I was the first to hold him, after the doctor and nurse. I'd read in one of those parental handbooks that a father should make eye contact with his newborn ASAP to begin forming a bond, and so from underneath the puff of my disposable surgical cap, I looked him straight in the eye, but his eyes lacked focus. Those big eyes, bequeathed by his mother. Twenty-one-and-a-half inches. Eight pounds, eleven-and-a half ounces. The nurse said we needed a name.

"I think he looks like a Wesley," I said to Marcy. It was a name we'd kicked around, but never settled on, thanks to Marcy's connection with Aunt Donna, the woman who made a life with Uncle Wes.

Slowly, she turned her head toward us and cracked a weary smile.

"I like it," she said. "Wesley Joseph."

Joseph is my middle name.

"Sounds like a winner," I said.

Late that night, after Marcy had some time to rest, a nurse brought Wesley back to Marcy's room to be with us. The nurse tucked him into a rocking hospital crib, right beside the couch where I was planning to spend the night. Marcy, alone in the hospital bed, finally dozed off, leaving me alone to rock my newborn son. Suddenly, I began worrying about what lay ahead for him, what his life would be like, and whether I'd be able to provide and care for him, control my ego for him, put his needs ahead of my own. As I lay there rocking him in the quiet hospital room, I was overwhelmed with uncertainty. I'd never been so frightened in my life.

Marcy was determined to stay at home with her only son for as long as possible, so she took an extended maternity leave and a year later I found a reporter's job at the *Harrisburg Telegraph*. Harrisburg's cost of living was cheaper and it was an attractive job for a young, one-income family. And because it's the state capital, Marcy knew she could easily find another public relations job when she was ready to go back to work. We looked for a home—not an apartment, but our first *home*—in suburban towns such as Hershey and New Cumberland, and were finally intrigued by a listing on Chestnut Street in Misty Hill. The home was in our price range, just barely, a red-brick Colonial built during the Truman administration. Driving through the neighborhood, as the white steeple from the Methodist Church radiated in my rearview, we saw several girls and boys playing in front of homes with lush green lawns, well-trimmed hedges, and basketball hoops in the driveways. We noticed a grade school just a few blocks away, and we made an offer the next morning. We were plowing on with life, the three of us, no more worries about Marcy's misshaped uterus and whether it was a pear, a horn, an amoeba or whatever.

I guzzled my Lavish Lager, still unsure of how to answer Marcy's question. So I chose the direct route: "No, I haven't thought about another baby. Why, have you?"

"Sure," Marcy said, her big eyes turning plaintive. "We're both thirty-nine years old. If we don't have one now, when will we? Wouldn't you like to give Wesley a little brother or sister? I get so sad when I think about him growing up all alone."

"He's not alone. He has us."

"He won't always have us."

"I guess that's true, but what about your—you know, your uterus. Once a horn, always a horn, right?"

"That was several years ago," she said. "There are always big new strides in the medical field these days."

"Have you talked to your doctor about it?"

"No, but wouldn't Wesley make a great big brother?" Her eyes deepened, a heartfelt expression washing over her face.

"Yes, that's true."

"I'd really love for him to have a little sister. You guys share so much together, baseball and everything. I want a little girl."

"I see."

She slid her beer glass to the right side of the table, as if clearing space for something, even though we were only having drinks and needed no more space. Then she folded her hands together on the table, and I sensed she was about to fire something really salient my way.

"Wesley asked me recently if he'd ever have a little brother," she said. "He was so cute. He said he wouldn't be a mean big brother, like Moose's older brothers. I don't know how he knows those kids are mean, but that's what he said."

I felt a *wump* in my chest. Our only son had been asking for a brother? Jesus. The wump slid to my gut, where it mashed with the lager, remnants of a sausage lunch and something else that felt like fatherly guilt. This lift-my-spirits trip to Sudzies had somehow morphed into a woeful moment, the one when I realized that my young son already suspected, on some level, that his life could turn out lonely and empty.

"Why didn't you tell me that?" I asked, my tone more accusing than I intended.

"I just did," she said, unfolding her hands, as if that should settle it.

"No, I mean, when it happened, when he asked you for a brother. That's a big deal."

"I handled it."

"What did you tell him?"

"I told him that we have no control over whether a baby is a little brother or sister, and he was fine with that. He said he'd be a nice big brother whether it was a boy or a girl, and he was so sincere."

"Did you tell him we couldn't have another baby?" I asked.

"No. I don't remember exactly what I said. I think I said, 'We'll see.'"

"But we *can't* have one, remember?"

She lifted her eyes toward the yellow pendant lights above the bar, ignoring the question. She sealed her lips and trolled her jaw, a look of resolve seizing her face. I raised my glass to my lips, then pulled it back, my insides still too uneasy to stomach a swig of beer. As I placed the half-full glass back on the table, Marcy curled her eyes back toward me and loosened her lips, purposefully.

"I want to try," she said in a can-do tone.

"Just like that? You want to decide this over beers? What about my job? What about the miscarriage? We should think about this, and talk to your doctor."

"I *really* want to try."

Her face hung over the table, eyes beaming, every little freckle radiating warmth and love. I couldn't say no. I had to answer Wesley's plea for a sibling and trust in the medical profession and whatever advances it might offer for our uterus quandary.

"Okay," I said. "I'm in."

She drained her beer and banged the glass on the table.

"Let's go," she said eagerly.

I nodded toward my half-full glass and said, "But I'm not done with my beer."

"Excuse me?"

"Never mind," I said, correcting myself and taking one last swig. "Let's go."

We had an hour before the birthday party would be over. We drove straight home, threw off our clothes and jumped into bed. We kissed passionately for several minutes, but when Marcy reached between my legs, I was completely limp. She rubbed her fingers on me lightly at first, then tried pulling and tugging. Nothing.

"What's wrong?" she said.

"Just a little stress, I guess. No big deal."

"No big deal?"

"Keep trying."

Late-day sun peeked through the blinds, casting streaks of light across the iceberg-blue walls of our bedroom. I tried to ignore my surroundings and concentrate. Yet for some reason, I took note of the framed black-and-whites atop our dresser—Marcy and me on our wedding day, all three of us down the Jersey Shore, Wesley in his T-ball uniform. *Forget everything*, I told myself. *Concentrate*. Marcy reverted to finger-tickling. And then, clearly frustrated, she started tugging and pulling again. Finally, she quit and let out a huff.

"I can't believe this," she said, folding her arms across her breasts. Her face sank.

"I can't believe this either. Maybe God's trying to tell us something here."

"Am I still attractive to you?"

Such a dangerous question, and I knew it came from an honest place deep inside her, a place where insecurities festered. I also knew not to hesitate, even though the honest answer was *yes*.

"Of course."

She yanked the covers up and over her chest, unconvinced.

"Then what's the problem?" she asked pointedly. "Tell me the *real* problem."

"Stress, I think. It's got to be stress. My job, baseball."
"Did you say *baseball*?"

6

WHERE THE FUCK ARE YOU?

*H*illary Clinton came to Harrisburg the following week. It was a Friday, just four days before a Pennsylvania primary that was attracting national attention, and Clinton scheduled a rally on Commonwealth Avenue behind the state Capitol. Now that I was a reporter again, I was one of several staffers assigned to cover it. Despite the national ramifications and my fondness for politics, I loathed the assignment. I was assigned to do crowd interviews and rain was forecast, so I was not looking forward to standing in the rain talking to strangers who would surely repeat the same political platitudes I'd heard many times before. *She has a lot of experience....I like her stance on the issues....Blub blub blub....She'll even save the whales, the bald eagle, and the Canada lynx!* And besides, the Rockies were scheduled to play the next morning, which meant I couldn't stop thinking about baseball.

Police blocked off the street on both sides of the Capitol, and I staked out the line where people were waiting at checkpoints at the south end of the street. The steady rain didn't deter people from turning out by the thousands, and the folks I approached for an interview were eager to be quoted in the paper. I'd brought along a clear plastic bag to protect my notebook from the rain as I jotted down quotes, so the afternoon moved along without any serious problems. Still, I couldn't stop thinking about the fact that the rain meant our game the next day was in serious jeopardy. And because we were scheduled to play Terry Hipple's hapless Padres again, I knew we had a chance of earning our first win. Which I wanted. Badly.

By 4:30 p.m., I had plenty of usable quotes for my sidebar story on the crowd. Though Clinton wasn't scheduled to speak until 5 p.m., I figured she wasn't going to say anything that would change the opinions of the Hillary fans I'd already talked to, so I walked to my car, typed up my story on my laptop, and filed it. As stragglers rushed along the downtown streets to get to the rally before Clinton started speaking, I drove home and donned a poncho and a beat-up pair of Reeboks and walked over to the field to survey the rain damage. It was substantial: big, long puddles along the first- and third-base lines, and another at second base. Most coaches would have called a rainout, but I wanted to play. I checked my watch: 5 p.m. Our game was scheduled for 10 a.m. the next morning, which meant I had seventeen hours to get this mud pit in shape.

Though the rain had slowed to a drizzle, the puddles were too big to seep into the ground overnight. I grabbed an industrial-sized broom and a rake from the equipment shed and went to work on the puddles, sweeping and raking. I worked for more than an hour and figured the field had a chance of drying out by gametime, with a little more work in the morning and a little help from Mother Nature. I walked home sopping wet, my Reeboks caked with infield dirt.

Marcy was home and said my cell phone, which I'd left on the kitchen counter before heading to the field, had been ringing constantly for the past hour. I checked my messages and saw six from the paper's editor-in-chief, Walt McNutt. *Shit*, I thought, *did I miss something?* As I dialed Walt I went to the living room and turned on CNN, and saw a "Breaking News" bulletin and video of police handcuffing people in downtown Harrisburg.

"McNutt here," Walt barked into the phone.

"It's Nick Marhoffer."

"Marhoffer! Where the fuck are you?"

"Um...."

"I've been trying to find you for a fucking hour."

"Um...."

"We got a big fucking story here—a national story."

"I know," I said.

"Well, where the fuck are you? When I couldn't find you, I sent another reporter downtown, and I don't have many bodies to work with these days."

"Something came up," I said. "I...I had to come home."

"Home? You went home? You're supposed to be covering the crowd! I got union goons fighting with pro-life nuts in downtown Harrisburg, and the national media is all over it, and my own crowd reporter goes home? You've got to be fucking kidding me!"

"Um...."

"Get your ass over to the downtown magistrate's office—pronto. Everyone who got arrested is getting arraigned tonight. And my newspaper is going to be on this story like stink on shit. Got it?"

"Got it."

I showered quickly and drove back downtown. The streets were still clogged with post-rally traffic, but I got to the magistrate's office just in time. Eight people had been arrested—four Teamsters and four members of Pennsylvanians For Life, an anti-abortion group that was known to cause trouble outside clinics and other public events. While I'd been tending to the field, the PFL folks had set up on a corner north of the Capitol, with bullhorns and signs calling Clinton a baby killer. The Teamsters, loyal Democrats who never backed down from a fight, had responded by gathering on the opposite corner. After a few minutes of shouting back and forth, the two groups had collided. Nobody had been seriously hurt, but there'd been a lot of pushing and shoving and a few errant punches, and television cameras had captured the whole melee. When it was over, all eight were charged with disorderly conduct, the magistrate set bail at one thousand dollars each, and I was high on Walt McNutt's shit list.

I got home just after midnight, exhausted, yet I hardly slept. Once again, I was worried about my job—how long until Walt would forgive and forget, assuming he was capable of forgiving and forgetting—but at the same time I couldn't help fretting about the condition of the field. At 6 a.m., I gave up on sleeping and got out of bed. I looked out the window and saw clear skies. I made coffee and checked the weather forecast, which called for a nice day, then trudged back over to the field. The infield was still too wet and slippery to play on, so I went back to work with the rake. I was wearing the same muddied Reeboks, which by now felt like combat boots, and my feet started to ache. But by the time I finished raking, the sun peeked out and I felt a glimmer of hope. Yet I also knew this field needed just a little bit more help. So I went back to the equipment shed and stacked five bags of Quick Dry—a granular drying agent—on a wagon. At eighty dollars a bag, the Quick Dry was expensive for a Little League, and if Sam DiNardo knew I was using five bags in one morning he'd have gone ballistic. One bag per game was the league standard. But I didn't care. No one was around yet to see me using it, and I was willing to do whatever it took to get that damned field ready.

I spread the Quick Dry across the infield and whisked the empty bags back to my house to discard the evidence. I stuffed them in the bottom of my trash can, showered and dressed for the game. Three parents called to ask if the game was still on. "Of course," I said to each one. "Why wouldn't it be?" I walked back to the field at 9 a.m., just as the sun began warming the town. The infield dirt was turning to a nice, light brown. The morning sun and the Quick Dry were doing their job.

"Beautiful day," Terry said to me before the game. "I hear you're the man to thank for getting the field ready."

"Anything for Misty Hill baseball," I said.

"I feel bad for not coming over to help," he said. "But I had a long night at the diner, and I thought it was a lost cause after all that rain we got yesterday. I assumed we'd just cancel today."

"Let's play ball," I said.

"Sounds good," he said.

Wesley had his best game of the year, smacking two doubles and accounting for several outs on defense. Though in grown-up baseball one of his doubles might have been scored an error, because a little Padre outfielder basically watched the fly ball drop at his feet, we called it a double in coach-pitch. It was enough to remind me that Wesley had some aptitude for this sport, something I'd first noticed during our father-son catches in the backyard before he began playing T-ball, when he showed significantly better hand-eye coordination than I'd ever had. And we needed every run Wesley could account for, because we finally won a game, a 15-14 squeaker.

Yet surprisingly, I didn't feel much glee after the game, even though the Rockies themselves were jumping all over themselves—to the point where I had to calm them down on the bench and remind them to be good sports. The win consigned me with a much-needed sense of relief, but I also felt bad for Terry, whose team remained winless and didn't seem to have any hope of notching a victory. After all, Terry had been Wesley's first T-ball coach, and I knew what constant losing felt like, how it can pummel the soul.

I met Terry in the infield after the game and we shook hands amicably.

"I'm sorry," I said. "I know that was a tough one for you to lose."

"Oh, well. It was a close one," he said. "So that's good."

"This is a tough business," I said. "I thought the newspaper business was tough, but Little League is a whole different animal."

"Try running a restaurant in this economy," he said, and we both let out little chuckles.

"No, thank you."

"This isn't too bad," he said, changing the subject back to baseball. "The kids are having fun—I think. Or at least I try to make sure they have fun. We talk about it at practice—the fun part—and I remind them about it before and after every game. I think that helps."

"Good idea," I said, and suddenly I felt inferior. It seemed Terry was maintaining a healthier perspective than I was—just trying to have fun, and encouraging the kids to do the same. It was so simple, but I'd lost sight of that part of it somewhere along the way. Sure, I was rotating my kids, ensuring they got equal playing time, trying to teach each one of them the game. But I was letting it wear on me.

I gave Terry a hearty pat on the back and we parted. Then I visited the concession stand, where I found several Rockies sitting together at a picnic table and munching happily on their Player's Snack.

"So," I said, nice and loud. "Are we having fun?"

And they bellowed together: "Yeah!"

I couldn't help but think to myself, *Enjoy it while it lasts, boys.*

7
STAY THE HELL AWAY
FROM THIS WOMAN

A week of sexless nights went by. After I'd failed to perform in bed and do my part to bring another Marhoffer into the world, Marcy and I lived in relative silence. For the first few evenings, we went to separate rooms and read. One night I was stretched out on the couch re-reading Angelo Tannabaugh's classic book—his chapter on coping with losing appealed to me, particularly his ruminations on a biblical passage from Romans stating that "suffering produces perseverance"—as Marcy unloaded the dishwasher. And she unloaded it with vigor, slamming every drawer and cabinet as she stashed away each dish and handful of silverware.

"Do you have to close them so hard?" I asked innocently.

She didn't respond. I heard the clanging of another batch of silverware, then another *Bang!* of the drawer. Then the clatter of ceramic plates being stacked and another *Bang!* of the cabinet door. These bangs, I realized, were her way of sending passive-aggressive signals to me that she was still upset. I didn't say another word. I heard some rumbling in the trash can, then a *Bang!* of the pantry door. I heard the back door open, which meant she was probably taking out the garbage, and a moment later I heard her footsteps in the kitchen again and the back door closed with the most thunderous *Bang!* so far. The whole house rattled.

That night, I fell asleep on the couch watching political talk shows, and I joined Marcy in bed only after waking in the middle of the night to take a leak.

After a few days, the frequency of our conversations increased, but it was still small talk, the kind of brief but necessary conversations that keep a household running. *What do you want for dinner? Can you watch Wesley while I'm at my hair appointment? Your cell phone's been ringing for the past hour—hope it's not your boss.*

And then, when we returned home after notching our first win over the Padres, *Can you fix the latch on the back door?* I'd noticed the broken latch a few days earlier, but I didn't think much of it then. I'd managed to jam it into place and hoped it was one of those things that would end up fixing itself somehow. Besides, home maintenance was always a problem for me. It was another casualty of my lot in life: The children of bad dads are rarely blessed with maintenance skills.

Never had my dad taken the time to teach me how to fix things. In fact, I couldn't recall him putting much work into our house at all. He had, as best as I could remember, two approaches to home maintenance—call a professional or duct tape it. I remember him duct taping a leaky downspout, a loose refrigerator shelf, a cracked toilet seat, even a punctured tire on his shit-brown Ford (though the taped-up tire lasted barely long enough for him to drive to the shop). And then he'd pop open a beer and spend the rest of the day doing what he did best.

So when Marcy asked me to fix the latch, I was flummoxed. I went out and stared at it for a minute, then fiddled with it for another minute, trying to figure out exactly how the thing worked. But I couldn't. And I didn't want to call a professional door and window guy, either, and there was absolutely no way to duct tape it. So I conceived a temporary fix. I rummaged through the garage, found a sturdy piece of wood, measured it to fit in the groove behind the sliding door, and sawed it off. For the time being, at least, we'd lock the door by slipping the wood behind it to block it from opening. Before long, I hoped, the latch would fix itself.

And maybe my sex life would fix itself, too.

I had low expectations for our next game against the Braves, but I was also confident that Big Ed would let up at the end and allow us a couple of good innings. So I was in a half-decent mood. And the weather helped: It was a warm Tuesday afternoon in mid-May, primary Election Day. Down the street from our fields, the Misty Hill Community Building was brimming with blue and red political signs and hosting a trickle of after-work voters who were deciding on judges, school board members, tax collector, sheriff, and a sewer referendum.

Marcy got stuck at work and arrived in the second inning, still wearing her pinstriped black pantsuit and matching Anne Klein pumps. According to our life plan, she'd re-entered the job market when Wesley started kindergarten, and she'd landed a job with a top-notch public relations firm that specialized in legislative issues. I saw Marcy unfold her chair on our side of the field, far down along the third-base line. Normally when she arrived late she came to the bench to check in and give me a peck on the cheek, but not this time. After unfolding her chair, she plopped down in it and appeared ready to stay there for the duration.

I realized then that there were two beautiful women on my mind, and at that very moment they were on opposite sides of the same field. If I looked out to center field, I could see each of them at the same time on the outer edges of my peripheral vision. Marcy on the left, her lovely strawberry blonde hair brushing against her shoulders, her trim legs stretched out and crossed at the ankles, her arms folded in a way that seemed like some sort of angry signal to me. Tess on the right, chatting happily with a mom from the Braves, her Diet Coke bottle swaying gently with her hips as she talked, her big earrings and ruby lipstick glistening in the sun. For a moment, I found the whole scene kind of exciting. Almost enough to give me an erection—well, almost.

The Braves jumped out to a lead, but it never reached double digits, so as the innings moved along I felt like things could have been worse. The thought of leaving the field with a moral victory crossed my mind, until a Brave hit a lazy pop-up near first base in the top of the sixth. Wesley was playing first base at the time. We were losing by eight runs, so the play didn't matter in the larger scheme of things, but still, it must have mattered to Wesley. He dashed in and made a yeoman's effort to catch it, sliding feet-first in an attempt to snag it at his hip just before it hit the ground. But he didn't get there in time. The ball bounced off the ground, careened off his elbow and into foul territory. As the catcher chased after the ball, Wesley writhed in the infield dirt, holding his left elbow and bawling.

It didn't look like a bad injury to me—the ball wasn't hit hard enough to cause serious damage—but I ran onto the field and tended to him as if it were. I wondered if this new sense of tension in our life and all the losing on the field was starting to affect him. Or maybe it was just the nature of being seven years old, such a young age to know how to hold your composure when things go wrong. I figured his pride was hurting more than his elbow, and of course I feared that as a left-hander his pride was more vulnerable to wounding, so I bent over him and calmly rubbed his back, giving him a moment to collect himself. I asked him if he was okay.

"I'm not okay," he groaned, as dirty tears rolled down his cheeks.

"How about some ice?"

I helped him up by his good elbow, and we shuffled off the field together as parents on both sides chimed in with the obligatory applause for an injured player. Wesley finished the game on the bench, wiping his tears and holding an ice-pack on his allegedly injured elbow.

At the end of the game, as the parents packed up their chairs and the first wave of boys sprinted to the concession stand, Tess visited our bench. Wesley was there with me, on my right, still working up the courage to join his teammates at the concession stand. Tess approached from the right side of our bench and bent forward, a motherly gesture, so she was eye-to-eye with Wesley.

"Is Wesley okay?" she asked me as she looked him over. "He took quite a tumble."

"He's fine," I said. "I think he hurt his ego, mostly."

Wesley shot me a look that was part confusion, part embarrassment. I patted him on the shoulder, and he wiped my hand away, which I took as a sign that he was learning when he was being patronized.

"Oh, good," Tess said, just as Marcy appeared on my left.

Marcy held her chair firmly over her left shoulder, the knuckles of her left hand gripped so tight around the strap that they were white. In what seemed like one swift move, she veered past me, wrapped her right arm around Wesley and gave him a kiss on the cheek. She then stood erect, turned toward Tess and held her right hand out stiffly.

"Hi, I'm Marcy," she said to Tess. Her tone was deliberately cordial, with an edge of protectiveness. "I'm Nick's wife."

"Oh, I know," Tess said, shaking hands prudently. "Haven't we met before?"

"I don't think so," Marcy said promptly.

Ever since T-ball, Marcy usually sat alone at the games. She'd find a quiet spot of grass at the edge of the field and set up her fold-up chair and stretch out. She was too smitten with her own son to miss the game, but too uneasy around the other Misty Hill moms to interact with them. She labeled the doctor, lawyer, and lobbyist parents as cliquish and snooty. Marcy was a Jersey girl, from a blue-collar part of Trenton, and though we'd moved to Misty Hill when Wesley was a year old, she still didn't seem comfortable around the locals.

"Well, it's probably my fault we never met," Tess said, "because I'm sure I've seen you around. I'm Tess Sugarmeier, Carter's mom. I was just checking on Wesley. He took such a tumble."

Wesley must have sensed that adult stuff was taking center stage, because he finally asked to go to the concession stand. Marcy nodded yes and gave him another kiss on the cheek.

"It's nice to finally meet you," Marcy said to Tess. She said it with a sense of phoniness that only I could recognize—the pitch of her voice increased slightly and she tilted her head, almost as if talking to a dog.

"Likewise," Tess said. "Your husband's a great coach. He's so good with all the boys. I hope Carter can be on his team every year."

As I stood there between the two women, I was reminded of Rocco, my enchanting neighbor, and the complex web of women entangled in his life. I felt a rush of kinship, as if I'd finally been initiated into some sort of privileged rite of masculine passage, when you find out that multiple women are still attracted to you, even though middle age is right around the corner and your best years are behind you. I forgot, just temporarily, that I was married to one of these women, had a ring and a mortgage and a commitment to her, and a son in the arrangement as well.

I also forgot that Marcy and I had a history that gave her good reason to be distrustful.

———

We'd been discussing the color of the wedding party dresses while walking back to Marcy's apartment after a casual dinner on Walnut Street.

"I like black and gold," I said.

"What?" she said in a voice that sounded partly startled and partly annoyed. "That is the *dumbest* thing I've ever heard." It was the first time I'd seen how quickly she could turn sharply critical if something rubbed her the wrong way.

"Wait, hear me out— "

"No, no," she said. "That is so tacky and redneck."

Until then, I hadn't realized that Marcy's working-class background left her with an insecure side. Her dad was a sheet-metal worker in Trenton, and when his plant shuttered in the 1990s he bounced around in different crappy jobs. Dump-truck driver, contractor's assistant, then a clerk at Home Depot. Marcy's mom was a middle-school English teacher, the family's economic backbone, and Marcy earned her communications degree thanks largely to an academic scholarship at Villanova. Coming from a steel town myself, I knew how it could leave you with a permanent inferiority complex. But black and gold were the unofficial colors of my home region of Western Pennsylvania, the colors of the Pittsburgh Steelers, Pirates and Penguins, each winner of at least a couple of championships in my lifetime. To me, they were colors of hard-earned success, colors that proved that great things can emerge from anywhere—even from the shadows of a downtrodden steel town.

"I'm not having a redneck wedding," Marcy continued. "Where do you want to have it? A fire station up in the mountains? Do you also want plenty of Busch beer and pork rinds on hand?"

What I wanted to suggest was this: predominantly black with touches of gold. Marcy had already mentioned that she liked plain black for the bridesmaid dresses because it was sleek and would complement traditional black tuxedos. So why not dress it up with a little gold? But Marcy waved me off and sped up, walking several paces ahead of me all the way back to her apartment. I decided not to push my luck, though I was confident I'd get a chance to make my case when she was in a better mood. That night, however, we watched *Fargo* on HBO in relative silence and fell asleep without having sex. I didn't worry too much about it at the time, or for the following days; I figured it was just a temporary little spat.

Until my office Christmas party.

I was among the seven or eight staffers who partied until the end. And so was Marianne McGibbons, a little blonde from Northeast Philly with a dimpled smile and perky eyes. She sold ads at the *Reader*, and we usually only saw each other in passing in the stairwell. She dealt out friendly hellos as fast and often as a blackjack dealer doles out cards: "Hel-*lo*!" She must have been one hell of a salesgirl. And she had a reputation as a naughty Catholic girl who slept around.

We were hanging around the bar doing shots of Sambuca. It was a Thursday night at a second-floor bistro on Sansom Street, Otis Redding pumping through the stereo system: *Merry Christmas, baby, sure do treat me nice.* I hadn't seen Marcy for a few days. We'd had a short phone conversation that afternoon, and she told me she had extra work to wrap up before the holidays and was planning to work late. Have fun at your party, she said, though she didn't sound like she meant it. I sensed lingering bitterness over the whole black-and-gold spat.

So after I downed my second shot of Sambuca, I banged my shot glass on the bar, looked up and locked eyes with Marianne McGibbons. It felt like she'd been staring me down first. She was wearing a black sequined cocktail dress with ample cleavage for her sprightly breasts. Outside, the weather was warm for early December, but I had the impression she'd have worn that skimpy dress anyway. I smiled at Marianne and she smiled right back. Her dimples dazzled. Her eyelids danced. Someone ordered another round of Sambuca, and when I looked her way after plunking my next shot glass on the bar, Marianne and I were goggling each other again.

She slid onto the stool beside me and hooted, "Hel-*lo*!"

I could feel myself preparing to do something wrong, but I couldn't tell myself to stop. A woman's charms are a powerful thing, and I must have been more vulnerable to them than I'd ever realized. Let's face it, I was raised almost solely by a woman and I couldn't resist their attention. And booze dulls the conscience and exposes vulnerabilities. I thought about Marcy, but my first calculation was whether she'd find out if I misbehaved with this adorable little blonde. Highly doubtful. She'd been so pissy—and about what, a touch of gold in a wedding?—that she'd refused to show up at my Christmas party. Maybe the liquor poisoned my reasoning, but I wondered if I deserved a little pre-wedding fun.

Sometimes life doesn't give us a chance to save ourselves.

Marianne's eyes fluttered. Her dimples beckoned.

"You're the cutest girl in the place," I told her.

"You're awfully cute yourself."

"Wanna blow out of this popsicle stand?"

Marianne cocked her head and flashed a guilty smile. "Sure."

I tossed a twenty on the bar, took her by the hand and we grabbed our coats.

"I have a boyfriend," she said as we stumbled outside.

"So what?" I said, wrapping my arm around her waist. "So do I—a girlfriend, I mean."

"But we live together," she clarified. "So we can't go to

my place."

"Then we'll go to mine," I winked.

So we hailed a cab to my apartment, where I'd accidentally left the heat on high, despite the unseasonably warm temps, and we had the wildest, sweatiest sex I've ever had. Thanks, no doubt, to all the alcohol, I showed significantly more endurance than usual, and we did it in multiple positions: missionary, spoon, leg-lift, figure-eight, straddle my saddle, and when I finally climaxed we were in the face-to-face fandango. I rolled off of her into my damp sheets, feeling alcohol-induced sleep coming on hard and fast, but before I dozed off I heard her pick up my bedside phone and punch the buttons. She called a cab and dressed hurriedly.

"Sorry I can't stay," she said as she yanked on her black pumps. "But I have a very jealous boyfriend at home."

I woke up the next morning with dry mouth and a thudding headache, no pillows on the bed. They'd been thrown somewhere during our romp. My boxer shorts hung on the headboard. The guilt sank in heavy as I staggered to the kitchen sink and chugged a glass of water: *Oh, God, I just cheated on my fiancé.* That thought didn't mix well with the warm tap water and traces of Sambuca that still lined my stomach. I barfed in the sink.

The following weekend, Marcy slept over at my apartment after we'd resolved our dispute over wedding colors—we settled on plain black dresses and traditional black tuxes, though the groomsmen and I would wear white-rose corsages with a thin gold ribbon. We'd spent the evening at a bar on Rittenhouse Square, then made love and fell asleep and woke up late the next morning. Marcy had dozed off with her contacts in, so when she woke up she tried to blink the dryness out of them. One of her contacts popped out. She searched for it along the edge of the bed, then hopped out of bed and scoured the carpet. She was an all fours, still naked, alongside the bed, when she reached underneath for something. She gasped and sprung to her knees.

She held up a pair of lacey red underwear. The look on her face suggested she wanted to shoot me.

"Who the fuck do these belong to?"

With one glance, Marcy brought me back to reality. It was a quick and discreet look of warning as I stood between her and Tess, a look that turned to a glare, a look that said, *I don't want this woman around.* I realized then that these two women had spent just enough time on post-game pleasantries—fake as they were—and it was time to wrap up this conversation and split them up.

"Thanks for checking on Wesley," I said to Tess. "Now, I've got to get moving, got to get all this gear packed up and make sure everything's kosher at the concession stand."

"Of course," Tess said, and she waved at us both and walked away.

When Tess was about twenty paces away, Marcy turned her back and mumbled in a thick Jersey accent, an accent that I only heard from her when she was feeling feisty: "Bye, bye, and stay the hell away from my husband."

I realized then that Marcy wasn't so much angry at me as she was hurt by my failure to perform and do my part to expand our little family, and the rush that I'd felt moments earlier over my own masculinity dissipated. I remembered the night before the season when I'd had trouble getting it up while I was stressed about the drunk grandfather and foul-mouthed Little Leaguer, among other things. Marcy seemed to take it personally that night, interpreting my limpness as a sign that I no longer found her attractive. This time she reacted differently, more outraged at my comment about baseball than anything else, and so I hadn't put two and two together during the past week. But I should have realized that she was thirty-nine years old now, and the big forty mark was weighing on her mind, her self-consciousness running deeper.

No doubt, Marcy was still a beautiful woman, but she must not have completely realized it. Her face was still fresh, with only slight creases developing, and her body was still toned, with only a slight roll around her belly. Still, Tess Sugarmeier was strikingly attractive and appeared to be a few years younger than Marcy and me. Tess must have seemed like stiff competition, especially for a woman who couldn't figure out how to get her own husband stiff in bed.

With the equipment packed away, Marcy and I strolled joylessly toward the concession stand, just the two of us crossing the grassy field together. I was feeling beaten-down and blue, in no mood for further confrontation, but she still seemed to be in a cross mood. She told me everything she knew about Tess Sugarmeier, things she'd picked up talking to people around town, none of it good.

Tess's husband was Joe Sugarmeier, a powerful lobbyist in Harrisburg, and he was never home. He lobbied for gambling and fracking interests and worked nights and weekends, and he was often seen eating and drinking in downtown Harrisburg with lawmakers and their aides, sometimes the young female aides. No wonder Tess had her eye on other men. Tess had been a cheerleader in high school, and there was a rumor that she'd reconnected via the Internet with one of her high school sweethearts a few years back, and another rumor that she once made a pass at one of her married neighbors, and another that her breasts were fake. And on top of it all, she didn't even watch her son's games—she just jibbered and jabbered like she was at some big social event.

"You're gorgeous," I blurted out. "Do you know that?"

Marcy jerked her head toward me, clearly stunned.

"What?" she said. "Where did that come from?"

"You're totally gorgeous. You have no reason to be jealous of anyone. It's not your fault—you know, my problem. It's my fault. I'm sorry."

"Oh."

Her big eyes flashed, and I could tell her mind was racing but she didn't know how to respond to my sudden change in demeanor. She'd been poised for a fight and instead stumbled into an apology. And more than that—an apology that followed a sincere compliment about her good looks. I hadn't planned it that way, but it just came out, and it immediately struck me as the best way to forge a truce. Even for a tough public relations pro like Marcy, it was hard to do anything now but surrender.

"Have you thought about going to the doctor?" she asked, leering down at her flip-flops as we walked.

"No, not really," I said, blinking at my own dirty gray Nikes. "Well actually, yeah, once or twice. But it just happened once, and I'm pretty sure it's just stress, so I thought I'd give it a little time."

We stopped in a patch of grass about fifteen yards from the crowded concession stand, and I felt her gaze on me, so I lifted my head to meet it.

"It's happened more than once," she said. "This is the second time."

"Wait a minute," I said, cracking a smile as I sensed an opportunity to shift the conversation into lovable banter. "The other time was just a little delay. That shouldn't count."

"A big delay." Her eyebrows shot up as her eyes widened. She nodded knowingly.

"Okay, maybe. But I'm not counting that one."

"I am," she said, though at least she was smiling now, too.

8
WE CAN STILL HAVE
SOME FUN HERE

*I*n our season finale, we played Reggie Knox and his mighty Rangers again. It was a cloudy Saturday afternoon in early June, and I went into the game braced for a blowout. I kept reminding myself about Terry Hipple's mantra about having fun and swore to myself I'd hammer home the Fun message, especially after the game. I told my assistant, a helpful and pleasant guy named Gene Murchie, not to let me near Reggie Knox, no matter how he managed or what he did.

In the first, Wesley was playing second base when I saw him positioned too far to his right. By now I'd learned that Wesley, as a lefty, wasn't supposed to play second base, but I kept putting him there a few innings anyway, because it offered a short throw to first base and he was one of my more capable fielders. In coach-pitch baseball, I figured, any level of competence was a valuable thing, regardless of whether you're lefty or righty. I waved at him and called out: "Wesley, three steps to your left." As he shuffled over, he tripped over his own feet and hit the dirt. He didn't fall hard—it was more of a crumple—but he didn't get up. I called time and ran out to tend to him.

"My elbow," he cried.

"I think you're fine."

"No, my elbow."

"Get up and shake it off. I think you're fine."

"Okay," he blubbered, and climbed to his feet.

When the game resumed, Wesley was still playing up the elbow injury, nursing it with his other arm while fighting back tears.

"Wesley!" I screamed, and as the words came out of my mouth I sensed the edge in my voice, but I also I couldn't stop myself. "You're coming out of the game if you don't stop it. Now, shake it off and play baseball!"

Big mistake. Wesley started wailing. I called timeout, turned to my bench and told one of my reserves to run out and play second. "Get in here," I yelled to Wesley.

With two outs and the bases loaded, the batter hit an easy roller to second, but the boy who'd replaced Wesley was one of my weakest players, and he fumbled it. Two runners scored. I cringed: Wesley would have made that play. I turned and looked at Wesley as he sat on the bench, another ice pack pressed to his elbow, the familiar dirty tears streaked across his face. *Bad Coaching Moment*, I told myself. *Try to relax and have fun.*

Wesley re-entered the game in the second when it was his turn to bat. No surprise there: By now I'd learned that nothing cures a boy's injury—real or imagined—like his turn at bat. Wesley singled and scored a run, and I thought, *Okay, we can still have some fun here.* The score wasn't too bad yet. We were down 6-2.

In the third, the Rangers went on an offensive rampage. They scored seven runs, several on our errors. The seventh run scored when our third baseman, Trevor Murchie, my assistant's son, booted an easy grounder with the bases loaded. Trevor whipped off his glove, threw it on the ground, then kicked it into the grass. Trevor was normally a well-behaved and even-tempered kid, and I wondered if this long and frustrating season had gotten to him, too. I pulled him aside and told him he was benched for the next inning because of his little outburst.

Trevor was back in the game in the fifth when he smacked a double to left-center. The Rangers' center fielder bobbled it, and Trevor darted for third. The outfielder gained control and heaved it to third, and the third baseman scooped up the ball after two hops and tagged Trevor out. Trevor jumped up and stood on the base and started screaming, "I'm safe!"

"Trevor, come on in," I said. "You're out, pal."

"I'm safe!"

"No, you're out. You have to come in."

"I'm safe!"

"Listen, it was a close play, and you really hustled, but you're out. Let's go."

"I'm safe!"

I turned toward his dad, Gene, my loyal assistant, and said, "You want to try?" Gene jogged out to third and leaned into Trevor's ear. He whispered to his son for a minute, and Trevor responded by howling even louder, "I'm safe!" Gene waved for me to come out from the dugout. Reggie Knox came out of his dugout, too, and the three of us huddled around a hysterical Trevor at third base.

"He didn't get nearly enough sleep last night," Gene said, an apologetic look on his face. "He had a sleepover."

Reggie twisted his head in my direction and asked, "You allow sleepovers before games?"

"Um—I guess," I stammered. "I never even thought about it. How do you disallow them?"

"I tell my parents no sleepovers before games," Reggie said matter-of-factly.

"We're getting sidetracked," I said, and rubbed Trevor's

back. I told the boy: "I know that it's no fun getting out, buddy, but it's part of the game."

Trevor crossed his arms and locked them in place. He tightened his face and shook his head no.

"He's got to come off," Reggie said. "It would set a bad precedent to let him run."

"I know, Reggie," I said, annoyed at his rulebook attitude during a boy's meltdown. "I never suggested otherwise."

"I'm just saying," Reggie said.

"We'll just have to carry him off," Gene said, and Reggie backed away.

"Works for me," I said. "You grab his feet. I'll get him up high."

"Why do I have to get his feet?" Gene asked.

"You're his dad," I said. "If he starts kicking, it's your problem." Then I turned to Reggie and said, "You're not going to help?"

"You can handle it," Reggie said.

"Fine," I said to Gene. "Let's go."

Gene bent down and corralled his son's feet as I grabbed him around the shoulders, and we hauled Trevor away. He didn't kick much, but he twisted and jerked and continued yelling, "I'm safe!" When we set him down feet-first at the dugout entrance, he ran right back out to third base. Gene and I looked at each other, stupefied. Neither of us said a word, but we dutifully followed Trevor. And we carried him off again. This time we took him to Gene's car. We loaded him head-first into the backseat.

"I think we'll go straight home," Gene said. "I'm really sorry about this."

"Do whatever you have to, and don't worry about it," I said. "It's not like the game is on the line."

I felt numb. And I certainly wasn't having fun. Quite the opposite. But I also knew the sixth and final inning was right around the corner, and I knew Reggie would finally insert his weaker players in the infield, and so I knew there was a fair chance we could finish this dismal season by scoring a few runs, at least.

Our first batter in the sixth reached first on an error, but the second batter popped out to first. Our third batter reached base on a single, but our next batter popped out to shortstop. Then came Wesley, who drilled one at the third baseman. The fielder couldn't handle it, and everyone was safe. Bases loaded, two outs. We still hadn't scored a run in the inning, and anxiety lapped over me. After Wesley came one of my eight-year-olds, a big and lanky kid named Mason, and I knew he had a fair chance of knocking in a couple of these runners.

"Two outs!" I hollered, pacing, arms swinging. "Everyone's running on contact. The ping of the bat! Run hard!"

Mason slapped a hard grounder to the second baseman's right. The fielder stabbed at it and slowed it, and the ball trickled toward second base. I looked for Wesley, who'd been on first, hoping he could race to second before the fielder. But Wesley wasn't there. We had no runner in the base paths. No one. But I was certain Wesley had been on first. What the hell?

The second baseman gained control of the ball and looked around for someone to tag, but he seemed just as confused as I was. Finally, I saw Wesley running down the first-base line through the outfield. He appeared headed toward the bathroom, holding his crotch as he ran. Reggie yelled for his fielder to step on second base, but I didn't even bother calling for Wesley. After another shout from Reggie, the baffled little fielder stepped on second. Three outs. Game over. Season over. It ended just as my son reached the bathroom and darted inside.

For a moment, I felt anguished, and I dropped my head in my hands. Then came a rush of relief that the season was finally over, then the realization of exactly how it had ended. And I started chuckling. And soon I was laughing—loudly, and I couldn't stop. Something about the odd confluence of events—my own son's dash to the bathroom, after loading Trevor into the car, after Wesley tripped over his own feet—made me crack up. Parents began arriving in our dugout to greet their little Rockies, and some of them were laughing, too. Some were just shaking their heads. I still couldn't stop laughing. I scanned the small crowd, covered my mouth to hide my laughter, and did what I could to accept responsibility—like an adult. I simply said, "I'm sorry."

I was sorry for more than my laughing fit. I was sorry we'd gotten walloped so often, sorry their kids weren't going home feeling good about themselves. I was sorry for my Bad Coaching Moments, sorry I wasn't a Real Baseball Guy. But despite my mea culpa, the mood in the dugout was lighthearted—some of the Rockies were even giggling themselves, though I suspect they didn't know exactly what they were laughing at. They only knew some of the adults were chuckling, and of course, laughing is contagious.

I learned something valuable about coaching in that moment: Teams really can take on the personality of a coach. Mine had. And my own son, especially. I was sorry for that, too—sorry that I didn't realize it sooner. We'd become increasingly tense and emotional as this miserable season had dragged on, and then we finally erupted with an unexpected burst of giddiness at the end. I should have known better, should have seen it coming, should have adapted better. But I didn't. Sometimes experience is your best teacher.

After I packed our equipment, slung the bag over my shoulder and started toward the concession stand, Tess met me at the edge of the field.

"I know you guys didn't win much," she said, "but I want you to know that Carter enjoyed this season. Thank you for everything. I'm so glad you were his coach."

"He's such a nice boy," I said, not knowing what else to say.

She pulled a vanilla envelope from her purse and handed it to me.

"Just a little token of our appreciation," she said.

"You didn't have to do that."

"Yes, I did. I know he's not the best player out there, but I hope you coach again next year, and I really hope Carter can be on your team."

We parted ways, and I peeked into the envelope on the way to the concession stand, where Marcy was hovering over a picnic table of giddy Rockies. Inside the envelope was a thank you card with a one-hundred-dollar gift card to Red Lobster and a handwritten message: *Thanks so much for everything, Love, Tess.* Obviously, Carter's dad, whom I still had never even seen, earned a nice living as a lobbyist, and more likely than not, he spent little time at home. Not so obvious was this—What the hell was Tess's real message here?

I stuffed the card back in the envelope and tucked it in my back pocket, but as soon as I got to the concession stand Marcy started grilling me like a Philadelphia lawyer.

"What were you looking at over there?" she asked.

"What? Where?"

"You were looking at a card or something and your jaw dropped. You stuck it in your back pocket. What is it?"

"Huh?"

"Your back pocket," she said, reaching around my waist. "What's in there?"

I wiggled away so she wouldn't be the one to pull it out, and said, "Oh, this."

Left with no choice, I slid the card out of my pocket and shrugged both shoulders innocently. "Just a card from a parent."

She yanked it out of my hand. "Then why did your jaw drop?"

Her eyes bulged as soon as she read it. "What the hell?" she sniped.

"Shh," I said. "There are kids around."

For a second, I wondered if a strategy of naivete would get me out of this—act as if it was a completely innocuous gesture and my darling wife should offer up some bland and equally innocuous comment: *Oh, isn't that nice*! But Marcy was no dummy, and she'd already been attuned to where my eyes had been wandering and those waves of sexual tension that were whirring all around.

"Love?" Marcy spouted. "Why did she sign this 'love?'"

"I don't know. Some people sign all their cards that way, don't they?"

"Not to married men. And what does 'everything' mean? Why is she thanking you for 'everything?'"

"I don't know. Everything I did for the Rockies, probably."

"And the *love*?"

I threw my hands up in front of my shoulders, palms out, defensively.

"Tell me something," Marcy said, flicking the whole packet back to me, card and all, but the empty envelope escaped my fingers and twirled to the ground. "Why is it that some women in this town are so enamored with my husband but hardly even speak to me?"

I didn't bother answering as I bent down to pick up the envelope. Marcy had just flashed a mix of emotions that I wasn't accustomed to from her. At first I felt a crash of guilt: I'd hurt her. She was an innocent bystander who had reason to feel plowed over by an unthinking husband, and the memory of Marianne McGibbons may have given her reason to suspect the worst. But I didn't have time to self-loathe for long, because Wesley suddenly appeared in front of us, a dab of mustard on his chin, and added yet another layer of complexity to a horribly uncomfortable final post-game moment.

"Can Carter come over to our house to play today?" he asked innocently.

Now, complete distress. Wires in my brain crossed and sizzled. One wire carried the information about how eager we were for our only child to make friends, and though he'd befriended Cam the Cub Scout, another friend would be nice. The other wire transmitted this simmering animosity that Marcy was feeling toward Carter's mom—and by extension, me.

I stammered: "Umm—"

"No," Marcy snapped. "We're too busy. Play with Cam today."

Wesley's face melted.

"Maybe," I said diplomatically, "we can do something else fun today."

"But I thought we were busy," Wesley moaned.

Marcy curled her lips shut and stared off in the distance. Her unspoken message to me: You made this mess, so clean it up yourself, buster.

"Um," I muttered. "I guess we're too busy for some things, but not for others. Does that make any sense?"

"No," Wesley said flatly.

"I guess it doesn't," I said, but I didn't want to feel like the bad guy any longer, and I was also realizing there was no good way to end this. "But that's what your mom said, so deal with it."

We walked home single-file—Marcy first, followed by Wesley, me in the rear—and in complete silence. As soon as we got there, I chucked the whole packet from Tess in the trash, gift card included, and Marcy never asked about it again.

If only we could dispose of the intangible so easily.

Two weeks later, Father's Day weekend. We decided to get out of town. Things had settled at my job—the rumor mill had stopped churning with any more news of cutbacks—and we thought a little weekend trip would help us forget a stressful spring. As my Father's Day gift, Marcy bought us tickets to see the Pirates play an interleague game at Camden Yards in Baltimore against the Orioles, the same match-up as in the World Series in 1971 and 1979. Wesley had started showing an interest in history, so we drove to Baltimore on Saturday morning and visited Fort McHenry, where the Americans deterred a British assault in the War of 1812, and we booked a room Saturday night at the Lord Baltimore Hotel. The Lord Baltimore was a classic, Art Deco hotel where the Pirates had stayed for the World Series. I used the opportunity to introduce Wesley to some great names of Pirates history— Roberto Clemente, Willie Stargell, and Steve Blass. As we strolled through the hotel's grand lobby imagining we were rubbing shoulders with the greatest Pirates of my youth, Wesley seemed interested in the stories I weaved about those old ballplayers, even though he struggled to pronounce Clemente's name right. He said it more like "Clennety."

The next afternoon, a gorgeous Sunday filled with sunshine and high skies, we had good seats along the third-base line. For the first time in his young life, Wesley sat contentedly and watched an entire professional baseball game. Previously, he'd lost interest mid-way through and begged for visits to the concession stand, souvenir stand or bathroom—a couple times each. But on this day, the three of us sat relaxed in the warm sun at Camden Yards, with trickles of sweat on our skin, and examined the game and all of its little details—how the batters warmed up, where they planted their feet in the batter's box, where the fielders positioned themselves, and why the third-base coach kept making so many frenzied hand signals. Tied five to five, the game went into extra innings, but Wesley showed no signs of discontent. Instead, he snickered when I described the extra inning as "free baseball," and he was only slightly upset when an Oriole won the game with a run-scoring double in the bottom of the tenth.

At home that night, Marcy and I had slow, cautious sex, the kind young lovers have when they're still getting to know each other, the kind I had in high school in the backseat of an old Ford in the dark hills outside of Johnstown. Afterward, Marcy and I lay in bed naked and tired and chatted quietly, affectionately.

"So how did that happen?" Marcy asked, her tone pleasantly surprised.

"I don't know. It just happened."

"It doesn't just happen."

"I'm no doctor, but I really think it was just stress."

"Right," she said sarcastically. "Your baseball season's over."

"Not just that," I said. "Work's been better, too."

"So that was your first erection in what, five weeks? Six?"

"Actually, no," I said. "I had one in the middle of the night at the hotel last night."

"Oh, really?" she chuckled.

"I wanted to tap you on the shoulder and wake you up, but I thought better of it with Wesley in the bed across from us."

She giggled again, and we left it at that. Good thing she didn't pursue the matter further. I sure as hell didn't want to let on that I couldn't remember what—or whom—I'd been dreaming about when I popped that erection in the hotel.

9
CAN YOU TEACH A KID
HOW TO CATCH A BREAK?

On October 1st, the first day of the new quarter, Walt McNutt called me into his office, and I knew right away that he had bad news for me. A short ex-marine who wore a graying buzz-cut, Walt exuded no sympathy. He didn't bother straightening his tie or donning his suit jacket, as he often did for important business matters. His tone was matter-of-fact. Revenues were plummeting, and the economic forecast was bad, he told me. The global financial meltdown had begun just a few weeks earlier, and the stock market had crashed, and business executives were scrambling to cover their bottom line amid signs of a deep recession. For newspapers, the meltdown served up a double whammy because they'd already been losing money as readers and advertisers flocked to the Internet. My newspaper was laying off 10 percent of the newsroom, and this time I didn't have enough seniority to save me. In other words, the Great Recession punched me with its right fist just as the Great Newspaper Decline socked me with its left.

"And another thing," Walt said, his tone changing toward mild annoyance. "You never did give me a good explanation for why you disappeared during the Clinton rally. So there was no way I was going out on a limb for you."

So as the recession and newspaper decline delivered their one-two, I also got a kick in the shin thanks to my Great Obsession With Youth Baseball.

"I don't have a good explanation for that," I mumbled at Walt.

"What's that? Speak up," he said.

"Never mind," I said.

Walt gave me the whole day to clean out my desk and say my goodbyes, but before I did I called Marcy.

"Oh, God," she said. "I was afraid it was coming. Oh, God."

"It's okay," I said. "It'll be okay."

"What a bad day. I have a big meeting with a bitchy client in an hour, and now this."

"There's a severance," I said. "But it's not great. One week for every year I worked here."

"Better than nothing, I guess, but still. This is so shitty."

"I can collect unemployment for a while, at least. And we have your health plan."

"I know, but this is a terrible market for you to be looking for work in," she said. "I'll start putting out feelers for you. Are you okay?"

"I think so."

As I cleaned out my desk, another reporter named Wendy Rogers, a petite, unmarried forty-something, came out of Walt's office and burst into tears. Other reporters and editors quickly surrounded her, consoling her. I didn't want that kind of sympathy or attention, and I didn't want to see a whole day of scenes like that, so I hurried to pack my things—photos of Wesley and Marcy, a mini-tape recorder and a handful of mini-cassettes, award plaques from the Pennsylvania Press Association, a Steelers bobblehead—and I said some awkward goodbyes to my colleagues. It was late morning when I walked outside, and a warm autumn sun was beating down on the city. I resented the sun. This was a gloomy day for me—how dare it pretend otherwise? I loaded my things into my car and walked around the corner to the Harrisburg Brew Pub. I thought about calling someone for companionship— Rocco came to mind, partly because he was connected and personable and could rattle off at least a short list of options I could explore—but I felt like being alone. I ordered a beer and a jerk chicken sandwich and watched a television above the bar showing an ESPN talk show with the volume on mute.

I'd never lost a job before, and I hadn't prepared for this moment. I should have, but I didn't. I hadn't networked for other jobs, hadn't taken classes to prepare for another career, hadn't even thought much about what I'd do if the newspaper ax fell on me. Marcy had a good job, and maybe in the back of my mind I knew I could rely on that, and maybe that's why I never thought much about my second career. Because newspapers everywhere were in the same financial predicament, I knew the odds of finding another newspaper job were slim to none. I had absolutely no idea what I'd do next.

I drove home and took a nap, then walked over to Wesley's school at 3 p.m. I felt a need to be with my family and wanted to walk him home. I told him about my job, and he bombarded me with questions. He was old enough to understand something like this, and he seemed genuinely concerned. *How will we get money to pay our bills? Can you get another job? Will we have to move? Will I have to leave my school and my friends?* I told him that his mom still had a good job, and I'd find another one soon enough. No, we wouldn't move. In the meantime, I'd be home with him more often, which meant more time for things like hiking and fishing. When we got home, we grabbed our gloves and moseyed out back and played catch together. We didn't say much as we tossed the ball lazily back and forth. I knew hard times lay ahead, but after a while, as I broke a slight sweat in the afternoon sun while enjoying the sound of a ball smacking leather, things seemed just a little better, if only for those few moments.

When I put Wesley to bed that night, he had the same series of questions as when I'd picked him up at school. *Are you sure we won't have to move? Are you sure I won't have to leave my school and my friends?* I tried my best to reassure him, then crawled in bed with him and stayed there until he fell asleep. After I tiptoed out of his room, I found Marcy sitting on the front stoop in the darkness. The night was turning chilly, and she was bundled in a sweatshirt with a glass of chardonnay in her hand. I sat down beside her and noticed she'd been crying. For the first time all day, after realizing the full extent to which my family was affected by my job loss, I felt a flood of shame wash over me. I rubbed Marcy's back, and she wiped her eyes dry with her wrist.

"Everything will be fine—eventually," I said softly.

"You'll find something soon," she said. "I just know it. You're very marketable. I must have told a dozen people today to keep an eye out for something for you."

I knew something else was bothering her, but I didn't want to mention it; this wasn't the right time. She was now our family's only bread-winner, so we were faced with another reason not to have another baby. And because she would soon turn forty, she was now faced with the reality that we probably never would have that second child.

That night, many things thrummed through my head as I lay awake in bed, wondering what the future held for me and my little family. I thought a lot about my dad, Mick Marhoffer, the family drunk. He'd lost his accounting job at the steel mill when it shut down, then he almost lost his next job crunching numbers at the hospital, when his drinking problem was at its worst. My mom almost left him a few times. On some level, I'd known things were bad, even when I was young, but he was still my dad, and I accepted his flaws without casting judgment.

Like my dad, I'd lost my job in a dying industry. We had that much in common. But as I lay in bed that night fretting over my future, I realized that I did not want to be like him in any other way. None whatsoever. But I couldn't help feeling like a loser myself, a guy who'd just lost a modest job at a medium-size newspaper in a small city, a guy who was destined to catch the bad breaks in life, and what really, really bothered me as my head rolled back and forth across my pillow was the thought that my only son might turn out like me.

Can you teach a kid how to catch a break?

———————

Surprisingly, the next weeks and months went by quickly. I experienced a few severely mopey days after the initial jolt of losing my job, but then my mood improved to a steady state of moderate dampness, thanks largely to the realization that the old safety net, unemployment compensation, would keep our family afloat for a while and give me some time to transition to another job. I also found that days spent at home, searching job boards and doing domestic duties, were more pleasant than those days spent dealing with bastards like Walt McNutt. I busied myself by getting Wesley off to school in the mornings, loading and unloading the dishwasher, folding laundry and going on long runs. I mailed resumes out in bunches—to public relations firms, lobbying firms, and newspapers that had a bureau in the state Capitol. I also exchanged emails with old colleagues and contacts from the newspaper, and sometimes I'd meet someone for lunch around the Capitol. I had one lunch with a top aide to a senator, who Rocco had set me up with, but the aide told me that a budget crunch at the state level meant hiring was on hold in most offices, which left me only mildly disappointed because I wasn't sure if I was ready to go work for the government. If I was lunching with someone who wasn't a potential employer, such as an old newspaper friend, I might have a beer or two, and I'd come home and nap in the afternoon. I also clipped coupons and did the grocery shopping, and I canvassed Marshall's and T.J. Maxx for pre-Christmas bargains. Marcy and I had scaled back our spending in several other ways—dropping the premium cable package, depositing less in Wesley's college fund, eating out less, and buying cheaper brands of beer and wine—and we seemed to be getting by just fine.

My first job interview was in November with a public relations firm. It was a Philly-based firm with an office in downtown Harrisburg, and the director of the Harrisburg office was an old colleague of Marcy's. Her name was Sandy Gates, a leather-skinned, thirty-something overachiever who'd been a star legislative aide for Senate Democrats while in her twenties. Her office specialized in government issues, with clients such as the Trial Lawyers Association and several casinos. The interview was in Sandy's sprawling office on the top floor of the Strawberry Square office complex, and the whole office smelled like stale coffee. The interview seemed to be going fine until she raised the topic of damage control.

"So tell me," Sandy said in her gravelly voice, sipping from a large cup of Starbucks. "How would you handle this scenario: One of our casino clients is unfortunate enough to suffer a scandal—let's just say a top executive is charged with a crime, and the gaming board is considering whether to revoke his state license to work for the casino. The newspapers are covering the story intensely, and it looks very bad for our client. How would you mitigate the damage?"

I leaned back and rubbed my chin. I'd never thought

about something like this before. "Hmm," I said.

After a short pause, I added, "What's wrong with just telling the truth? Fess up to what the guy did and the casino's plan for dealing with him. I know it sounds simple, but I've always been a big fan of being straightforward."

Nodding agreeably, Sandy puffed out a little chuckle. "Sure," she said in a way that sounded as if she didn't really mean it. "The truth. We're always interested in telling the truth, but in a way that mitigates the damage. How would you mitigate the damage?"

"Mitigate the damage?" I said, accidentally letting a trace of sarcasm into my tone. "Well, what a term. I'd hope the truth would mitigate the damage. If not ... boy, I don't know. I would just hope the truth would do the job."

"Sure," she said, a touch of condescension grazing her voice. "I'm sure it would."

She set down her coffee and clicked her tongue, and I knew I wasn't getting this job. I also knew I didn't want it.

At home, Marcy was eager to hear all the details about the interview. She came home from work and plunked her purse on a kitchen stool and instructed me to tell her everything as she yanked a pack of chicken breasts from the fridge. I withheld no detail, not even my fumbling of the question about mitigating the damage.

"I should have known Sandy would ask that," Marcy said. "She is so by-the-book. I'll help you come up with a better answer for that question. We'll come up with a killer answer."

"I'm not sure I want a better answer to that question," I said.

"Why not? You'll need one." She pulled a knife from the drawer and started cutting the fat from the chicken on a wooden block.

"I'm not sure I want a job like that. I can't spin for a living—or lie."

"It's not lying," she said, and sounded offended. "And

you know better than that. Why would you say something like that?"

"I'm just saying—it's not for me."

"I know a lot of old newspaper people who go into public relations," she said testily. "And so do you. It's a natural career path. Don't be so high and mighty."

She was hacking at the fat now—finishing each slice with a *Clat!* on the wood block.

"Don't take it personally, but I don't think I have the right mentality for it."

"Then tell me," she said, slamming the knife on the counter. "What the hell do you think you're going to find?"

My eyes bulged, and though I was relieved the knife was out of her hands, I still found myself backing away. "Good question," I said.

10
BAD FAMILY MOMENT

*S*o there was damage that needed mitigation in my marriage. Though Marcy had been supportive through the early stages of my unemployment, my rejection of a public relations career changed all that. Her personality turned chilly, just as it had when I'd had trouble getting it up for her. Once again, our conversations were mostly relegated to small talk. *When are you going grocery shopping? What about that Nerf gun Wesley wants from Santa? Can you pick up some toothpaste while you're out? Oh, and don't forget trash bags.* And every now and then, she'd resort to banging drawers and doors again.

Our sex life changed again, too. I'd had so much extra energy during the first couple weeks of my layoff that we'd rediscovered a healthy sex life. We'd ratcheted up our lovemaking to four or five times a week, sometimes twice a day on weekends—using condoms, thanks to the double whammy of unemployment and an unreliable uterus. But the tensions that crept into our marriage after my interview with Sandy changed that, too. I slept on the couch most nights, and we had no sex whatsoever for the following couple of weeks, and when we finally did, the weekend after Thanksgiving, it was quick and quiet, almost as if Marcy wasn't really into it.

A few days later I was driving home from Staples just before dinnertime with a new supply of high-quality resume paper and business envelopes, feeling particularly glum, unwanted and pessimistic about the future. So I decided to drive by Tess's house. Not stop in or anything—just drive by. See where she lived, how she lived, maybe catch a glimpse of her, unpacking groceries or something. Maybe get a friendly wave, one of those surprised-to-see-you-in-the-neighborhood waves. Maybe pull over and chat, maybe.

I turned into the mini-mart on Main Street and asked a grumpy Pakistani clerk for a phone book, and he shot me a look that suggested I might use the information inside to defraud someone's grandmother or kidnap someone's baby. I flashed an innocent smile, which seemed to convince him that I wasn't a scammer or kidnapper, though perhaps he pegged me for a frustrated husband/unemployed newsman/novice stalker who couldn't stop flirting with and fantasizing over another woman. But even if he did, that must not have concerned him, because he forked over the book and I looked up Tess's address and found it listed under her husband's name: Sugarmeier, Joe...125 Hilltop Circle. I hopped back in the car and headed straight up there.

Hilltop Circle sits along Misty Hill's eastern perch, with a view of the Harrisburg skyline and the Capitol's green-and-gold dome in one direction, and our town's rooftops, backyards and pious steeple in the other. The homes are goliaths, built around a winding bump in the earth with a historical marker that goes largely ignored these days, all that remains of a hastily built earthworks fort meant to protect Harrisburg when Lee invaded Pennsylvania. The homes are either stately, post-Civil War beauties with wraparound porches and gingerbread trim, or sprawling, red-brick contemporaries, which, if it weren't for their double driveways and protruding front foyers, would look as if they were designed to mix in with the originals. Number 125 was one of the latter, with giant weeping willows draped over each corner of the front yard and a large, black-metal "S" hanging on the house, which struck me as Joe Sugarmeier's way of marking his territory, like a dog pissing on a tree.

It was dusk when I drove by, and while a couple of the homes were lit up with laces of red or white Christmas lights, Number 125 was fastened up and dark, being that time of day when lobbyists and other Capitol bigwigs were either enduring one last meeting or embarking on a new round of schmoozing with happy-hour drinks or an overpriced meal. As I crept past in my Honda, I wondered where Tess could be—nabbing a few things at the grocery store for dinner? Or, if hubby was still downtown doing lobbyist duties, maybe she took Carter to Subway or Arby's, or maybe, just maybe, she dropped the boy at a friend's and went out to toss back a few glasses of wine?

I fought back a desire to stop in front of her house, and instead motored to the end of the block and circled back, driving more slowly on my second pass, during which I noticed a little blue signpost warning me of a home-alarm system. After I passed the second weeping willow for the second time I felt a shiver and realized the late-day cold was seeping into the car, and so I flicked on the heater, and as soon as it coughed on and I turned my attention back onto the street, there she was—Marcy! Power-walking on Hilltop Circle with Felicia Spinelli. And coming right at me.

Marcy saw me. There was no doubt. Through the windshield, we made eye contact as soon as I'd redirected my eyes toward the street. I had no time to react. No time to devise an escape route or consider whether she recognized my titanium-toned Honda with the "Journalists

Do It On Deadline" sticker on the front bumper. Of course she did. We locked eyes. She waved first. I waved back. They kept power-walking. I kept driving.

And I drove straight home, all the while trying to think of how I'd explain what the hell I was doing up there in Tess Sugarmeier's neighborhood. Would Marcy even know that Tess lived up there? It sure didn't help that they had that big metal "S" attached to the front of their house. I decided to keep it simple—just tell her I swung by to check out the view and kill some time, and play dumb if she mentioned Tess. Maybe it wasn't the best plan in the world, but it was the best I could come up with on short notice.

I was at the kitchen sink when Marcy blew through the front door. I figured if I cleaned up a few breakfast and lunch dishes that were languishing in the sink, I might avoid her total and complete wrath. I heard her let out a *brrr*, to no one in particular, and head toward the closet to put away her fleece. I decided to break the ice.

"How was your walk?" I asked.

"Cold, but good."

No mention of why I was driving past the Sugarmeiers' house. Instead she peeked into the kitchen and asked, "When you're done with those dishes, would you go next door and get Wesley? He stayed at the Spinellis' while we walked, and I have to go to the bathroom."

"Sure."

Then suddenly she asked, "What were you doing up on Hilltop Circle?"

As I opened my mouth, I flashed back to my interview with Sandy Gates, the one that started this round of marital strain, the one in which I'd come off as Mr. Holier Than Thou, asking, "What's wrong with telling the truth?" But, knowing full well what would happen if I told the esteemed truth, I held that thought for roughly a second before the words came out of my mouth in a big, fat lie.

"Oh, I just took a little detour, you know, to check out

the view."

"Mmm," she said dispassionately, then tramped upstairs and shut herself in the bathroom, and I realized there was enough lingering tension over my job problem that she never even bothered to connect the dots.

―――――――

At 7 p.m. on the first Thursday in December, the proud parents of Misty Hill's third grade flooded the school cafeteria for the Science Fair. Mrs. Van der Torne, the longtime third-grade teacher who was nearing retirement, apparently assigned the spots randomly, and the dumb laws of chance placed Wesley at a table beside Carter Sugarmeier. So I found myself smack in the middle of the two boys and their projects—and their mothers. Tess and Carter on my left, Marcy and Wesley on my right.

The room smelled like leftover green beans mixed with expensive perfume and cologne. Most of the parents were dressed nicely—moms in their best Talbots winter wear, dads still in their suits and ties from the workday. As usual, however, Carter's dad was a no-show.

With Marcy's help—a significant amount of it—Wesley had made a simple electric circuit. It was mounted on a cherry-stained block of wood, a battery, resistor and switch connected by wire. Behind it was a professional-quality tri-fold board explaining the flow of electricity and the key parts in layman's terms—electrons, conductors, and insulators—with each outlined in an elegant black font. An impressive project from mother and son. Still, Marcy seemed edgy. She'd had a bad day at work, where she lost a client to a rival PR firm. And there in the middle of the Science Fair, as she rotated her head anxiously to check out the booths around us, or lifted herself onto her tiptoes to scan the projects in the rows in front of us, she gave me the impression that the other projects were adding another, unwelcome sense of competition to her day.

Carter, probably with a significant amount of help from Tess, had turned in an insect collection, and it was one heck of a bug cache. Thirty insects, from your common bumble bee and stink bug to the splendid blue dasher dragonfly and eastern tiger swallowtail. They must have been collected over the course of the entire year, all sealed in little baggies and framed in a nice, wooden shadow box, which must have cost at least fifty bucks at the craft store, and each bug had a little card underneath explaining what it was.

"Who has the best project?" Carter asked his mom innocently, but loud enough that we could hear at the next table.

"You do, of course," Tess said.

Wesley's face dampened, and Marcy, already feeling threatened by Tess's presence, must have felt like she'd just received a slap in the face. She looked positively stung.

"That's not true," Marcy said to Wesley, shaking her head aggressively. She turned her voice up one notch louder than Tess and added: "Your project's the best."

Carter's face drooped, and Tess rubbed his back. "You heard me, honey," she told him. "This bug collection takes the cake."

"I wish they judged them," Marcy said to Wesley, another notch louder, another layer of insistence in her tone. "Because your project would take the gold."

A jolt of tension crossed the room as parents and kids in other rows heard her. Heads turned.

Tess, still caressing Carter's back, poked her head toward Marcy and said, "Let's not do this."

"Let's," Marcy snarled.

Bad Family Moment, for sure.

"Listen," I said, trying to inject some levelheadedness. "They're both great projects. Everyone deserves a lot of credit here."

"Don't be such a diplomat, Nick," Marcy snapped. "Which one is better?"

I stammered, "Well, as I said—"

"Choose one," Marcy insisted.

"I ... I can't."

"Choose one!"

Mrs. Van der Torne appeared at my side, patting both hands in the air, attempting to settle things down. A broad-shouldered woman with a shock of silver hair, she clearly had years of experience breaking up spats at recess and sending kids to the principal's office.

"Now, now," she said, her voice sounding authoritatively calm. "Everyone completed great projects, so let's not compare."

She waved Tess and Carter to the left and waved us to the right. "Why don't we all move along so we can see all of these other great projects."

"Yes, *let's*," Tess said, mocking Marcy's lines from a moment earlier.

Marcy zipped her lips and fired a look at me. As if this was all my fault. Then she pivoted on her heel and moved along, just as Mrs. Van der Torne had instructed, and Wesley and I followed. The rest of the crowd turned their heads back toward the projects before them, or stepped aside if Marcy came their way, all pretending to mind their own business, and nobody said a word to Marcy the rest of the evening.

Around town, it quickly became known as the Science Fair Smackdown. A couple of days later, Rocco told me he'd heard all about it, and Felicia told Marcy the same thing. Some of the various retellings, however, were not completely accurate. In the version Rocco heard, Marcy asked Tess to step outside. But that apparently didn't happen in the version Felicia heard, because that would have angered Marcy even more. So I never told her about the version that reached Rocco's ears.

But the local grapevine wasn't my biggest problem after the Smackdown. My problem was what had actually happened, and how I'd handled it. Maybe another man, eager to keep the peace at home, would have handled it differently. Maybe another man would have said something or done something to appease his wife, regardless of what it meant for the other mom and her boy. As for the other mom, what can I say? Standing near Tess in the cafeteria once again, I felt like there was some sort of magnet force drawing me toward her. There was no way I could bring myself to say anything that would have offended her.

But Marcy. After the Science Fair, we drove home in silence, and she stormed into the house, slammed her purse down on a chair, tromped upstairs to our bedroom and never came back down. I helped Wesley get ready for bed, and shortly after tucking him in, while I was brushing my teeth in the bathroom, I heard her sneak across to his bedroom to say goodnight. A moment later, I heard our bedroom door close, and I followed her inside, where she was settling under the sheet, lying on her hip with her back turned toward my side of the bed. I crawled in beside her, hoping the best strategy for soothing things over was to minimalize, pretend it was no big deal. I reached across her hip and slid my hand underneath her nightshirt. Makeup sex?

Nope.

She seized my arm, with her thumb locked on the soft underside of my wrist, and squeezed those little wristbones so hard that it hurt.

"Ouch," I said.

"Sleep on the goddamned couch."

Maybe I should have understood that Wesley was *her* only son too, and she probably felt the same sense of parental anxiety at the fair that I often felt on the baseball field. Maybe I should have recognized that Marcy also harbored feelings of outright jealousy toward Tess that seemed to be morphing into mistrust toward me, and deep down she was still that self-conscious overachiever from blue-collar New Jersey who hadn't forgotten my misbehavior with Marianne McGibbons. And maybe I should have understood that the public nature of the scene contributed to the feeling that I'd betrayed her yet again. If we were to ever end up in counseling, this would surely come up.

So I slept on the couch.

The next night, too. And the next.

Meanwhile, Marcy did not say a single word to me. She communicated through Wesley. *Honey, will you ask your dad to take out the trash? Will you tell your dad that his dinner is ready?* At dinner, we would eat quietly, except for the occasional question that Marcy or I would pose to Wesley about his day at school. When we finished, Marcy would start clearing the table and say to Wesley, *Honey, would you ask your dad to load the dishwasher?*

Two nights after the Smackdown, as I tucked Wesley in, smoothing his blue baseball-themed sheets across his tummy, he was mopey. He lifted his head from his pillow, peered up at me with those big eyes which reminded me so much of Marcy's, and asked, "Why are mom and you mad at each other?"

"Ah, buddy," I said. I forked my fingers through his hair reassuringly as I tried to conjure an appropriate answer. After a moment, I said, "We're not that mad at each other. We just need a little time to work through something."

"Will you get a pivorce?"

"A what?"

"A pivorce. One of the girls in my class said her parents are getting one. She said it happens to a lot of parents."

"Do you mean a *di*vorce? No, buddy, we love each other very much, and we love you and our little family. We're sticking together, I'm sure."

"Do a lot of parents get a divorce?"

"Not a whole lot, but a good many do. Too many, I think. But don't worry, buddy, because I'm sure we're sticking together."

I planted a kiss on his forehead.

"I really hope you don't get one," he said sadly, and he turned those big eyes on me once again.

"Me, too."

The next day, Marcy embarked on her reconciliation efforts, slowly. She started talking to me directly, though it was still just domestic small talk—*Will you check the garlic bread and stir the sauce?* The next day, it escalated to the point where she asked me to do something with her, albeit domestic—*Will you help me fold this laundry?* I took that as a test, her little way of gauging whether we could still work together on things, so I folded as well as I could, and by the next day, we were having full-fledged, polite conversations again, though we never directly addressed what had occurred at the Smackdown.

We had makeup sex the following night. Afterward, Marcy wrapped her arm across my chest and snuggled up to me.

"Did you enjoy that?" she asked.

"You mean the sex? Of course."

"Good, because I'd like you to keep something in mind," she warned. "If you'd like to continue having it, you better keep your distance from that Sugarmeier tart."

Part of mitigating the damage in my marriage involved refocusing my job search. I doubled my efforts to find another newspaper job, mailing resume packets to editors across the state who might want someone to man their own news bureau in the state Capitol, but that effort went nowhere. A few days before Christmas, an editor in Altoona told me he was interested, but his budget was too tight right now. Check back next summer, he said. When Marcy came home from work that day and I told her about my phone conversation with the Altoona editor, her lips tightened and she turned her head, avoiding eye contact.

"Keep trying," she said tersely. Her tone turned heavily sarcastic as she added, "You're too *pure* to do anything else, remember."

I let it go without responding, and she thumped out of the room, apparently satisfied with the message she'd sent me. We hardly spoke for the rest of the night, and I slept on the couch.

I started out on a five-mile run the next morning, heading away from Hilltop Circle, because I didn't want any Tess-related complications seeping into my thoughts, but it easily stretched into a six miler and then a seven miler as I tried to make sense of my career and my marriage. While Marcy and I had been through rough spots before, this one seemed trickier to navigate, and every mile helped me ponder another angle. Obviously, I'd insulted Marcy deeply, and inadvertently drawn a new line that separated us. I'd sent her the message that I didn't respect her career, which she must have interpreted as disrespect for her personally, all while she was bringing home the bacon. I didn't know how to explain to her that I'd chosen to become a journalist twenty years earlier because I thought it was important work, and I wanted to do something important again and was having a hard time perceiving public relations work as important. And because I'd been running a lot again, I'd also been rereading the works of guru Angelo Tannabaugh, and passages like this were racing through my mind: *Don't listen to others; listen only to yourself—your heart. No matter what you must endure—and if you're lucky, it won't be much worse than bloody socks and gut-wrenching cramps—do what your heart tells you to do.* I also didn't know how to tell my wife that in my family men tended to die young, and now I was forty years old and afraid that I too was destined to die young, and I was bound and determined to listen to my heart.

For Christmas, I'd splurged on one gift for Marcy, a five-hundred-dollar necklace that I'd found on sale for two hundred dollars at Macy's. I'd paid for it with my Visa card, hoping it would help smooth things over. Marcy was not a jewelry addict like some women, but she had a modest jewelry collection, and I thought the necklace was perfect for her. It was fourteen-karat gold with a little, crystallized ball layered with diamond chips. It was the last thing I gave her on Christmas morning, after Wesley had opened all of his gifts and she was still sitting on the living room floor, which was littered with rolled up wrapping paper, mini football helmets and Nerf bullets. She looked surprised when I handed her the small, wrapped jewelry box.

"Ooh," she said flatly when she opened it. "I like it."

Then her lips pursed—not as tight as they normally did when she was mad at me, but just enough to signal that a Christmas necklace wasn't going to fix things between us. She stood up and sauntered over to me, gave me a little peck on the cheek and said, "Thank you." It wasn't a real kiss; it just seemed to be her attempt to be polite. All three of Wesley's grandparents were due to arrive by lunchtime—Marcy's parents from Trenton, and my mom from Johnstown—and so that was that.

Marcy's parents arrived first, and as they hauled presents into the house, they seemed more mismatched than usual, even though they'd been married more than forty years. Marcy's mom, now retired from teaching English, looked fresh and prim in her knit slacks and red snowman's sweater. Her dad, still working part-time at Home Depot, was hunched and cranky in his red-and-black flannel shirt. Even in front of Wesley, he couldn't stop cursing, a bad habit that had gotten worse as he'd aged.

"Jesus H. Christ," the old man said as he dropped a pile of presents in the living room. "My goddamned back."

"Dad, watch it!" Marcy scolded.

"Oh, Jesus," he mumbled.

My mom, who'd never remarried after Dad died, arrived a half hour later. She'd driven alone from Johnstown, a three-hour trip that made me somewhat nervous because she would soon be seventy. But Wesley was her only grandson, and she insisted, and there was no snow in the forecast to deter her. She smelled heavily of cheap hair spray and lemon hand cream, and she tried to convince Wesley that all of the presents she brought were actually from Santa, who'd made a special stop in Johnstown. But Wesley, who'd been questioning Santa's existence all month, was especially skeptical about an extra stop at Grandma's.

"Why doesn't he stop at all the grandmas' houses?" Wesley asked.

"He makes a special stop for boys who are extra good," Mom replied.

"How does he have time for extra stops?"

"He works quickly."

Wesley looked unconvinced.

"The boy's no dumb ass," Marcy's dad grumbled.

Marcy's parents left just before dark, but my mom spent the night and drove back to Johnstown the next morning. She'd slept on the couch after watching old sitcoms late into the night, with the volume turned up too loud, and even though I was upstairs in bed the muffled voices of George Jefferson, Jack Tripper and Mr. Roper haunted our house and kept me from sleeping well. After she was gone, I was eager to get out of the house. Marcy's parents had given me an ugly sweater from Boscov's, so I wanted to return it, even though I knew the stores would be a zoo. After waiting in line at the return desk for about two minutes, I felt a tap on my shoulder. I turned to see Tess Sugarmeier.

"Hey there, coach," she said in a chirpy tone. "Happy Holidays! Did you have a good Christmas?"

"As good as possible," I said, trying not to disclose too much personal information. "You?"

"Fabulous. What are you returning there?"

I showed her the sweater, a green V-neck with a baby-blue paisley design.

"Ugh," she said. "Definitely deserves to go back where it came from."

"And you?"

"Oh, I'm not returning," she said. "I was over at the jewelry counter, looking for those after-Christmas bargains, and an excuse to get out of the house."

"I hear you," I said.

As soon as I said it, I realized that her claim about having a "fabulous" Christmas was probably untrue, probably just a word she threw around this time of year without thinking about it.

"Listen," I said, motioning toward the long line in front of me. "I can do this later. Would you like to go get a cup of coffee or something?"

A relieved look brushed over her face.

"Yes, perfect," she said. "I could really use one."

"Starbucks?"

"Perfect," she said.

I tucked the sweater under my arm and we headed out of the store together. As we walked through the perfumed air of the fragrance counter, chatting casually about our kids, I felt comfortable beside another woman for the first time in weeks. I checked my watch: just after 1 p.m.

"Oh, hell," I said. "I could use something a little stronger than coffee. How about a drink?"

"Whew," she said instantly. "Sounds good to me."

11
IN A BAR AT 1:30
IN THE AFTERNOON

$\int$he wore a tight, charcoal Ralph Lauren turtleneck that accentuated her pert little breasts. Her lipstick was a soft shade of burgundy, and she wore a diamond snowflake necklace and silver hoop earrings. I wondered if either the necklace or earrings had been a Christmas present, but I didn't ask. I wore a gray hooded Steelers sweatshirt and faded jeans, but was at least relieved that I hadn't simply thrown on sweatpants before leaving the house.

We'd chosen Sudzies, the brightly lit new brew pub, and it was mostly empty. There were a few twenty-somethings at the bar, but all the tables were empty. We were at a small corner table in the bar area, underneath a framed black-and-white photo of a cart and buggy lumbering down Misty Hill's Main Street in the late 1800s, and I was not at all concerned about being spotted with another woman. I'd always felt comfortable at Sudzies.

"So tell me," I said, feeling relaxed and confident as I

took my first sip of Lavish Lager. "Was your Christmas really that fabulous? I get the impression it wasn't."

"What gave it away?" Tess said, sipping her pinot noir.

"Let's see—we're in a bar at 1:30 in the afternoon, on the day after Christmas."

"Yep," she chuckled. "That would be a dead giveaway."

"Rather not talk about it?"

"I don't mind talking about it," she said. "In fact, I'd prefer to talk about it while I have a glass of wine in front of me. You know Joe, right?"

"Actually, we've never met. I wouldn't know him if he fell from the ceiling right here and spilled my beer."

"Really?" she said, sounding only slightly surprised. "Well, I guess that explains it, or at least part of it. He's never around during the week, hardly around on weekends, always has a legislator to schmooze or a client to see, then Christmas comes around and he has to take charge of everything. Must be a lobbyist thing—they're used to controlling the agenda, I think. He's been driving me nuts for two days now."

"Yeah," I agreed. "Must be a lobbyist thing."

"And that's not the worst of it," she said, wrapping both hands around her glass, as if she needed to steady herself. "He's always texting someone, and usually sneaks into another room to do it. Doesn't think I notice, but I do. Doesn't know I've heard the stories about the so-called Capitol culture, where even lawmakers sleep with those cute young aides. So sometimes I wonder if I'm his only Christmas bunny."

"I'm sorry," I said.

She shrugged—a heavy shrug, the gesture of someone who'd grown accustomed to dealing with crap. She reached into her purse for the tube of burgundy lipstick and touched up her lips.

"It makes you wonder," she said, "how many people get married for the wrong reasons. Money, security, appearances. Even good looks or good sex. Isn't it amazing how some people can jump into a big decision like marriage for all the wrong reasons? Don't you wonder about it sometimes?"

In actuality, I hadn't. I was always convinced I was in love with Marcy, until life dropped job problems and this beautiful but lonely Little League mom in my lap, and I hadn't bothered to think about the bigger issue of why some people marry in the first place. But I was so enthralled by Tess's mention of good sex that I didn't want to discourage this line of conversation.

"I suppose," I said mildly.

"Even right here in Misty Hill," she continued, "in our so-called perfect little town, I'll bet there are so many people who married for the wrong reasons."

I nodded and sipped my lager.

"What about you?" she asked. "Why are you in a bar at 1:30 in the afternoon on the day after Christmas?"

"You know I lost my job, right?"

"I did not," she gasped. "Oh, my God."

"Newspapers are dying, but that's another story. We're getting by. Marcy's still working at the PR firm, but things have been tense around the house. I don't want to make her sound like a total bitch, because some of it's probably my fault. Maybe. I don't know."

I paused, contemplating whether to delve into the whole matter.

"Rather not talk about it?" Tess asked.

I took a swig of beer and said, "Maybe after one more of these."

We ordered another round, but we never returned to the issues of my job problems or our marital woes. Instead, we talked about Wesley and Carter and their teachers and baseball. We gossiped about some of the other parents in town, and Tess knew her fair share. She told me who'd left their wife and who had cancer. Reggie Knox had left his wife, and everyone who'd heard it thought it was odd, because Reggie seemed to have political aspirations and being a divorcé might doom those. I was really saddened to hear who had cancer—a guy named Ben Huffnagel, who'd been in charge of field maintenance for our Little League for years. Though I didn't know him well, he seemed like such a good guy. He had lung cancer. I remembered that he smoked heavily, and would even sneak one at the fields sometimes despite a smoking ban in our league.

"Life is fragile and short," Tess said. "Remember what Warren Zevon said before he died—enjoy every sandwich."

She tilted her wine glass toward me in the form of a toast, took a tipple and added, "And every sip of wine."

Could there be a more attractive woman in this world? A more fun, understanding and empathetic one? I felt such a riveting connection to her at that moment that I wanted to enjoy more than a drink or a sandwich with her. I felt the urge to touch her. Any part of her. Face, legs, shoulders, elbows, fingers, you name it.

I thrust my right hand across the table and cupped it, palm up.

"What do you know about palm reading?" I asked. "I'm wondering if any of these lines mean there's good health and a good job in my future, or if I should just bag it and move to Vegas."

"Let me see," she said, hunching forward, grasping my open hand with her left, cracking a frisky smile. "I was a gypsy fortune teller in a previous life—didn't I tell you that before?"

"No, but I was a private eye," I quipped, "which is how I knew you were a fortune teller."

Her hands were soft and lithe, her fingernails a perfect and polished candy-apple red, the kind of hands that always let Old Lady Kenmore do the dishes for her. As she traced my palm with her right forefinger, slowly and delicately, I felt blood rushing under the crotch in my faded jeans.

"This is your heart line," she said. "I'm a little rusty, but I think yours means one of two things. You have trouble relating to others, or your heart always breaks easily. Could be either one."

"I see."

"And this is your head line," she continued. "Like I said, I'm rusty, but I think it's predicting a productive life for you, which is good news on the job front."

"Got it."

"And this is your life line. If I'm reading it right, it's predicting vitality, which is a good sign for your health."

I felt vital, all right. I also felt a rush of guilt: We'd inched too far toward something we might really regret, and wasn't I the wretch who started it? So I pulled my hand back, nodding agreeably, as if I was content with her playful prognostication, and did what most men do when they suddenly want to switch things up—I checked my cell phone.

"It's almost three o'clock," I said in a tone that suggested I had something important to do at three—pick up this or drop off that.

For a moment, we both fidgeted.

"We should probably go," she said. "As much as I'd like to, I can't spend the whole day out cavorting."

"Yeah, I should get going, too."

"Let me get the tab," Tess said.

"No, let me," I said, reaching for my wallet. But there was only a five-dollar bill in it, plus the credit cards.

"I insist," Tess said, pulling a pair of crisp twenty-dollar bills from her wallet.

I didn't want to put the tab on a credit card, because Marcy would probably see the bill, and I didn't want any evidence of this little matinee being mailed to my house. So I didn't argue, and Tess grabbed the tab and dropped it on the bar along with the twenties.

Walking out to the parking lot, the strain of guilt that had me whipping out my cell phone ten minutes ago dissipated, and I felt like a teenager on a first date. Part of me wanted to start smooching, take her somewhere and rip her clothes off. But no, I thought. *I can't!* My mind was tied up with complications—I was a married man, and we really had nowhere to go.

A hotel? Maybe she'd pay for it. I couldn't, for sure. And I sure couldn't suggest we go to my house or hers. My mind zoomed back to another time and place—to high school, when we'd drive into the woods outside Johnstown and park and fool around in the backseat. The thought of driving a grown woman into the woods made me laugh to myself for just an instant.

But no. It didn't matter. I'm a married man, I reminded myself, with a son. *A son!* I thought about the Sambuca-fueled night when I'd rolled in the hay with Marianne McGibbons, and all the turmoil that ensued, and I was reminded of how easy it is to get into trouble and how much fortitude it takes to stay out of it.

We'd parked in adjoining spaces—her Lexus SUV beside my reliable little Honda—and we stopped in the space behind the two vehicles. She reached in her big purse for her keys, and I dug both hands into my jeans pockets. But I still didn't know what to say—goodbye, or let's go somewhere and fool around. She broke the silence.

"We should do this again," she said. "Soon."

"Sure."

"Even coffee, if it's too early for a drink."

"That'll work."

"Call me," she said. "I'd tell you to text me, but I don't want to be like Joe. You can just call the house—he goes back to work tomorrow, which means he won't be around for the next 364 days. Believe me."

"Sounds good," I said, and yanked a hand out of my pocket and waved goodbye.

As we both climbed into our cars, I wasn't sure if I was relieved or disappointed.

There was a reason people in town were chattering about Ben Huffnagel's lung cancer: It had progressed rapidly since the fall. In early January, Sam DiNardo sent an email to all the families in the Little League relaying the sad news of his death. Ben, who owned the Misty Hill Auto Body Shop, was forty-eight and had three sons, one of whom was twelve and still played Little League. Another was a sophomore in high school while the oldest was twenty and helped Ben run his shop. Ben had been the field maintenance director in our league for the past twelve years, since his oldest son was eight years old. It was a time-consuming job, requiring frequent mowing, weed-whacking and other thankless, dirty labor. In his email, Sam called Ben "the back-bone of our league, and a man to whom every child in our league is indebted."

I decided to go to the funeral. Though I didn't know Ben well, I felt a connection to him from the league. Besides, I was unemployed and didn't have an excuse not to go. The funeral was on a bitter cold Wednesday afternoon at the Methodist Church on Main Street, and I was one of several Little League dads who'd turned out. Ben was a Misty Hill native, and the church was packed. I sat in the back with a group of guys from the league, including Sam, Big Ed and Terry Hipple. Even Reggie Knox had found time to get away from his job as deputy secretary of corrections, though he showed up a little late and squeezed into our pew right beside me.

Afterward, the guys from the league gathered outside. We could see our breath in the January air, but we didn't talk much. I felt an odd sense of camaraderie with the other guys, even though we'd competed against each other and argued forcefully at times, and it made me wonder how men feel after they go away to war together. I felt a pinch of guilt for comparing Little League to war, then I reminded myself I was at a funeral, a funeral for a good man, a father and husband, and I didn't feel so bad.

"I wish I could have a smoke," Big Ed said. "But I'm afraid it's not appropriate."

"It's not," Sam said sharply. "So don't."

"I was just saying," Ed said.

"Who's going to maintain the fields now?" Terry Hipple asked, as if trying to change the subject.

"It might be hard finding someone," Sam said. "It's a lot of work, but let's not think about that right now. We'll talk about it soon enough."

"Hey, Nick," Ed said. "What about you? Have you found a job yet?"

"I haven't," I said dully.

"Let's not talk about that right now," Sam said.

"I didn't know you lost your job," Reggie Knox said, his tone sending out a rare note of sympathy from him. "I'm sorry."

"Yeah, last fall."

"Wow, I heard about cutbacks at the paper," Reggie said. "But I didn't know you were among them. Do you have any leads?"

"Not yet."

He dug into his wallet and pulled out his deputy secretary card.

"Listen," Reggie said, handing me his card. "Things are tight at the state level, too, but if you want me to circulate your resume, just let me know. I'm sure there are some PR openings somewhere."

I was a little surprised by Reggie's gesture, but also touched, so I didn't want to respond by telling him how I felt about PR.

"Thanks," I said. "I'll keep it in mind."

With that, we said our goodbyes and disbanded. A week later, Sam called me and asked if I'd consider being the new field maintenance director.

"Think it over if you want," Sam said. "I know it's a lot of work, but you did a great job as a commissioner, and

I'm sure you'd do a great job at this, too."

"I don't need to think it over," I said. "I'll do it."

12
IT'S GONE TOO FAR

The backseat of Tess's SUV was spacey and comfortable—gray leather seats, ample leg room and tinted windows. Geez, I thought, if only we'd had backseats like this when I was young! It was dark outside, and though I was oblivious to exactly where we were parked, I knew it was the end of a trail that led into a patch of woods, and we'd see any cars coming from a hundred yards away.

We'd started smooching in the front seat then moved to the back, where I wrapped my right arm around her shoulder. Though we'd hurried into the backseat, we kissed slowly, patiently. Kiss like a grownup, I told myself, and we did. Her lips were full and sweet, and we used our tongues lightly and sparingly.

With my left hand, I gently traced the outline of her hip. She was wearing those tight, low-cut jeans again, and just tracing her hip gave me a sense of the contour of her body. Inside my own jeans, I was rock hard, pressing against my zipper, but in my head I kept repeating the words *be patient*. So I pulled my hand back slightly and ran only my fingertips along her hip, then down to her thigh, and then I alternated full hand and fingertips along her thigh and hip before moving my hand up higher.

I placed my hand on the side of her stomach for a moment and held it there. Patiently. She wore another snug, dark-colored turtleneck—I'd forgotten which color—and her belly was nicely toned with just a small roll around her waistline. Wow, I thought. I moved my fingertips down to her hips, then back to her stomach, back to her hips, and then with one sweeping movement I went from her hip to her stomach to her breast.

I cupped her breast in the palm of my hand and then stopped. It was smallish, but not too small, and firm. After a moment, I ran my fingertips around her breast in circles, then cupped it again. Meanwhile, she rubbed my chest with her right hand. She pressed firmly, as if massaging it, then moved her hand downward and stopped at my belt buckle.

With both arms, I shifted her body to the right and reached around her back and underneath her turtleneck. I pulled back and stopped kissing her as I seized the back of her bra strap with both hands. Take your time, I told myself, and don't fumble. I was careful to squeeze both latches together, and the strap came undone. As she reached underneath her shirt to slide the bra off her shoulders, I looked out the back window to be sure no cars were coming down the trail. It was hazy outside, but there were no headlights in sight.

Second base, I thought.

And then, with a start, I woke up.

Initially, I wasn't sure where I was. Soon that foggy feeling disappeared and I realized I was in bed beside Marcy, lying face up. She was on her side, turned away from me and sleeping soundly. Inside my pajama pants, I was hard. Through the cracks in the blinds, I could tell it was still dark outside. Our room was just as dark, and quiet. It was a Sunday night. I glanced at the clock on the nightstand, and the red digits read 3:49.

I lay there for a minute and wished I could go back to my dream. I closed my eyes, hoping to fall back to sleep immediately. No such luck. So I opened my eyes and stared at the ceiling for a minute. Inside my pajama pants, I was still as hard as a calculus exam.

I looked over at Marcy. The covers had slid down to her waist, and I could see her strawberry blonde hair spread across her back. She wore one of my old gray T-shirts, as she'd done for years. I tapped her softly on her left shoulder.

She didn't move at first, so I tapped her again, a little harder this time. She let out a little groan and slowly rolled over to face me.

"Huh?" she moaned, lifting her head off the pillow.

"Want to have sex?" I whispered.

"Huh?"

"Do you want to have sex?"

She rubbed her eyes and looked at me with disbelief. I expected her to check the clock, but she didn't.

"No," she said, her tired voice also conveying a sense of annoyance. "Go back to sleep."

She plopped her head back on the pillow, rolled away from me and yanked the covers up to her shoulder.

"Okay," I said. "Sorry."

I lay there several minutes, hoping my erection would soften, and it did. But I knew I wouldn't be able to fall back to sleep anytime soon, so I got out of bed and went downstairs. I stretched out on the couch and turned on the television. I clicked around and finally stopped on C-Span, which was showing a book talk by Mitchell Michaels at the Heritage Foundation. A dorky-looking guy with thinning hair and a whiny voice, Michaels had written a book titled *Why Capitalism Still Rules*, and he was ranting about why business executives get a bad rap for their high salaries and hefty bonuses.

"A lot of people forget what it takes to make the wheels of capitalism move," Michaels said, waving his hands furiously. "And some people have this feeling that making money for a big corporation is somehow evil, but what they forget is that it's what makes us productive. Those people who think they're too pure to do what the corporate bigwigs do, that they have too much heart or soul to simply go out there and make money, those are the people who forget the importance of productivity, and those are the people who are dragging us down as a society."

Was I a drag on society? Sprawled uselessly on the couch, I took stock: I was, after all, unemployed, reluctant to jump into a new career I wouldn't like, thanks to my damned heart and soul, and as a consequence it had strained my marriage, and hey, it was even worse, because let's not forget I'd just lost a perfectly good erection, which my wife wanted absolutely nothing to do with, even though erections weren't all that easy to come by these days. But hey, who could blame her, considering this latest erection was caused by a dream about another woman. I changed the channel, driving my thumb into the remote button as I said out loud, "I fucking hate Mitchell Michaels."

While Marcy went to work the next day and Wesley was at school, I tinkered around the league's maintenance shed. It was late January, and though it was too cold to start either of our mowers, I wanted to get out of the house and take an inventory to see what I needed to get the fields ready when the weather warmed up. I'd thought about calling Tess that morning for coffee, but decided against it. I didn't want to seem too eager to meet again, and was also afraid I'd be tempted to tell her I'd dreamt about getting naked with her in her backseat.

Though the shed was dirty and smelled like some combination of oil, cigarettes, dead grass and mouse droppings, it brightened my mood, diverting my thoughts from my troubled career and tense marriage. Instead, I was focused on bags of mound clay and drying agent, mower blades and sharpening tools—and sweeping out the cigarette butts that Ben Huffnagel had left behind. Nothing warms the soul on a January day like working for the local Little League.

I spent half the afternoon in the shed and walked home in time to meet Wesley when he got home from school. I helped him with his homework, played a few games of ping-pong in the basement, and made dinner. I'd gotten into the habit of making dinner on most nights, even though I couldn't make much. But I had a small repertoire of easy dishes that worked for a little family on a weeknight—pasta, tacos, meatball sandwiches. Marcy called and said she was running late, so we started eating without her.

"What are we having?" Wesley asked, sliding into a seat at the small table in our breakfast nook.

"Turkey meatball sandwiches."

"Ah, no."

"Yeah," I said. "Why? What's wrong?"

"I'm sick of turkey meatballs." He made a snub-nosed face.

"Since when?"

"Since now."

"Don't complain," I said, shoving his plate in front of him.

"And what is a turkey meatball, anyway? It doesn't make any sense. Why not chicken meatballs, or pepperoni meatballs?"

"It's a meatball made out of turkey meat. It's better for you than ground beef. Your mom and I like to buy food that's better for you, and besides, they're pre-made, so all I have to do is cook them."

He eyed his sandwich warily.

"You better eat it," I said, sitting down beside him with my own plate.

He sneered at it for a few more seconds, and Marcy walked in the front door.

"Mom!" Wesley called out, as if tattling on a friend. "Dad made turkey meatballs again."

"What's the problem?" she said, hanging her coat on the back of a chair.

"Dad keeps making turkey meatballs, and I'm sick of them."

"Honey, there's not much else your dad can make," she said matter-of-factly. "And besides, this is the first time he made them this week."

"But it's only Monday," Wesley said.

She shook her head dismissively and looked at me, a sign she was about to change the subject.

"More importantly," she said. "Guess who I bumped into today?"

"Who?" I asked.

"Reggie Knox. I was at lunch with a client and saw him downtown. He says he offered to circulate your resume around the state."

"He did," I confirmed.

"When?"

"We talked after Ben Huffnagel's funeral," I said. "It was a nice little talk, actually."

"Well?" she asked, hopefully.

"Well what?"

"Did you give him your resume?"

"Not yet," I said, biting into my meatball sandwich.

"Are you going to?"

I finished chewing and said, "I haven't really thought about it."

"I think you should," she said in a matronly tone.

"Okay," I said with a little shrug, and took another bite.

"And if you don't," she said firmly, "I will."

The next morning, I called Tess to see if she wanted to meet for coffee, but there was no answer and I didn't leave a message. I figured she'd have caller ID and would know I called, but I still wasn't comfortable leaving my voice on tape at her house. As soon as I hung up the phone, I felt guilty about calling her. I started a pot of coffee and sat at the counter while it brewed. I thought about how beautiful Marcy had looked in this same kitchen just an hour earlier as she headed off to work, wearing her high black boots with a long black skirt and sweater vest. As I watched the coffee drip into the pot, I wondered if I'd forgotten how good I had it at home, and if I'd already started something with Tess that I couldn't turn off so easily.

That's it, I told myself. *Don't call her again. It's gone too far, and it's time to fix your own marriage.*

Buzzing from caffeine, I spent the morning trying to rejuvenate my job search. I posted my resume on some new Internet job sites, even though I doubted that any employers would ever check them, and I sent out a round of emails to old colleagues asking them to keep their eyes open for me. I also emailed the editor in Altoona who'd expressed interest in opening a Capitol bureau, saying I wanted to "check in" on his plans. He replied with a short email that afternoon, saying little more than "no change in status here."

I decided against sending my resume to Reggie Knox, though I knew Marcy was serious about doing it herself. If she had some time to cool off, I thought, I could talk to her rationally about how much I wanted to find another newspaper job. The time had come for us to have a serious sit-down, and I spent the next couple days mulling over strategies for it.

But when Marcy came home from work that Friday, I wished I'd initiated the sit-down sooner. She slammed the door behind her, dropped her purse on the floor and fell back against the closed door. It was a raw day, cold and rainy, and Wesley and I were holed up in the living room re-organizing his baseball cards. Marcy looked pale and wind-beaten, her eyes strained and her hair messy.

"Wesley, honey," she said calmly. "Go up to your room for a minute."

"Why?" he said.

"Because I asked you to."

"I don't want to," he said.

"What's wrong?" I asked, and immediately wondered if she'd seen Reggie Knox again. "Bad day?"

"Wesley, please," Marcy said.

"Fine," he said, and stomped upstairs.

My mind raced with reasons why I hadn't given Reggie my resume, plus everything I'd done that week to revive my job search. Then I decided this was the time to initiate the sit-down. It wasn't the perfect time, but I apparently had no choice.

"Come on in and sit down," I said. "I think we need to talk."

She didn't reply. She was still propped up against the door, looking down at her black boots and shaking her head with that haggard look on her face. Finally, her jaw locked and she lifted her head. She looked straight at me, accusingly.

"Do you want to tell me what you were doing in a bar with that slut?"

13
I TOLD HIM TO SHOOT YOU

Unbeknownst to me, this is what had happened:

While I was sipping lager and dallying with Tess, Larry Swanger came into the bar to have his growler jug refilled. Larry had a daughter in the same grade as Wesley, but we were barely acquaintances. Sitting with my back to the door, I never saw him. If Tess saw him, she either didn't recognize him or, being the wife of an absentee husband, didn't worry much about being spotted in a bar with another guy. Larry must have been in the bar only about five minutes, just long enough to get a refill of his holiday ale and catch a glimpse of Tess playfully reading my palm at a corner table.

Larry's wife was a close friend of Jane White, who was a close friend of our neighbor, Felicia Spinelli. So when Larry told his wife about his Nick-and-Tess sighting, she eventually told Jane, who eventually told Felicia. And then Felicia—after spending a week or so agonizing over what to do with the information, all the while totally ignorant, or at least in some sort of denial, over the heavy irony involved, considering her own husband was the town's number-one womanizer—eventually invited Marcy over to her house, ostensibly for an after-work glass of wine and idle chit-chat. Only the chit-chat wasn't so idle.

Marcy explained that entire chain of events to me after she threw her coat on the living room recliner, sat down across from me, straightened her hair and collected herself. She spoke in a restrained and measured tone, sitting erect, her hands folded tightly, as if they might do damage if she let them loose. And she kept looking straight at me with that accusatory stare.

My first inclination was to deny it. To say something like, *You heard wrong.* Or, *Someone got their facts screwed up.* But I didn't. I sank into the couch and confessed.

"Listen," I said. "It's not what you think. Believe me, there's nothing going on between Tess and me. It was a totally innocent, totally platonic thing."

"You think I was born yesterday?" Marcy said.

"No, no. But we just talked. That's it. I know it looks bad, but you have to believe me."

"Oh, sure," Marcy said, her tone turning sarcastic. "My husband, who's been flirting with this other woman for the past several months, and obviously has a thing for her, leaves me behind and goes out drinking with her, and I'm supposed to believe it's no big deal. Totally innocent. Is that what you said? Totally innocent. Sure, I'll believe that."

"Okay, look," I said, trying my best to sound reassuring. "I know how it sounds. I really do, but I don't know how else to explain it. We just talked."

"Is that so?" she snapped, the sarcasm warping into distrust. "I heard you were holding hands and making gaga eyes at each other. In fact, after Larry Swanger saw you, he told the bartender you two should get a room."

"No, that's not true. We weren't—well, she read my palm, if that's what you mean by holding hands. But it was just in fun."

"Oh, really. She read your palm, huh? In fun? What else did you and that palm-reading bimbo do together that was fun?"

"I didn't mean it that way," I said, sinking further into the couch. "I swear, all we did was talk."

"Why do you even need to talk to her? Huh? I don't understand why you would even need to talk to her. I'm not buying your goddamned story."

"It's not a story," I said, the words trickling out hopelessly. "We just talked about ..."

And I realized this was complicated territory, too. What was I supposed to say: I wanted someone to talk to other than my own wife? I let out a deep sigh and said, "We just talked."

"No problem," she said, her tone heavily sarcastic now. "None at all. In fact, feel free to go out with other women whenever you want, read each other's palms, get a room, whatever. I can always stay behind. What do you need me for, anyway? Besides our only income."

"Oh, boy," I huffed. "I know things have been tense between us lately, and I know we probably should have tried to talk this out sooner."

"You mean, before you started an affair."

"Good God, it's not an affair. You have to believe me."

She stood up, wheeled away from me and said, "I absolutely don't have to believe you. I'd like you to leave. I don't even want to see you right now."

So I spent that night at the Wayside Inn, a little red-brick motel with mustard-yellow doors, circa 1950, on the edge of town. But first I'd stopped at Sudzies, because I wanted some beer and welcomed the pub's faux sense of hominess, and I also felt a strange need to return to the scene of my crime. On a Friday evening, the well-lit bar was much more crowded than the day after Christmas, but I found an open spot at the bar to order a growler jug for take-out. As I waited for the bartender, I checked out the corner table where Tess and I had sat. A well-dressed young couple was at the table, which was partially hidden by a beam that buttressed the end of the bar, and I realized how easy it had been for Larry to slip in and out without us noticing him. I envied the couple, because they seemed too young to worry about being seen in a bar, still too young to have a complicated life.

At the motel room, which cost thirty-nine dollars and smelled like an old vacuum cleaner, I propped the pillows on the bed and watched TV while I drank my beer from a plastic motel cup. I couldn't settle on a single show, and instead surfed channels constantly all night. Even after finishing off the growler, I couldn't sleep. It was close to 3 a.m. when I finally dozed off during a CNN piece about climate change. My last thought of the night was how severely the climate had changed in my own corner of the world, but I was confident that I'd eventually convince Marcy that nothing happened between Tess and me, at least nothing physical, and it was just a matter of time until she came around. That's why I'd packed only one change of clothes and my toothbrush. All night long, another question that really nagged at me was, how the hell would I explain my absence to Wesley?

But I also knew this: The next day was the first Saturday of February, which meant it was the first day of signups for the spring baseball season, and a new beginning. Only I didn't know exactly what was beginning.

The front door was chain-locked when I got home the next morning. With a Styrofoam cup of mini-mart coffee in one hand, I'd unlocked the door with my key but couldn't get past the chain.

"Hey guys, it's Dad!" I yelled into the house.

No response.

"Guys, come on!"

Still no response.

"I know you're in there."

From behind the door came Marcy's voice, soft yet stiff: "Nick, I told you I don't want to see you right now."

"You told me that yesterday," I said.

"I meant it indefinitely," she said coldly.

"Come on, Marcy. I told you this was all a big misunderstanding. And besides, today is sign-up day for baseball. You don't want Wesley to miss that, do you?"

Silence.

Then I heard the chain come off and I pushed the door open. As soon as I entered the doorway, I was pummeled with a round of orange Nerf bullets—*thwap, thwap, thwap.* I heard Wesley laugh uncontrollably from behind the couch.

"Mom told me I could shoot you as much as I want," he said as his laughter died down.

"I'm sure she did."

The barrage of Nerf bullets left me with the impression that Marcy had said nothing to Wesley about our predicament. So my only concern for the moment was Marcy, who turned away from me in her pink terrycloth bathrobe, tightening the belt as I stepped cautiously into the house. I couldn't see her face at first, but her hair was a mess. It was almost 11 a.m. I'd slept late, and I suspected she had, too. Wesley was still in his pajamas.

"Baseball," Marcy muttered, just loud enough so I could hear. "Damn baseball. I can't do anything without baseball entering the equation."

"Wesley, why don't you get dressed," I said as he crouched behind the couch again. "Baseball sign-ups are at your school gym this morning. We'll go over and sign up."

He took aim and fired another round. I let the foam

bullets hit me in the chest—*thwap, thwap, thwap*. As soon as his chamber was emptied, he said with a naïve cheerfulness, "Okay. I'll get dressed now."

While Wesley was upstairs changing, I followed Marcy into the kitchen. She poured herself a cup of coffee, leaned back against the counter and finally turned toward me. Her face was pale with dark circles under her eyes.

"Listen," she said. "Take him to baseball sign-ups, but then bring him right back home. Do you hear me? I have a lot to figure out right now. *We* have a lot to figure out. But I don't want it to affect Wesley, so take him to sign-ups this morning, and nowhere else."

I nodded.

"I suppose you're going to want to manage his team, too?" she asked.

"Of course."

She looked down at her feet and muttered out loud again: "Baseball, baseball, baseball. Why does it complicate my life so much?"

"What did you tell Wesley after I left last night?" I asked, because I wanted to be certain about where I stood with him.

"You heard him," she said, stomping out of the kitchen and leaving me behind. "I told him to shoot you."

Indefinitely. The word rattled around in my brain as I drove Wesley to the school gym. It was such a tough word to take, loaded with whole new meaning. She hadn't said it yesterday—I was sure of it. I remembered clearly what she'd actually said. *I'd like you to leave. I don't even want to see you right now.* A man doesn't forget those types of statements. And now she'd changed her stance. Or maybe clarified her stance. Either way, it hurt and it worried me, because I knew from experience that Marcy was no pushover when it came to matters like this.

After I'd fessed up about whose underwear Marcy found in my apartment, she wiggled into her jeans and turtleneck, scooped up her sweater and jacket, and stormed out. She slammed the apartment's front door and yelled, "Fuck you!" through the closed door. I didn't chase after her. Instead, I sat alone in bed, head buried in my hands, her "Fuck you!" reverberating in my head. The next afternoon, Marcy sent me a brief email saying only that she'd cancelled all the arrangements and the wedding was off, adding another "Fuck you" at the end.

That night I went to her apartment and knocked on the door, but if she was inside, and she probably was, she never replied. I knocked twice the next day, but still, no response. Then I started calling, once a day, but no pickup. I left voicemails with messages such as: "Marcy, please, I really love you and I really want to talk this out."

After several days of calling once a day, I decided to give her some space, but I kept calling once a week. She kept dodging me.

I missed her. Missed the way she made any happy hour or casual dinner something to look forward to, missed the way we chatted late into the night, whether we were scarfing down pizza at 2 a.m. or lying in bed after sex. Missed all of those lovely little freckles and the way she looked at me with those big hazel eyes—yes, even when she was ticked at me.

For two months, I tried varying my call times, thinking I might catch her when she didn't suspect it was me, and I varied my voice messages. I started asking about her and saying things like, "I hope you're having a good week." And for two whole months, she wouldn't pick up. I was beginning to believe my chances of ever reconciling with her were nil.

Maybe I wore her down, or maybe she was haunted by the thought of remaining single, as she was about to turn thirty. Whatever the reason, Marcy finally picked up the phone.

"You sure are persistent," she said.

Surprised that she'd finally picked up, the only reply I could muster was, "Yeah."

"I can't believe I'm even talking to you," she said.

"I miss you," I said.

A pause. "Of all the things you could say to me right now, that's probably one of the best."

"And I can't tell you how sorry I am."

Another pause. "And that's probably one of the things you *should* say to me right now."

"And I still love you."

Longer pause. "I see."

We met for a stroll in Rittenhouse Square—and "maybe a late lunch?" as I'd phrased it over the phone. "Maybe," she'd said. It was a Saturday in February, unseasonably warm, and the sun was out, the city bustling, people in sweatshirts and windbreakers hanging out in the parks and walking their dogs. The stroll went well, even though we started out talking like an old divorced couple. She asked me how I was doing; I said okay. She asked about things at the paper; I said they were okay. No mention of Marianne McGibbons. She told me that she'd been on two dates in the past several weeks and each was a disaster. One was with another PR guy—a "pathological narcissist," as she put it—and the other was with a young lawyer who couldn't stop talking about his old girlfriends.

We strolled some more, all the way down to Old City, and the conversation slowly became friendlier. When we passed a corner newspaper box for the *Reader*, she stopped and eyeballed the cover story, one of my stories about a crooked developer and his political connections. "That Nick Marhoffer," she cracked, "what a hack." Soon we came upon a classy old tavern called the Society Hill Hotel, and she agreed to that late lunch. We ate gourmet cheesesteaks and drank Yuengling drafts, and I suggested we go out the following weekend. She hesitated.

"I think you're having a nice afternoon," I said.

"I am, but—I don't know."

"How about two more Yuenglings? I'll bet I can talk you into it then."

"Don't be so sure. I can hold my beer."

"Just one of the reasons I love you," I said, and she laughed and agreed to go out the following Saturday. Although she did caution me, "It will just be a date."

We chose the same joint, Society Hill Hotel. Why not? It just seemed right—tasteful and comfortable, and squeezed into the corner was a piano bar that filled the place with jazzy tunes on weekend nights. We both ordered the same gourmet cheesesteaks and downed Yuenglings again, and it no longer felt like we were an old divorced couple. We talked about newspapers and PR, the Clintons and the Gores, Julia Roberts and Lyle Lovett, and the single life. When I walked her back to her apartment, I knew not to press my luck. I leaned in for a kiss, just a peck on the lips, nothing too heavy. She acquiesced. And as I pulled away, she grabbed a fistful of my shirt and yanked me back in, and we kissed passionately.

"I can't believe I'm doing this," she said. "But I have to admit, I missed you, too."

She led me inside and took two beers from her fridge, but they sat untouched on the coffee table as we kissed again on the couch. Soon she led me into the bedroom, where we had makeup sex of the first degree. Twice. The next morning, as we lay in bed together, we officially decided to make another go of it, with one caveat: Neither one of us would mention Marianne McGibbons ever again.

As I drove Wesley to baseball signups, past the well-built, red-brick homes of Misty Hill, with the white steeple of the Methodist church hovering, I was reminded that we'd moved into one of the nicer and more stable neighborhoods in central Pennsylvania. These were cozy, tree-lined streets where the homes had stood for three or four generations. They had spacious front porches with Amish-made rockers, neatly stacked piles of firewood and snow shovels leaning against the house at perfect angles. I hadn't forgotten that Tess saw it as a town full of secretly unhappy people who'd married for the wrong reason, but even so, it sure didn't feel like the type of place where men got kicked out of the house for carousing in bars with other women.

"Dad, where did you go last night?" Wesley asked from the backseat as we approached his school.

"What, exactly, did Mom tell you?"

"She cried a lot last night."

I paused, brooding.

"I see," I finally said as we pulled into the school parking lot. "And what did you do?"

"Mom let me sleep in your bed."

"That was a good idea. I'm glad she did that."

"Where did you go?" he persisted.

I pulled into a space and shifted into park. I took a deep breath and turned toward the backseat to face him. As a newspaperman, I believed in telling my son the truth. As far as I could remember, the only things I'd ever lied to him about were the existence of Santa Claus, the Easter Bunny, and the Tooth Fairy. He sat there, motionless, still strapped into his seatbelt, looking back at me with his mother's big hazel eyes.

"I stayed at a motel, pal."

"Which motel?"

"The Wayside Inn."

"Do they have a pool?"

"No, and besides, it's February."

"Why did you stay at the motel?"

"Mom and I are having some trouble, and we thought it was best."

"Are you getting a divorce?"

Oh, boy. I took my time answering.

"Neither one of us has mentioned that," I said. "It's hard to explain, but we're not getting along very well right now, but we still love each other, and I think we'll work it out, and we still love you. We both love you a ton. Believe me when I say that. It's why we came here to sign you up for another great baseball season."

"Are you staying at the motel tonight, too?"

I paused again, then let out a deep sigh. The word *indefinitely* popped back into my head.

"I guess so."

14
AVOID THE STENCH

So my marriage was on the skids, I had nowhere to stay, no job and no real prospects. I didn't even have a checkbook. Marcy and I had joint checking and saving accounts with only one checkbook, which she kept in her purse and guarded dearly. I took stock of what I had: my trusty little Honda, a cell phone, one bag of dirty clothes, and a wallet. And inside my wallet were two credit cards, each with a ten-thousand-dollar limit, and I knew now that I'd need them. I also had some sort of relationship going with another woman, albeit a married woman, though I wasn't exactly sure what our relationship was. I knew, however, that this wasn't the time to try and figure it out.

I went back to the Wayside Inn on Saturday afternoon and told the clerk I needed a room indefinitely. The clerk was a twenty-something girl with a pierced lip and some sort of snaky tattoo running down her neck. I tried to negotiate a rate lower than thirty-nine dollars, telling her I might be there a while, but she said I'd have to check with the manager on Monday morning. So I gave her my Visa card and asked for a room that might smell better than the one that stank like old vacuum grit.

"They all smell the same," she grumbled.

"If you can just give me a different room," I said, "I'll take my chances."

This is what it's like, I thought, when you get kicked out of your house, when you hit bottom: Your first goal is to avoid the stench, and you hope things improve from there.

She gave me Room 119, a corner room, and it smelled better. Before settling in, I went to Sudzies and had my growler jug refilled, but I couldn't drink much. After one plastic cup full of beer, I was wiped out. I fell asleep early, my jug sitting on the nightstand, and slept wonderfully. There's something oddly comforting about knowing you've already hit bottom and have nowhere to go but up. I woke up the next morning feeling surprisingly refreshed and walked across the parking lot to the Denny's. I feasted on the breakfast buffet, all the while trying to figure out the best way to approach Marcy again—and exactly what to say.

Should I call first? Or just drive over? Should I wait a day or two? Show up in the morning? Or evening? I decided to call on Sunday evening, because it had been a disaster when I'd showed up in person the previous day, and I was hoping she'd figure me back into her plans with the work week looming. So I did, and was surprised by her tone: businesslike, not curt. It was almost like she was expecting to hear from me, which at first I interpreted as a sign of encouragement, but I soon realized I had no reason to be encouraged.

"I made plans for Wesley after school," she said. "Felicia Spinelli is going to watch him until I get home from work. I'll leave in the morning at 8:45, and if you want to come get more clothes or whatever, I'd like you to come then. I've thought about baseball, too. I know you're going to coach his team, and I don't want to deny him anything if I don't have to. But practice won't start for another month or so, and so we don't have to figure that out right now. I'm sure we can work something out."

"Marcy, you have to listen to me..."

"Where are you?" she asked.

"The Wayside. Where did you think I'd go?"

"I thought you might go to your mother's in Johnstown."

"Actually, I never even thought of it. But Marcy, you have to listen to me. Nothing happened. I mean it. I wouldn't lie."

"I've thought about that, Nick. I've thought about a lot of things the past couple days. And you know what: Something did happen. Even if you never had a physical relationship with that woman, and I'm still not sure I believe that you didn't, but even if you didn't, you still had a relationship. It's called an emotional relationship, which in some ways is even worse than a physical relationship. So something did happen, and you have no idea how hurt I am."

"What did you call it? An emotional relationship? Is that an Oprah thing?"

"Don't be glib."

"I'm not trying to be glib. I'm just confused."

"Oh, yeah, well I'm *very* confused. And hurt. Very, very hurt."

And with that, I stopped pleading my case.

"Okay, listen," I said with a heavy sigh. "Let Felicia watch Wesley this week. I'll come by tomorrow for more of my clothes, and I'll check back with you soon."

"Come get your clothes, but don't check back with me. As I told you earlier, I don't want to see you."

On Monday morning, I stopped in the Wayside office to see the manager about a better rate. He was a skinny guy in his early thirties with a goatee and a cheap tie, and when I first saw him I was confident I could get him down.

"How long will you be here?" he asked dryly.

"Indefinitely."

"Can you give me a sense?"

"I wish I could, but I don't know what else to say, except indefinitely."

"Hmm," he said, scratching his goatee.

"How about twenty-nine dollars a night?" I asked.

"Hmm." He paused. "I don't think so. That's pretty low."

"How about thirty-four? Meet me halfway."

"Hmm." He paused again. "Okay. Sounds like you'll be here a while, at least. I can do thirty-four."

From there, I went home to get more clothes. Marcy was at work and Wesley was at school, and it felt strange being in our empty house with permission only to gather clothes. An outsider in my own home. I thought briefly about doing something dastardly—rearranging the furniture, perhaps. Or preparing a big dinner, a wine-and-candles kind of thing to surprise Marcy when she got home. I soon came to my senses, and realized it might only create an added complication. So I packed one more bag with my running gear and a few more changes of clothes; I didn't want to take all of my clothes, because I didn't want to acknowledge that I could be gone that long. Then I left.

I felt the need to talk to Rocco—partly for some male companionship, but mostly because his wife had Marcy's ear—so I called him at his Capitol office and asked him to meet for beers after work. He suggested Lumpy's, an old Harrisburg bar that was a short stroll from the Capitol. Just after 5 p.m., I parked on State Street, in the shadow of the green-and-gold Capitol dome, pumped a few quarters into the meters and meandered down Second Street to Lumpy's.

It was a tiny haunt, a green-brick building that

remained inconspicuous among the trendy and splashy downtown eateries that had sprung up on Second Street over the past several years. Inside, the bar was mostly empty, just a couple guys in shirts and ties at one end of the bar, and one scruffy guy at the other end who wore a red hooded sweatshirt and looked as if he'd spent the afternoon sleeping in the alley. Even when it was empty, Lumpy's felt like it could come to life at any moment, as if the mirrored walls and the long mahogany bar could tell stories after hearing decades' worth of political chit-chat, rumors, trickery and chivalry. I immediately felt comfortable there, knowing the walls had heard much juicier stories than mine, and so I sat down in the middle of the bar, ordered a Yuengling draft and started a tab, figuring Rocco would pick it up.

I was on my second draft when Rocco blew into the bar, his blue tie undone and charcoal trench coat flapping at his sides. He apparently knew the two guys in shirts and ties who were there when I arrived, because he patted one on the back and said, "Hey, gentlemen." His eyes scanned the rest of the bar, which had filled up somewhat with more guys in ties, but he didn't acknowledge anyone else. He draped his coat over the stool beside me, gave me a hearty pat on the back, sat down and let out a cheery, "What's up, neighbor?"

Of course, he knew what was up. And he knew that I knew that he knew. Which is why, while I'd been sitting there sipping my draft and waiting for him to finish up his business at the Capitol, I felt conflicted about seeing Rocco. On the one hand, I envied him and wanted his company. Some masculine part of my psyche—could it be simple male ego?—wanted to be just like him, wanted to be popular with the guys and the girls while cruising through life giving everyone what they wanted, whether it be state-funded park projects or a quick, semi-discreet boffing after a game. At the same time, I was beginning to resent him, and not just because he was making me wait for him in a bar on a lonely Monday. And it was, I was certain, more than simple jealously. It was, finally, my recognition that his life was basically one big lie, the worst sort of political life, where public appearances directly conflicted with private realities. He was, as far as I knew, our town's number-one adulterer, all while living a chuckling, back-slapping life with a beautiful, yet ignorant, wife. Meanwhile, I'd had a few drinks in a bar with one woman—and admittedly, flirted with her way more than I should have—yet I'm the one who got kicked out of the house? I thought briefly, not seriously, about this spectacle: climbing atop the immaculate steeple of the Misty Hill Methodist Church and shouting to the whole damn town, *Listen everyone, I'm not the adulterer around here— it's Rocco Spinelli! You have to believe me!*

As soon as he sat down, Rocco nodded at the bartender and pointed at my draft, a signal that he'd have the same. I wasn't in the mood for any breezy neighbor talk or boozy guy talk, so while the bartender poured Rocco's draft, I cut right to business.

"Listen," I said, hunched over my pint glass, my head tilted toward him. "You know what happened with me and Marcy, I'm sure. I was hoping you'd talk to Felicia for me about this big mess I'm in."

"Yeah," he said as his beer arrived. "I hear you're sticking it to Tess Sugarmeier."

"Wrong—totally wrong," I said, knowing I sounded impatient. "We went out for drinks one day. That's accurate. And we've been a little too friendly lately, even though I know that Marcy's always been terribly jealous of her. But Marcy and I have been having problems ever since I lost my job. So it's complicated. But I never touched Tess."

I reminded myself that I needed him as an ally and regained my sense of patience. "Honestly," I continued. "I'd tell you if I touched her, but I didn't. I really didn't."

"Jesus," he said after his first sip of beer. "It does

sound complicated."

I nodded agreeably.

"That Tess is really hot," Rocco said.

"Oh, believe me, it's been tempting."

"So nothing happened? Nothing at all?"

"I'm being straight with you."

"How do you know Felicia will listen to me?"

"I don't."

"To be honest, I doubt she will," Rocco said, as if he didn't even want to try. "She'll figure I'm just your buddy trying to get you out of the doghouse. Women have this thing—there are moments they trust men completely, and others they don't trust us one iota. This is one where they don't."

Maybe Rocco was an expert on when women do and don't trust men, or maybe his own marriage was forever complicated by issues of trust, whether the two of them knew it or not, but either way I realized his heart wasn't in this for me, and it suddenly seemed like a longshot.

"Will you try?" I asked.

"Sure. Of course."

"Thank you," I said earnestly.

"Where are you staying?"

"The Wayside. It sucks."

"Sounds like it," he said. "Don't worry, I'll talk to Felicia. See if we can't get this straightened out."

I swallowed a gulp of beer, which didn't go down well. It forced out a big burp, which I covered with my hand, and left me with a slight throbbing in my chest. I felt dismal and weak from head to toe, and I knew Rocco would let me down. At least he picked up the tab.

———

For the rest of the week, I mustered the energy to go on long runs in the morning and dallied around the Misty Hill Public Library in the afternoons. Because the Wayside had no computers, the library computers were my only way to connect with the outside world, to check e-mail and surf listings on job sites. I had just arrived at the library on Thursday afternoon when my cell phone rang. It was the school nurse, calling to tell me Wesley was sick.

I drove to school and was promptly directed to the nurse's office, where I found him lying on the cot beside the desk. He had one arm propped behind his head and another across his stomach, and his big eyes looked sad.

"What's wrong, bud?"

"He says he has a stomach ache," said the nurse, a formidable woman fairly deep into middle age.

"Yeah," Wesley groaned. "A stomach ache."

"You can take him home for the rest of the day," the nurse said. "I think that's the only thing left to do at this point."

"Okay. I can do that."

"He doesn't have a fever, and doesn't show any other symptoms," the nurse said. "In fact, this is the third straight day he's been in my office complaining about a stomach ache, and the past two days he said it subsided after lying on the cot for a while. But not today. Perhaps some TLC will do the job."

"I see," I said slowly, processing the facts. "I think I know what's going on."

"Yes?" the nurse asked.

"We're having some trouble at home—my wife and me. I'm sure Wesley's upset, so I think you're right about the TLC."

"In that case," the nurse said, "there is a school counselor. If problems at home are affecting his performance in school, we can set up an appointment."

"Plus," I said, "he's an only child. And he's left-handed, too."

She shot me a quizzical look and asked, "What does being left-handed have to do with anything?"

"I've read that left-handed people are more likely to

suffer from an inferiority complex."

"I think that's an old wives' tale," she said matter-of-factly, and I felt silly for mentioning it. Maybe some of my concerns over my only son weren't warranted, or even completely rational, but this wasn't the time to dwell on it.

The nurse patted Wesley's wrist and said, "Try the TLC today, and let's keep an eye on him."

"Come on," I said to Wesley, helping him off the cot. "Let's go home."

"But I thought you can't come home," Wesley said.

"It's not that simple, pal. But we'll get you home and settled."

"What's THC?" he asked.

"Not THC. It's TLC, and don't worry about it."

I waved goodbye to the nurse and made a mental note about the counselor. I put my arm around Wesley's shoulder as we left school. Halfway across the parking lot, I asked him if he was feeling better yet.

"A little," he said.

"I have an idea," I said. "If you're feeling up to it, why don't we drive out to Jake's Sporting Goods? We can get your baseball pants and spikes, and maybe a new glove. I think your old glove is probably going to be too small this year."

"Yeah," he said. "It is too small."

"So it sounds like you're feeling better."

I called Felicia Spinelli and told her about the alleged stomach ache, and that Wesley wouldn't be going to her house after school. She sounded wary, and I was certain she'd be making a frantic phone call to Marcy next, but I tried not to care. He was still my son, and I knew I was doing the right thing. Wesley was trying on a pair of Adidas spikes in Jake's shoe department when my cell phone rang.

"What's going on?" Marcy asked abruptly.

I relayed the facts to her calmly, yet still felt a bit like a child abductor.

"I'm still his dad, Marcy, so don't act like this is a big deal. I'm doing the right thing here, and he obviously feels fine now."

"I'll be home at 5:15 sharp," she said. "I expect he'll be home then, too."

"He will," I said, and we hung up on each other.

Wesley liked the size four Adidas spikes and a Rawlings glove—and thankfully we had no trouble finding a lefty glove—and as we started toward the checkout aisle I realized that Marcy would probably be the first one to see the credit card bill from our visit, and I suddenly wanted to shock her. I wanted to ring up as much as possible and imagine her gritting her teeth as she eyeballed the bill. My little way of saying, *I still have a say*.

"How about a new bat?" I asked Wesley. "And batting gloves?"

Yes and yes. What else was he going to say?

"Oh, and a cup! How could I forget a cup? We should see if you're ready for a bigger one. Am I right?"

———————

I pulled up to the house at 5:15 and saw Marcy waiting on the stoop with her coat buttoned tight, scarf wrapped around her neck and arms folded across her chest. Even from the driveway, I could see the watchful look on her face. Wesley tumbled out of the backseat with his two overstuffed Jake's bags and ran toward the front door. Marcy bent down to hug him, as the expression on her face turned warm and motherly. I was five paces behind Wesley, but she ignored me.

"How's your stomach?" she asked him.

"I'm all better," Wesley said, digging into one of the bags. "Look what I got!"

He whipped out his bat, a black Louisville Slugger, and Marcy jumped backward defensively, as if he were about to swing it at her.

"Take it easy with that," Marcy said, then finally turned her eyes toward me.

"How did you pay for that?" she asked.

"Visa."

"I see," she said, and patted Wesley's shoulder. "Run inside, honey. I want to talk to Dad."

As the screen door banged behind her, she asked, "Are you still staying at the motel?"

"Yes."

"And how are you paying for that?"

"Visa." My short answers left me with a slight sense of satisfaction. I was offended by her reaction to Wesley's alleged stomach ache, which seemed to suggest that I'd overstepped my bounds, and I felt defiant. I did not want to reveal any more than necessary.

"I see." She paused. "You know what? I can't think about that right now. How did the school contact you?"

"Cell number."

"I see."

I turned to leave, but then remembered what the nurse had told me about counseling for Wesley, so I turned back. And as I turned back, I felt confrontational, the old newspaperman on a mission once again.

"By the way," I said. "I was talking to the school nurse, and she said they have counseling available for Wesley if things between us start to affect his schoolwork, and I told her we'd keep it in mind. I think we should consider it."

"I'll have to think about that," she said coolly.

"And another thing," I said, "I understand that *you* don't want to see me right now, but you can't make that decision for Wesley, and you don't have the right to keep him away from me. I built the last eight years of my life around him, and I should be able to see him more often."

"Maybe," she said in a sassy, in-your-face tone, "you should have thought about that before you started seeing what's-her-name."

"For Christ's sake," I said, my voice rising. "I told you I

never touched her, but if you don't want to believe me, fine. But I want to see my son!"

I wondered if the neighbors could hear me, but I didn't care.

"Don't talk to me in that tone, not after what you did to me."

"I'm totally serious, and I'm not backing down."

She locked her jaw and narrowed her eyes. I locked my own jaw and stared right back in her face.

"I made arrangements with Felicia," she snapped.

"I don't care. Arrangements can be changed."

"Fine," she said, and I was surprised to hear that word come out her mouth. "You can come see him on Fridays. I'll tell Felicia you'll pick him up at her house after school. But I want him back here by 7 o'clock."

It wasn't much, but it was a small victory, one that I hadn't been expecting, and so I took it.

"Fine," I said, turning to leave. "Tell Felicia I'll be there every Friday."

15
DON'T THINK WITH
YOUR PENIS

I settled into life in Room 119: breakfasts at Denny's, afternoons at the library and evenings at Sudzies, bellied up alone at the bar. At the library, I checked out books by the armful—how-to books on coaching baseball; biographies on great leaders such as Lincoln and Churchill; even a relationship book titled, *Win Your Ex Back in Ten Easy Steps.* Yet as I leafed through the books, usually while propped up on my saggy motel bed, three or four pillows stacked against the nicked-up headboard behind me, I found myself thinking about Tess Sugarmeier. I wondered which woman might be thinking about me—my wife or her—and which one figured into my own future. As far as I could tell, each was unhappily married, and the odds on each seemed about fifty-fifty.

As hard as it was some days, I kept mustering the energy to run, and one weekday morning I saw Felicia Spinelli, alone in a patch of frozen grass, hovering above her small easel, painting a small corner of the winter landscape in Oak Park. She wore furry boots and a bulky ski jacket with the hood pulled over her head, yet from the trail I was on I could still see her profile—petite and pretty Mediterranean features with a look of perpetual disappointment on her face, which made me wonder if, even on some subconscious level, she knew her life and marriage were so much more complicated than they appeared on the surface. She was a South Philly girl who'd grown up in the same rowhouse neighborhood as Rocco and married him young—which may or may not have explained Rocco's tendency to stray—but she lacked Rocco's gregarious nature and always seemed to prefer being shut off from the tidy, suburban culture in which she now lived.

I slowed my pace to a shuffle jog, because I wanted to stop and talk to her but first had to convince myself it was a good idea. Clearly, my plea to Rocco to talk some sense into her, and by extension, Marcy, had fallen on deaf ears, so I felt the need to make the case myself. I wanted to personally explain that I never actually cheated on my wife, that the afternoon I'd had drinks with Tess was a big mistake, but not quite as big as it seemed. I also wanted to ask about Wesley, to see how he seemed when he came home in the afternoon and went to her Ethan Allen-lookalike house instead of mine.

As I shuffled down the trail, I realized that Felicia didn't see me. Or if she did notice the figure of a lone jogger somewhere out of the corner of her eye, she didn't realize it was me. Her eyes were glued to her little canvas, and I suspected that's how Felicia preferred to go through life—as if she didn't notice all the shit going on around her, and only wanted to see the stuff that's beautiful enough to paint. I decided it would be pointless to stop, so I picked up my pace and ran past her, through the maze of oak trees in winter, which, I was quite certain, wouldn't have any joggers in Felicia's painting.

And then Valentine's Day, which came and went. I let it come and go, because things were too complicated to try to include either of the women in my life in any way. I spent the night according to my new routine: a pulled-pork sandwich and a few lagers at the bar at Sudzies, followed by late-night cable news until I dozed off. Lying in bed watching Chris Matthews jabber about the dismal state of the new Republican Party, I imagined Marcy crying herself to sleep with Wesley in bed beside her, and Tess and her husband going through the motions—a bout of emotionless sex, perhaps, with the obligatory dozen roses sitting in a vase in their living room.

I missed seeing Wesley every day, being there in the morning and seeing his messy hair and sleepy eyes, and in the afternoon, when he came home from school and dropped his backpack in the middle of the living room floor, and I would inevitably say, "Is that where that belongs?" And to an extent, I missed Marcy—or at least I missed how things were before. I missed the smell of our house in the morning—hazelnut coffee and toasted Pop-Tarts—and the feel of our cushy bathroom rug under my bare feet. I missed the cocoa butter soap that Marcy splurged on, and the vanilla-scented candles she'd light in the house at night. And Wesley's night-time routine, perfected at age three: a hug and a kiss for Marcy and me and a prayer that began, "Now I lay me down to sleep..."

By comparison, the people I encountered most in Room 119 were a pair of maids—an older Latino woman named Luciana on Monday through Friday, and a young Russian woman named Sophya on Saturday and Sunday. Luciana was efficient but never smiled. She gave me a fresh bath mat every day, while Sophya had a quick smile but sometimes forgot the bath mat. It was nice to get a new mat every day because they were cloth and bunched up easily and remained damp after one use, and I had few pleasures in life in Room 119. Besides the bath mats, the towels were rough and the soap bars were small and heavily perfumed. And while Room 119 smelled better than my first, it still smelled of some vague combination of furniture polish and cheap air freshener. Perhaps worst of all, the walls were thin. I often heard people in 118 or 120 talking loudly on the phone, or coming back drunk at 2 a.m. and arguing over TV choices or pizza orders.

One afternoon I came home from the library and heard moaning coming from Room 120. It was a female voice— low and sultry. *Oh, God*, I thought. *Do I have to listen to this?* Soon I heard a male voice. "Yeah, baby, yeah." Then both voices rising together. The woman: "Ooh, ooh. Right there. Ooh." The guy: "Yeah, baby, yeah." Then the headboard banging against the wall: *thud, thud, thud.* I checked the clock. It was 4:05 p.m.

"Ooh, ooh."

"Yeah, baby."

Thud, thud.

"Ooooooh!"

"Yeahhhhh!"

When I heard them leave five minutes later, I hustled to my window and peeked out the drapes, hoping I'd recognize them, hoping the guy was Larry Swanger, and the woman was Jane White or Felicia Spinelli—anyone who'd spread rumors about me. Or could it be Rocco and one of his extramaritals? But no. The 120 lovers were two thirty-something strangers who hurried into separate cars and drove away without even a kiss goodbye.

So life in Room 119 was depressing me, wearing me down. I often felt tired, and wondered if I should stop running as much in the mornings or drinking as much in the evenings. While in the library in the afternoons, I found myself napping, closing my eyes for a moment while stretched out in one of the orange leather chairs that had sat in the exact same spot for twenty years, then waking up an hour later with spittle dripping from my chin.

Three days after Valentine's Day, eager for some personal interaction with a woman who wouldn't treat me like the plague, I called Tess. I asked her out for coffee, suggesting a quaint, corner coffeehouse in Misty Hill called the Java Hut. I arrived just after 9 a.m., when the place was still crowded with stay-at-home moms who'd dropped off their kids at school. There were no tables available, only a few vacant seats at the counter, so I grabbed a counter seat and ordered a house coffee. I draped my jacket over the seat beside it to save it for Tess, and she came in ten minutes later, dressed in a snazzy gray sweatsuit with hot-pink stripes, looking fresh and beautiful, as if she'd just left a salon. She also wore her big hoop earrings and soft pink lipstick.

"Hey there, coach," she said cheerfully.

I picked up my coat and patted the seat, and she sat down.

"How's life?" she asked.

I immediately wondered if she knew the answer to that question, but I decided not to be a downer.

"Hanging in there," I said casually.

She ordered a tall skinny latte, while I asked for a refill of house coffee.

"I trust you had a good Valentine's Day?" Tess asked.

Whoa, I thought. *She's in no mood for idle chit-chat.*

"That would be a long story," I said, trying to be vague. "How about you?"

"Is that all you're going to tell me? Mine was okay, but go ahead. I have time for a long story."

I realized that the news about me being kicked out of the house apparently hadn't made the rounds yet. I took a big swig of coffee and said, "I'm not sure I feel like getting into it."

"You don't have to," she said as her latte arrived. "I don't want to pry. How about the job search? Any news there?"

"Not really. There's an editor in Altoona who wants to open a Capitol bureau, and I keep exchanging emails with him, but he's having trouble fitting it into his budget right now. Cross your fingers for me."

As I crossed the fingers on my left hand, Larry Swanger's wife appeared in the doorway, and we immediately made eye contact. Though she was one of the gossip-mongers who'd spread the word about my afternoon of drinks with Tess, I hardly knew the woman. I didn't even know her first name. She was a mousey woman with salt-and-pepper hair, and as she averted her eyes from mine and sought out her friend at one of the tables, I knew that Marcy would soon find out that Tess and I had been here together, too. My heart sank.

I watched Mrs. S. wiggle her way between the tightly packed tables and thought, *Fine, rat me out again, you little bitch. I've got nothing left to lose.* Tess seemed oblivious to her—and to all the other women around us—almost as if she wanted her louse of a husband to find out about our little coffee date. While I tracked Mrs. S., Tess touched up her lips with her pink lipstick.

"So you're sticking with newspapers?" Tess asked.

"I don't know what else to do."

"I'm sure there are a lot of things you could do."

"Maybe. I looked into public relations, but it's not for me. I don't have the right personality for it."

I wanted to change the subject, the whole tone of the conversation, the whole feel of my morning, not to mention my life. I raised my eyebrows whimsically and said, "Maybe I'll write a book. About Little League baseball. Boy, do I have some good stories to tell."

"Seriously," she chuckled.

I looked back at Mrs. S., who sat down at her friend's table with her back turned to me. Yet I was happy with my little crack about a baseball book, satisfied that it had its intended effect, if only on my line of conversation with Tess, and I tried to forget about Mrs. S. and whatever she might say about me, because sometimes you realize there are things you simply can't control.

"What about teaching?" Tess asked off-handedly. "I think you'd make a great high school English teacher. Have you thought about that?"

My eyes were still stuck on Mrs. Swanger's scrawny back, so I didn't completely process the thought. "Teaching, huh?" I said half-heartedly. "That's an interesting thought."

Tess set her mug on the counter and cocked her head my way, as if she'd just realized she had something serious to discuss.

"I mean it," she said. "It might be hard to face the reality of a second career, but a lot of people change directions mid-life. People do all sorts of things. Some people start businesses, some people teach. You have to think about what options might be out there that fit your personality. Yes, it might mean that you have to update your skill set, go back to school or something, but I think you have to be open to it and think outside the box."

I pulled my eyes away from Mrs. Swanger and started processing what Tess was talking about.

"And besides," Tess continued. "I hear half the English teachers at the high school are ready to retire, and high schools love to have male teachers. It's an advantage to be a man, I think."

Finally I processed it. I plunked my mug on the counter and felt my eyes widen. Yes, this was a really good idea. After all, I worked well with kids, albeit younger kids, and it certainly seemed like important work: molding young minds. Though I didn't have a teaching certificate, I had a journalism degree and a writing background and it sure sounded like something worth looking into. Why hadn't I thought of it before? And why hadn't Marcy, whose own mom was an English teacher?

And Tess. Maybe, I thought as she raised her cup to those lovely lips, she had as much substance as style.

Maybe I'd gotten another peek into her personality this morning as I tried to yank myself out of the post-Valentine's doldrums: Not only was she beautiful and easy-going, but reasonable and smart. She wasn't simply a gabby ex-cheerleader. Maybe she was, in fact, the right person in my life at the right moment. And if Mrs. S. goes blabbing about seeing us here together, so what?

A new career path—teaching! The idea, along with my second cup of coffee, gave me a jolt. My mind raced, thinking about how to find a college program where I could get certified, perhaps even working as a substitute in the meantime.

"I think," I said optimistically to Tess, "you just gave me something to look into today."

"I'm glad," she said, and we nodded in unison at the worth and wisdom of second careers.

We finished our coffee as the Java Hut began clearing out. Mrs. Swanger hadn't budged, but I no longer cared. I fished in my wallet, which had ten dollars, so I was able to pay the tab this time, thankfully. I dropped it on the counter before Tess objected, and she didn't even try to pay.

As we strolled out the door together, Tess asked, "So you're going to coach baseball again this year?"

"Yes, of course. I'm looking forward to it."

"I *really* hope you can get Carter on your team again."

As we moseyed through the parking lot, past a shiny SUV, an old Volvo and a new Volvo, I had a caffeine high and sense of hopefulness about exploring a new career, so I decided suddenly to pry deeper into Tess's life. I wanted to know more about the woman who'd just given me the best idea I'd had in a while and a much-needed shot of optimism.

"Can I ask you something personal?" I asked her.

She didn't hesitate, even seemed a little curious. "I suppose."

"Does your husband know we meet like this?"

"Like what?"

"You know, like this. For drinks and coffee."

She looked at her watch.

"Let's see," she said. "It's almost 10 a.m., so Joe's been out of the house for three hours, and I just hope he's had his pants on the whole time. Does that answer your question?"

I felt sorry for her, and I wondered for the first time if she was genuinely interested in me, an unemployed forty-year-old man, or if her motives were more complicated. Perhaps she just wanted to make her husband jealous, exact some sort of relationship revenge. How could I tell?

"Did you see Larry Swanger's wife in there?" I asked.

"Yeah, her name is Sheila. So?"

"Marcy and I are ... well, I guess you'd say we're in a trial separation. Isn't that the term for it—a *trial* separation? I don't know what else to call it. Anyway, when you and I went out for drinks last time, her husband was in the bar, and thanks to them, word about it got back to Marcy. But that's not the only reason Marcy and I are separated. We'd been having some problems. I'm not sure if it's temporary or not, and I don't know why I'm telling you this, but I am, so there you have it."

As soon as I finished blurting that out, I knew exactly why I told her: I wanted the terms of everything to be clear. I wanted her to know exactly what I was up to, and I wanted to know exactly what she was up to.

"I'm sorry to hear that," Tess said without conviction. "Where are you staying?"

"The Wayside."

"Is it nice?"

Maybe her question was a hint that she'd like to head back to my room to find out, but this wasn't the time for me to push things any further. Not only was I unclear about what I'd be getting into, I was eager to get to the library and research that next career. And again, I remembered that sweaty night with Marianne McGibbons, two reckless twenty-somethings jumping into bed with no sense of consequences, and I reminded myself that what I did when my pants came off could affect the rest of my life. Now, at age forty, with my marriage on the rocks and a beautiful and apparently willing woman asking about my cheap motel room, I told myself, *Don't think with your penis right now.*

"It's not bad," I said, pulling my car keys from my pocket. "Let's do this again soon."

"Love to," she said.

I went straight to the library and logged onto one of the computers. With a simple Google search—*teacher certification Pennsylvania*—I was off and running. Penn State had a program, which was offered at its branch campus in Harrisburg. *Shit,* I thought, *could it be this easy? And why,* I wondered again, *didn't I think of this earlier?*

It wasn't all that easy, of course. There was the whole matter of tuition, no easy task for someone unemployed and living in a motel. I sat back in the rickety library chair and rubbed my chin and mulled options for how to pay the tab. Financial aid? Possibly. My savings with Marcy? Probably not. Hmm.

There was, of course, one other option, one that I hadn't relied on for anything in quite some time: My mother, living alone in Johnstown, with a half-decent retirement and surely some savings stashed away.

16
MOM

My dad made a lot of mistakes in his short life, but he also made at least two wise moves: He married a good woman and remained a loyal Democrat until the day he died. As a Democratic committeeman in an old steel town, he'd call off from his number-cruncher job every Election Day to work the streets, handing out fliers and offering the old folks a ride to the polls. Of course he'd drink too much at whichever Election Night party he went to, but at least he earned the respect of the local politicos for his politicking. And when he died my mom was rewarded: She was offered a job as a secretary to Congressman Jack McDevitt, a crusty Vietnam Veteran and so-called Blue Dog Democrat. It was a decent job for her. She put in her twenty-five years and got her pension, and in a burned-out steel town like Johnstown, that wasn't so bad.

I drove to Johnstown on the last Saturday in February, after spending Friday evening with Wesley. I'd taken him to Arby's for dinner, because they accepted credit cards, then to an arcade for an hour—a hyperactive hour full of bells, whistles and screaming children. Yet it was the perfect antidote for a boy who was struggling to understand his parents' damaged relationship, because he'd perked up at Arby's as soon as I suggested the arcade, and he remained in good spirits the entire evening. When I took him home, I followed him inside to tell Marcy about my plans. It was the first time I'd seen her since our argument on the front stoop. It was 7 p.m. and there was a single glass of red wine on the counter. Marcy was still dressed for work—a red sweater vest and long black skirt over her black dress boots. The dark circles had disappeared from underneath her eyes, and her fresh complexion had returned. I was reminded just how pretty she was.

"I've made a decision," I said.

She looked perplexed, but also as if she was unsure about exploring this line of conversation with me. "About?"

"My job, or rather my career. I'm getting my teaching certificate. For teaching English."

"Where? High school?"

"Or middle school, I suppose."

"Hmm."

The look on her face suggested she might be intrigued, but she remained detached and a little chilly. She picked up her wine and took a sip. Finally she said, "That's interesting."

"To tell you the truth, I'm really excited about it."

"How does one get their teaching certificate?"

"Penn State has a program, and they offer it here at the Harrisburg campus. I'm driving to Johnstown tomorrow to tell my mom. I'll need her help to pay for it."

She nodded as she took another sip, and a trickle of wine spilled down her chin. She wiped it quickly and seemed a little embarrassed. I wondered if she'd been out drinking after work, but decided not to ask.

"Teaching, huh?" she said. "That *is* interesting."

It was a dreary drive to Johnstown. The skies were gray and the snow banks in western Pennsylvania were bigger and sootier than those in Misty Hill, and everything else in Johnstown seemed dirtier, too. It seemed that way every time I visited: the streets more littered, the old shingled houses a little more slumped. As I pulled into town from Route 56, I longed even more for the onset of spring, and among other things, the start of baseball season in Misty Hill.

I didn't call my mom to tell her I was coming. She still didn't know that Marcy and I were separated, and I wanted to tell her about the whole situation in person. I knew she wouldn't take it well, and would fret about how often she'd be able to see her only grandson under the circumstances.

I pulled up to Mom's house on Potter Street at dusk—just in time, it turned out. Mom was on her way out the door, bundled up in a thick coat and knit-green scarf, with Marty Feigenbaum, a widower who lived three doors down. He wore a red-and-black checked jacket and an orange hunting cap. Mom closed the front door behind her and spotted me as I started up the steps.

"Oh, my goodness!" Mom said. "Look who it is—but where's Wesley? Where's Marcy? You didn't come alone, did you?"

"Hi, Mom." I dropped my bag on the porch and gave her a casual, hello-type hug.

"Oh, my. What's wrong?"

"Why do you always say that?"

"Because I've lived a long time. Where is Wesley? Please tell me you didn't come home without my grandson."

I shook Marty's hand and said with a little wink, "Hi there. Are you two going somewhere?"

"Out for hot dogs, and then a Chiefs hockey game," he

154

said, a bit defensively.

"We're not going anywhere until you tell me why you're here by yourself," Mom said.

"Marcy wanted some alone time right now. That's all. No big deal."

"Alone time?" Marty said in a dumbfounded tone.

"I've had alone time for twenty-five years," Mom said. "What a ridiculous concept."

Marty sneezed and wiped his face with his coat sleeve. Mom turned a shoulder to him, a pretend-it-didn't-happen look on her face.

"So where's Wesley?" Mom asked.

"He's at home with Marcy."

"That doesn't sound like alone time," Marty said.

"I guess you're right," I said. "But it is what it is. Now, you two go ahead. Don't let me hold you up."

"No," Mom said, shaking her head fervently. "Come with us. We'll get a third ticket. They're easy to get. The Chiefs never sell out."

"No, really," I said. "I'm not in the mood for hot dogs and hockey. You two go. I'll be here when you get back."

She and Marty gave each other a look, one of those *I don't know what else to do* looks that older parents get accustomed to.

"I had a bad feeling when I woke up today," Mom said, crossing her arms.

"You say that all the time," I said, picking up my bag. "Now, go ahead. Is there anything to eat inside?"

"Leftover chicken."

"That sounds good."

As I shooed them off the porch, Mom turned and said, "We're leaving after the second quarter, so we'll be home early."

Marty didn't protest. He only said, "It's second *period*. There are no quarters in hockey."

"Sounds good," I said. "Have fun."

I ate the leftover chicken and drank a can of Coors

Light from Mom's fridge and decided to go out for a few more beers. I felt like staying in the neighborhood, so I walked down to Al's Place. Meandering down Potter Street in the dark, I passed two boarded-up homes and tried to remember if either was newly abandoned, but I couldn't be sure. Potter Street sloped downward toward a wing of the steel mill that had been shuttered since the late 1970s, and the neighborhood was eerily quiet. Al's Place sat directly across the street from the fenced-off mill, and from the outside the pub also looked battered. The letters on Al's neon sign were almost completely faded, paint was peeling off the window panes and the mortar between the bricks was chipping out. Inside, the place was half-empty and dark. Yet it also had a familiar feel: My father had brought me with him many times and allowed me to sit at the bar and eat peanuts and drink 7-Up when I was little. The peanuts were still there, but the crowd seemed rougher. The bartender was a twenty-something woman with stringy hair and a hooded sweatshirt that read "Wildwood Senior Week, '96." She was on her cell phone when I bellied up for a beer, and she seemed in no hurry to serve me.

When she finally flipped her phone off, I ordered a bottle of Iron City beer, then another, and then another. I didn't talk to anyone, just watched a college basketball game on the TV above the bar—Pitt versus Connecticut. I felt strangely at home, like I belonged, like I deserved this wearisome place. I was unemployed with a broken marriage, and I guessed half the other guys in the bar were at least one or the other. Two seats down from me was a fifty-something guy in a yellow Steelers sweatshirt, drinking Budweiser drafts and shots of Jim Beam. Beside him was a forty-something guy in a green camouflage shirt who tried flirting with the bartender, but she clearly wasn't interested. And at the end of the bar was a sixty-something guy in an orange hunting jacket who seemed to be enjoying the other guy's failed attempts to flirt with the bartender. When the guy in orange smiled, I saw he was missing a couple of teeth.

Though I had little cash on me, I could afford five beers, which only cost a total of ten dollars. I left a dollar tip and walked home with a pleasant beer buzz. My mom was home when I got there, but Marty was not. She was putzing around the dining room, lighting candles and straightening things, as if she were expecting visitors.

"There you are," she said. "I wondered where you were. I'm worried about you."

"Don't be," I said, dropping my jacket on the arm of the sofa. "I'll be all right. I'm a survivor."

"Survivor, hell." She picked up my jacket and hung it on the coat rack in the dining room, then gave me a gentle scolding: "This is where coats belong—remember?"

"What about you?" I said. "Seems like you've got yourself a boyfriend."

"Hooey," she said. "I'm too old for a boyfriend. Too old for a husband, too. That's why I said no when he asked me to marry him."

"He asked you to marry him?"

"Last year. But I shot him right down."

"You never told me."

"I shot him right down."

"How about that?" I said. "My love life's a mess, and my mom's is sizzling."

"Stop it," she said. "We're just friends. We spend time together, that's all. And you're changing the subject. Why are you home? Not that I'm unhappy to see you."

I went to the kitchen and reached into the refrigerator for a Coors Light, and she followed me. She asked me to get a beer for her, and I did. I sat down at the kitchen table, which was covered with a green-checkered tablecloth, the same type of tablecloth that had hung over that table for decades. She asked me to open her beer— her fingernails always made it hard for her, and so I did. Finally, I felt ready to tell her my whole story. In the

Marhoffer household, the kitchen table was always where the serious business of family life was discussed.

"Listen," I said with a little sigh, "things between me and Marcy are bad right now. Losing my job put extra strain on our marriage, and I've been staying in a motel. I still see Wesley, though, so don't worry about that. Maybe we can still work things out—I don't know."

"I *knew* it," she said, shaking her head for emphasis. "I just knew something was wrong. And so that's why Marcy tells me to call you on your cell phone whenever I call your house."

"Yes, that's why."

"I never liked her," Mom said bitterly. "Those people from New Jersey. And her father—he's so vulgar. You should have heard him at Christmas, and right in front of Wesley, too."

"That's not important right now. And don't say you never liked her, because I know you did. But listen to what I have to ask you."

She held her beer steady and eyed me warily. I laid out my plans for a teaching career.

"So you need money."

"Yes, I need money."

I took a swig of beer. She wrapped her second hand around her can and held it even steadier. I decided to sit quietly and let her process everything. In that bright and quiet kitchen, I could see her haggard face clearer, and her familiar smell glossed over me: the same cheap hair spray and hand cream, this time mixed with a touch of hot dogs and beer. Her face was surrounded by a mound of stiff silver hair, done up every Saturday morning by the same hairdresser for thirty years. Her skin was leathery, her eyes reddish and tired—the eyes of a woman who'd dealt with a lifetime of hard luck and loneliness, yet managed to persevere.

She rolled her eyes sideways, then downward, then sideways again. She lowered her chin and let out a little huff. All the while, she kept both hands wrapped around that silver can. Finally, she lifted her head and looked at me squarely.

"So, an English teacher," she said.

"Yes. I think I'd be good at it."

"I think it's a great idea."

"Thanks."

"Whatever you need," she said. "Count on me for whatever you need."

"Thanks again."

"When do I get to see my grandson?" she asked pointedly.

"Good question," I said. "I'll have to work on that."

I slept in my old room that night, on a squeaky mattress that I'd had since high school, and beside the same nicked-up mahogany dresser, circa 1970. Long ago, my mom had ripped down my posters of Terry Bradshaw, Pink Floyd and Led Zeppelin, but she'd left my sports keepsakes on top of the dresser: gold trophies from track and cross country seasons, and three framed photos of my cross country team, most of us with a mane of hair, and me in the back row, the tallest, with thick glasses and bad skin.

As I lay in bed, I realized how few signs of my dad remained in the house. Gone were the razors and pocket combs, the worn-out paperback crime novels, the scratchy beer mugs, the black-and-gold coffee mug, and of course the brown bottles of Imperial whiskey, which were always poorly hidden on the top shelf of the kitchen cabinet. I wondered what I might find if I were to rifle through Mom's closet—if any of his clothes or shoes remained, or the starchy dress shirts and knit slacks and pointy black shoes. They were probably gone, I thought, just like most everything else that belonged to him. I didn't know exactly when his stuff began disappearing; it seemed to happen slowly, over time, just like memory fades.

The only sign of my dad, besides some old tools in the

basement, was a family photo of the three of us. It remained prominently placed in the center of the living room mantle, as if it were Mom's official way of recognizing she was once married. Maybe that's all he deserved, one photo. It was a portrait photo, which now had a slightly faded look, taken while I was about a year old. I sat on my mom's lap in a maroon jump suit with wide eyes and chubby cheeks. She was seated, wearing thick horn-rimmed glasses and a sky-blue paisley dress with short sleeves that turned up at the edges. My dad stood behind us, shoulders firm, wearing a thin black tie and gray jacket with a handkerchief folded in his breast pocket. His black hair was thick and slightly ruffled on top. His face was thin and he had these tiny circles under his eyes; it would be years until his face turned fleshy and the circles dark and heavy. And in the photo he had a little sparkle in his eye. He wore an expression on his face that was proud and hopeful: a young man and his small family, before life wore us down and split us apart.

I'd never felt out of place in Johnstown without a dad. It was a gritty town where everybody's life seemed scarred by something. Bobby Dawkins' dad walked with a bad limp and drew worker's comp for years after his leg was crushed in a mill accident. Greg Sellinger's dad was also a drunk, the type who would disappear for days at a time on his benders. The Carvers and Freidmans, who lived at the bottom of the street, were both divorced, and Mrs. Friedman married Mr. Carver a year after Mr. Friedman committed suicide at hunting camp. Then there were the unemployed dads. After the steel mill closed, it seemed like half the dads in town were unemployed.

As I dozed off, I wondered: What would Marcy's house look like in ten years, and what would Wesley's dresser look like? Would there be any signs of me? Would Wesley feel like he belonged, wherever he lived? And how clear would his skin be? Most importantly, how often would I get to see him?

I left late the next morning, after Mom made a big breakfast and we talked more about the teaching certificate, Wesley, and even the upcoming baseball season. I told her all the details about my arrangements to see Wesley every Friday, and that I'd signed up to manage his team again. I invited her to visit on Opening Day on the first Saturday in April, figuring that was a sure-fire way to see Wesley. Then, sobered up and stuffed full of bacon and eggs, I was eager to leave, mostly because I didn't want to feel like I belonged there any longer.

17
THE ANGELS

Draft Day fell on the first Sunday in March. The coach-pitch managers gathered at Terry Hipple's diner and squeezed around the extra-large corner table. We littered the table with our notebooks, clipboards, pens and pencils as Terry ordered two pots of coffee and a plate of doughnuts. The windows offered a view of the west end of Main Street, with a Friendly's and a pair of antique shops, aging maple trees with bare limbs hovering over the sidewalks, and royal-blue banners scripted with "Misty Hill" hanging from the street lamps. I'd loved Misty Hill, but now I felt out of place. It felt too stable, at least on the surface. My life was anything but. I wanted a healthy life full of hugs and kisses and children's shouts of joy, and I envied the men I was sitting with, because I suspected they enjoyed at least two of the three. I was absolutely dying for baseball season to start.

The cast of coaches was mostly familiar: Big Ed and Terry Hipple were back, as was Reggie Knox, whose twins graduated to the next age group but would now be coaching his youngest son, who just turned seven. There were two newcomers, both Real Baseball Guys. Both were lawyers, too. One was Scott Hossinger, known around town simply as Scottie Hoss, a corporate lawyer who'd played high school ball in Misty Hill. The other was Al Andrews, who'd been Reggie Knox's assistant coach the previous year. Known as Little Al, he was a short and chummy defense lawyer who'd played second base at a small college in Lancaster County. Sam had also installed both newcomers on the league board as part of his ongoing effort to pack the board with as many Real Baseball Guys as possible. And because Terry was already serving as secretary and Reggie as treasurer, the coach-pitch division now represented the block of power on the Misty Hill baseball board. Little Al was named player agent, in charge of handling disputes that arose involving the players, and Scottie Hoss was named vice president, responsible for little more than running league meetings in the president's absence. And in Misty Hill, vice president truly was a ceremonial post because Sam DiNardo never missed a meeting.

Sam was also there to oversee the draft, and he'd ordered changes for the upcoming coach-pitch season. The first change was the draft itself. Until now, teams in the younger divisions had been compiled mostly through random assignments, but coaches had also been allowed to request certain kids, and competitive guys such as Big Ed and Reggie Knox had abused their requests to stack their teams. Sam had installed the draft after receiving several complaints from parents who were upset about certain teams running rough-shod over the others, so I was hoping the draft would bring parody to coach-pitch baseball.

The other change was even more impactful—real pitching. There'd been significant soul searching among the league leaders in the offseason after Misty Hill's twelve-year-old all-star team, coached by Rocco Spinelli, was knocked out in the first round of the district tournament. How, they wondered, can we develop our younger ballplayers better, avoid such embarrassments in the future? Their answer: Introduce the boys to real baseball sooner. So in the coach-pitch division, each game would now consist of only one inning of coach pitching. The other five innings would be real baseball, kid pitching to kid, with stealing permitted. Nobody seemed to recognize the irony that the coach-pitch level would hardly include any coach pitching.

As the coffee and doughnuts arrived, we began poring over sheets of boys' names as if studying for a final exam. Only Big Ed dug into the doughnuts. Our first order of business was to assign the managers' kids to their teams, because managers automatically got their own kids. It seemed strange when Sam said, "Nick, you get Wesley." He said it casually, of course, then quickly moved on to the next guy. But it triggered an imaginary scene in my mind, one that I'd dreamed about at least once—or would you call it a nightmare? I'm sitting in Family Court at a big wooden table, with Marcy at the opposite table, a silver-haired judge on the bench. The courtroom is gray and cold. Marcy, with a smug look on her face, is accompanied by a high-powered lawyer in a black pinstriped suit. Not me—I'm alone at my table. The judge rubs his chin and winks at Marcy and her lawyer before staring me down. Oh, God, what does he say? Who gets Wesley?

Sam DiNardo plopped six numbered slips of paper into his hat and passed it around the table. I drew the first pick, and I couldn't believe my luck, because my life at that point suggested that good luck had abandoned me forever. I was also granted first choice of team names, and one of the options was the Angels. I liked the notion of being a called an Angel. For a change. God knows, at least one person in my life considered me a Devil now. So I chose the Angels and was relieved when none of the guys cracked any bad jokes or offered any other comments about my choice, a sign they didn't recognize the irony there, either.

In the first round, I picked Moose. No, I didn't like the kid, but yes, I wanted him on my team. I wanted to win some damn games, and I knew if I didn't take him, another manager would scoop him up and be well on his way to stacking a team that would once again thump mine. It's strange how our feelings for someone can fly straight out the window when the matter at hand is winning Little League games.

Next, I chose Johnny Joust, a speedy little eight-year-old who'd played on Big Ed's potent team the previous year. I didn't know much else about Johnny, except that he was an aggressive and heady ballplayer who seemed a nice complement to Moose.

"Whew," Big Ed said. "I'm glad you're stuck with Johnny. His dad is a *major* pain in the ass."

"How so?"

"His dad," said Sam DiNardo, "is an old friend of mine, so watch what you say."

"Ah, come on, Sam," Ed said. "Everyone knows he's the most obnoxious guy in the league. I hear his wife won't let him coach because he can't control himself at the games."

"Why didn't I know that?" I said, racking my brain to picture the guy.

"He coached one year of T-ball," Ed explained. "And then his wife made him quit. I hear she withheld sex from him for three months until he finally agreed not to coach anymore."

"That's enough," Sam said.

"She won't even let him sit in the bleachers," Ed continued. "Makes him stand behind the outfield fence."

"Enough," Sam said with a wave of his hand.

"Johnny's a good kid, though," Ed added diplomatically. "Got just enough of his mom's personality."

"His mom's hot," Scottie Hoss said. "They live around the corner from me, and I'd take her kid. I want as many kids with hot moms as I can get."

There were chuckles all around.

"That's *it*," Sam said, visibly annoyed. "Next pick."

In the third, I tried to forget about Johnny's dad and focus on the list of kids, and I chose Trevor Murchie. Trevor was a solid all-around ballplayer, and I figured his meltdown at third base the previous year was an isolated incident, and I knew I could count on his dad to be my assistant again. In the fourth I chose a chunky eight-year-old named Gus Bloom, because I knew he could hit with power and should make a strong catcher. After four rounds, I had a good nucleus of eight-year-olds and felt like I had a team that could hold its own. For the next several rounds, I chose kids with a reputation for at least one skill, be it hitting or fielding, or a rep for good behavior. When the eleventh and final round came up, I had the first pick, and Carter Sugarmeier was still on the board.

With the image from my courtroom nightmare still fresh in my mind, my first inclination was to avoid Carter. I imagined Marcy's lawyer calling Larry Swanger to the witness stand, where he'd recall seeing Tess with me in the bar on the day after Christmas, and then I imagined the lawyer calling Larry's wife, who would recall seeing Tess with me in the coffee shop. Then my thinking changed, as I realized my marriage was probably doomed no matter what, and I thought that drafting Carter would be the best way to stay in good with the one woman who was still willing to see me. But then my thinking changed yet again, as I remembered the tone in Marcy's voice when I'd told her I was pursuing a teaching career, and she'd said, "That *is* interesting." Maybe Marcy was leaving the door open a crack for me. Maybe, just maybe. Or maybe not. I had absolutely no idea.

"Come on, Nick," Big Ed said, as I realized I was

brooding too long over my pick. "It's not like any of these kids will make or break your team. Just pick one."

"Okay, okay," I said. Besides Carter, I'd been eyeing Sean Keezel, a chubby eight-year-old with a reputation as one of the friendliest kids in town.

"Make your pick," Sam said. "Or I'll make it for you."

"Okay," I said. "Sean Keezel."

Scottie Hoss picked next, and he didn't hesitate.

"I'll take Carter Sugarmeier," Scott said. "That kid's mom is *hot*."

———————

When I called the parents of my new players that evening, I waited to call Johnny Joust's last, because I didn't want to deal with his dad. Finally, I took a deep breath and dialed. A man answered, and I assumed it was Johnny's dad, Dan Joust.

"Hi, this is Nick Marhoffer," I said. "I'm Johnny's baseball coach."

"Hang on," the guy said, his voice a strange mix of gruffness and disappointment. "I have to put you on with my wife."

I heard muffled voices in the background, and a minute later a woman came on the line. "Hello?" she said in a voice as sweet as caramel. "This is Cindy Joust."

"I'm Nick Marhoffer, and I'm coaching the Angels this season, and Johnny's on my team, and I'm calling to give you all the details about practice and everything."

"Oh, hi," she said, every syllable as sweet as the one before. "Johnny is really looking forward to baseball season again. So let me grab a pen."

I gave her all the details—practice times, uniform needs, my cell number. When I finished she said, "Everything sounds great. I'll make sure everything is taken care of, and if you need anything else, anything at all, you give me a ring. Let me give you my cell number."

And just like that, my reservations about dealing with Dan Joust, the Notoriously Obnoxious Dad, were allayed. It was clear to me that Cindy Joust knew how to keep her man in line. If the guy wasn't even allowed to talk to me about practice times and such, she obviously kept him on a short Little League leash. I hung up and said to myself, "Whew."

That Friday, Moose showed up at our house.

I was there to pick up Wesley for an evening at the arcade, and I was standing in the foyer when I heard a light knock on the front door. When I opened it I was dumfounded to see Moose standing on the stoop with his glove on one hand and a baseball in the other, his red Angles cap on his head and a hello-neighbor look on his face.

"Is Wesley here?" he asked, not a trace of discomfort or awkwardness in his voice, not a hint that he was the boy who'd completely spurned my son when he'd asked to play with him a year earlier.

"Yeah, I think he's in the bathroom. What's up?"

"Can he play?"

"I'll ask him," I said cautiously. I turned inside and yelled upstairs: "Hey Wesley, Moose is here. He wants to know if you want to play."

Wesley's little voice scurried out from behind the bathroom door: "Tell him I'll be down in a minute."

Marcy, who'd been cleaning up a pile of dishes, must have overheard the exchange; she drifted from the kitchen toward the front door, head cocked and eyebrows raised, holding her dish towel out as if she might snap it at anyone at any instant.

There was a flush upstairs, followed promptly by the thump-thump of Wesley's footsteps in the hallway.

"Not so fast," I yelled up the stairwell. "Did you wash?"

"Oops." A thump-thump-thump in the other direction.

I leaned out the front door and informed Moose, "He'll be out in a minute."

Moose nodded. It was a nod that revealed a complete lack of self-consciousness on the boy's part, a nod that signaled that he never felt the need to apologize for anything he'd said or done before, a nod that said, *I yam what I yam and I yam what I yam.*

Wesley barreled down the steps, blew by Marcy and me, grabbed his glove, donned his Angels cap, and darted out the front door. I caught the screen door before it slammed so I could listen to whatever plans these two numbskull eight-year-olds devised. They stood chest-to-chest on the stoop and eyeballed each other as if they weren't sure whether to wrestle or hug.

"Hey," Wesley said.

"Hey," Moose said back.

I interjected, "Why don't you guys play out in our backyard?"

Moose gave another nod, lips bunched out, an affirmative. Wesley responded with his own nod, of the sounds-good-to-me variety, and off they went, circling around the house to our big backyard.

As soon as I let the screen door slap shut, Marcy said, "What the fuck?"

"Let's go to the back window and watch," I suggested.

"Yes, let's."

We hustled into the kitchen, where the back window looked out on the yard. I took the post on the left side of the window, Marcy took the right post, and we spied on the boys as they lobbed a ball back and forth and chatted amiably—about what, I had no idea.

"So let me get this straight," Marcy said, clutching her dishtowel beside her hip like a weapon she was holding in reserve. "Wesley's on Moose's team now, and that makes him good enough for Moose to play with him. Do I have that right?"

"That sounds pretty cynical."

"No it isn't. It's spot-on. This kid Moose is a little shit."

"First of all," I said as one of Wesley's throws fell at Moose's ankles, forcing him to scoop it up like a pro, "he's not little. He's built like an eight-year-old brick shithouse."

"I'd rather Wesley play with kids like Cam. Cam may be a dorky Cub Scout, but he's a nice kid. I want Wesley to be around nice kids. Your judgment's clouded right now because you're so thrilled that Moose is on your team."

"I don't know," I said. "They're eight. Can you judge them by their social skills at this age?"

She cocked her arm with the dishtowel, and I recoiled, but she swung it back to her side, no harm done.

"I know one thing," she said bitterly. "I'll never forget that day when Wesley asked Moose to play and the little shit completely blew off my son. No mother would ever forget that."

"Me neither," I conceded. "But people change, right? So kids change, too, right?"

"Little shit," she insisted, her eyes trained on the backyard, where the two boys played nicely for a half-hour. I was happy to postpone our visit to the arcade while the boys played and I lounged on my own couch for a change, even though Marcy spent the entire half-hour catching up on laundry and vacuuming and paid little attention to me. Then Moose's mom called, asked us to send him home for dinner, thanked us for having him over, and promised to return the favor sometime.

18
THE WORST SHOULD
BE BEHIND ME

There are two highly coveted spots in every batting order, at least as far as Little Leaguers are concerned: the leadoff and clean-up hitters. Wesley, the son of a distance runner, was growing into a fast kid, and he knew it, and he wanted to be the leadoff hitter. Badly.

Our first practice was on a chilly day in mid-March, and Wesley was the first player there, ten minutes early. I was tickled to see him walking down the little trail that led to our field, wearing his red Angels cap and a gray Pirates sweatshirt, his black bat bag strapped across his back, two bat handles, old and new, sticking out of the top. I'd seen him the previous Friday, as always, but for some reason he looked bigger and older all of a sudden. A serious little ballplayer.

He met me in the dugout, clipped his bat bag to the fence, unpacked his glove, put it on and smacked it with his fist. He was ready to play ball, and seemed completely unfazed by the fifty-something temperatures.

"Hey, buddy," I said, squeezing his shoulder. "Ready for another great season?"

"Yep," he said, smacking his glove again.

"Let's start warming up in the outfield," I said, grabbing my own glove. "Easy throwing, ten yards apart. Everyone else should be here soon."

"Today at gym class," he said, "I won the fifty-meter dash."

"Great."

"So can I be leadoff hitter?"

"As I told you on Friday, we'll have to see. I think you'll definitely hit high in the lineup, but I heard Johnny Joust hit leadoff on his team last year, so we'll have to take a look at him, too."

"I'm faster than Johnny," he said plaintively.

"I'm not sure about that, but you are definitely fast, so that's a good thing."

I didn't want to tell him that I'd practically made up my mind, and Johnny Joust was already penciled in to hit leadoff, especially now that the coach-pitch level would resemble real baseball. I'd spent the past couple weeks asking around town about the kids I'd drafted, and everyone said Johnny was a spark plug, a fiery, freckle-faced little kid with a knack for getting on base and getting home. Wesley, I figured, could hit second.

The next few weeks of practice went by quickly, because time always seems to fly after baseball season starts. Even when I wasn't running practice, I was tending to the field or watching The Weather Channel in my motel room so I knew when to schedule or cancel practice. It was a cool but relatively dry spring, and only two of our practices were rained out. And those chilly March practices confirmed my belief that Johnny should hit leadoff. But to be absolutely sure, I timed the boys running around the bases on our last practice before Opening Day. Sure enough, Johnny had the best time at 12.9 seconds; Wesley was next at 13.1.

Opening Day was damp and unseasonably cold. It had rained the previous day, so it took thirty minutes of raking to get the field ready to play. As planned, my mom came from Johnstown, and Marcy's parents came from Trenton. Thankfully, Marcy and all the grandparents sat together in the bleachers beside our dugout. Everyone was bundled in a jacket or hooded sweatshirt, and my mom draped a black-and-gold blanket over her lap. In our broken family, I realized, baseball appeared to be the only way to get everyone together.

We played Scottie Hoss' team, the White Sox, which meant Tess was there, too. I spotted her at the beginning of the game, wearing a pink North Face jacket and mittens, and even on this raw day she brought a bottle of Diet Coke. She sat in the bleachers across the field, both mittens wrapped around the bottle. She was chatting pleasantly with the parents around her. We made eye contact.

After an instant, though, she veered her eyes away. And then she shifted on her bleacher seat, turning a shoulder toward me. I don't know what I was expecting—a wave? a smile?—but I was surprised she turned away from me so quickly. Could she be upset with me for something? I hadn't called her for a few weeks, but that was only because I was busy with baseball matters and conflicted about whether I should be pursuing her or Marcy, and I knew I'd see her soon enough. Then again, maybe I was reading into her body language. Maybe Tess didn't mean anything by it, or maybe she had the good sense not to flirt with me at a game with the rest of my family in attendance—good sense that I'd never shown.

I toed the dugout dirt underneath my feet and decided I should concentrate only on baseball for six innings.

After the lone first inning of coach pitching, which under Sam's new rule did not count toward the final score, Johnny Joust led off with a single to right. I promptly gave him the steal sign, an ear wiggle. I'd put a fair amount of thought into what our steal sign would be, because signs were a completely new concept to these youngsters and the ear wiggle seemed unmistakable. On the first pitch to Wesley, Johnny obeyed the sign and swiped second with ease. Wesley dribbled the next pitch down the third-base line, where the third-baseman fielded it cleanly, and Johnny had the good sense not to run. The third baseman didn't even attempt a throw to first, and I had runners on first and second with nobody out. Nice start to the season, I thought.

On the very next pitch, with Moose at the plate, Wesley took off from first. I was stunned because Johnny was still on second and I hadn't given *anyone* the ear wiggle. The catcher, arm cocked, ran down the third-base line, more concerned with Johnny than Wesley. Johnny didn't budge—he held his ground on second while Wesley slid into the base. The catcher promptly realized we had two runners on the same base, and he ran across the infield, arm still cocked, ready to throw if necessary.

"Wesley, get back!" I yelled. "Get back to first!"

Then chaos. Players and coaches shouted wildly from the dugouts. Parents screamed from the bleachers. Above it all, I heard a guy waving and yelling furiously from beyond the outfield fence, and I immediately knew it was Dan Joust, the Notoriously Obnoxious Dad. He was short and stocky with buzz-cut red hair. "Stay there, Johnny!" he shouted. "Stay there!"

Johnny remained glued to second base, and as Wesley stood up, Johnny gave him a shove toward first base. But Wesley didn't go back. His eyes darted from first to second, and then he gave Johnny a shove toward third. As Johnny shoved Wesley toward first again, the catcher arrived at second, arm still cocked.

"Tag them!" Scottie Hoss yelled to his catcher. "Tag them both!"

And so he did. Wesley first, then Johnny. Johnny had the right to the base, and he'd never left it, and so he was safe, but Wesley was out. He dropped his chin to his chest, a dejected look on his face.

"All right," I said, trying to keep my composure. "Hustle off, Wes. We'll get 'em next time."

"Good job, Johnny!" Dan Joust yelled from the outfield, after all the other shouting died down. "Keep your head in the game!"

As I tried to ignore the N.O.D., I noticed from the corner of my eye that a woman approached him, gently took his arm and led him back to a set of folding chairs. She was attractive—petite and spry with a Dorothy Hamill hairdo—and was Johnny's mom, no doubt. It was pretty clear to me that after that one outburst, Cindy Joust had easily gotten her man under control.

My eyes shot across the field to the bleachers where Tess sat. We made eye contact again. And once again, she turned her eyes away after just a second. In the midst of this craziness on the field, I felt a pinch of hurt. It would have been nice to get a warm smile from someone, anyone, a smile that said, *It's just the first game, so it's okay.* And I knew Marcy wasn't ready to send any warmth my way. It also would have been nice to know I had someone to talk to after the craziness ended, and in Tess's case, talk about more than kids and baseball. I wanted to thank her for her insights into second careers and her idea to pursue teaching, let her know how things were moving along. But no. Not today. I scanned back across the diamond to where Marcy sat with my mom and in-laws in our bleachers, and strangely, she seemed to be staring me down. But why? Watching to see if I could avoid a Bad Coaching Moment? Or whether, in a difficult moment, I looked toward Tess?

Good God, I thought, my life was complicated. Might

as well get my head back in the game.

With Johnny as our lone runner on base, Moose doubled to left, and Johnny scored easily. But our next two hitters struck out, and so we took a 1-0 lead, which would have been a bigger lead if Wesley hadn't been so damned eager to steal second base.

"You have to wait for the steal sign," I said to Wesley in the dugout. "You can't steal a base with another runner on it."

"But I'm *fast*," he said, choking up. "I'm just as fast as Johnny."

"I know," I said, patting his shoulder. "But you have to be patient. You'll get your chance. Now buck up. Let's play good defense and shut these guys down."

Which is what Moose did. Sam's new rule also included instructions for the umpires to expand the strike zone significantly so these youngsters didn't walk most batters—anything from the shins to the shoulders was deemed a strike—and the result was a lot of swings and misses. Moose pitched two scoreless innings, allowing just two hits to go with six strikeouts, and when we came up to bat in the fourth the score was still 1-0, and we had the top of the order coming up.

Johnny doubled down the right field line, then stole third on the first pitch to Wesley, who then drew a walk after the Sox's pitcher threw him four pitches in the dirt. With second base open and Wesley dying to steal a base, I gave him the ear wiggle on the first pitch to Moose. The catcher, once again obsessed with Johnny at third, didn't even attempt a throw to second base, and Wesley finally had his first stolen base.

Whew, I thought, *the worst should be behind me.*

But on the next pitch to Moose, Wesley took off again. Yet Johnny was still on third, and there was no open base for Wesley! Again! And again, chaos ensued.

The catcher darted down the third-base line with the ball as Wesley arrived and he and Johnny jostled for position on the base. "Wesley, get back!" I yelled, to no avail. Soon the catcher, who by now was an old hat at this game of Two Runners on the Base, tagged Wesley out. And Wesley's chin fell into his chest again.

"You've got to get this down," I said to him as he walked off the field. "You can't steal a base with another runner on it."

"But I'm *fast*," he said, moping.

"Stealing bases is about more than just being fast. You have to know the right time to go."

"But I'm *really* fast."

"Sit down and talk to Coach Gene about it," I said, hoping Gene Murchie would have better luck than me. "And try to *listen*."

Moose followed with a liner to center field, and Johnny scored easily from third, giving us a 2-0 lead. But once again, it was our only run of the inning, and we'd lost the opportunity to score more.

After pitching three scoreless innings—thanks to nine strikeouts—Moose appeared to tire in the fifth, lobbing the ball right down the middle of the jumbo strike zone. And the Sox got to him, scoring three runs in the fifth and adding an insurance run in the sixth. We didn't score in the final two innings, thanks to six straight strikeouts, and we lost, 4-2.

In the dugout afterward, I reminded my Angels that it would be a long season, full of ups and downs. Just keep plugging, I said. They nodded in unison, but still had long faces. Wesley looked the worst, eyes moist with tears, nose dripping. Most of them perked up, however, after I told them to hustle over to the concession stand for their Player's Snack.

As I gathered my gear, I noticed Tess at the entrance to the other dugout, holding her half-full Diet Coke shoulder-high as she chatted with Scottie Hoss. They appeared to be flirting, and I felt a pang of jealousy. I knew Scott was married, to quite an attractive woman, and so I figured they wouldn't take it too far. But it would have been nice to talk to her, clear up whether she was irked at me for some reason. But this wasn't the moment, not with my entire family in tow. I convinced myself that I was reading into Tess's shirking body language and I'd see her in friendlier environs soon enough. After all, if she were that ticked, she never would have made eye contact with me at all, right? Yet I also thought that drafting her son might have been wise, because I could have used a little flirting myself at that moment.

My own family—Mom, in-laws and estranged wife—waited beside the concession stand for Wesley and me. The weather had warmed up a bit, and each of them had their jackets draped over their arms. Wesley corralled his nachos in his arms, and I had my equipment bag strapped over my shoulder, and when we met them all three women made an obvious attempt to pick up his spirits.

"Great game, buddy," they said, almost in perfect unison, and took turns hugging him.

As Marcy's mom administered the last of the three hugs, my emotions veered into old territory, one that reminded me of juice bags and the joy of T-ball—I felt a tinge of the warm-and-fuzzies. Maybe, I thought, the old clichés about baseball really are true: Maybe baseball really can bind a family together.

Then Marcy's dad opened his mouth.

"Jesus Christ, boy," he barked, "you got to learn how to run the damned bases!"

And Wesley started bawling.

19
YOU SHOULD WRITE A BOOK

*T*ime for a beer. After the White Sox game, after Wesley dried his tears and I sent him and Marcy off to their separate new lives and directed the grandparents back to the turnpike, I stopped at Sudzies. It was mid-afternoon and the bar was mostly empty. The bartender, a genial guy with a blonde ponytail named Chuck, had plenty of time to hear the story of our painful first game as I nursed my Luscious Lager.

"I'll bet you have a million stories like that," Chuck said, his arms crossed as he leaned against the back of the bar.

"At least a half million," I said dryly. "I should tell you about last year, when I served as a commissioner—one of the coaches was a grandfather with a drinking problem. And then, in the last inning of the last game, my son is on first base, and as soon as the ball's hit he does a beeline to the bathroom. He was out, by the way, for running out of the baseline. Technically, that's the correct call when the ball's in play and a kid runs to the bathroom instead of the

179

next base."

Chuck giggled. "You should write a book."

I didn't answer. I actually thought about it for a moment. I'd joked about it before but never seriously entertained the idea. But I couldn't—not now. I'd just mailed my application to the teaching certification program at Penn State, and I was pretty confident I'd be accepted for the fall semester. At the same time, I'd applied to the Misty Hill School District to be a substitute teacher in the fall, so I was committed to my next career as a teacher.

"I'll have a full plate soon," I told Chuck. "But maybe someday."

Chuck was summoned by two guys at the other end of the bar who wanted refills, and I was left to ponder what to do about Wesley and the Angels. Considering it was early in the season, maybe I could switch Wesley and Johnny for the second game and give Wesley a shot at hitting leadoff. Why not? It might boost his spirits while giving me a chance to look at another lineup. Nothing wrong with juggling the lineup early in the season, I figured. And nothing wrong with giving your son a vote of confidence, especially while his parents are split up and he really needs one. It occurred to me that was the main reason I got so deeply involved in this sport in the first place—it was my son's best and favorite sport. I was there for him.

At 8:05 on Monday morning, my cell phone rang. I was in bed watching CNN, and while reaching lazily for my phone, I accidentally knocked over a half-full growler of beer. But when I saw Tess's number listed on my phone, I felt a rush of excitement and forgot about the puddle of day-old beer forming on the carpet. I'd given her my cell phone number earlier, but this was the first time she'd used it.

"Hi Nick," she said matter-of-factly. "It's Tess. I was wondering if you're busy this morning."

"Not at all."

"Feel like meeting for coffee?"

"Of course," I said.

"Java Hut?"

"Sure. Can you give me about forty-five minutes?"

"It's a date," she said.

A date. The words thrilled me, erasing any concerns I'd had about her giving me the cold shoulder at our first game. Her tone wasn't overly warm, certainly wasn't suggestive, but still. *A date.* Those were the words she chose, and she must have had a reason.

———————

I sprang out of bed and stepped in the beer puddle, then grabbed a dirty T-shirt from the opposite bed to mop it up. I promptly shaved and showered and chose a nice pair of khaki shorts and a blue Polo shirt. I asked the maid, Luciana, to make up the room as soon as I left. I warned her about the beer spill but also asked her to go light on the air freshener, which tended to overwhelm the room. She responded with a dour nod, but she was the efficient one, so I was confident she'd have it ready before I returned—or hopefully, before *we* returned. The cold weekend temps had subsided, and it was a cloudless day with just a touch of morning chill in the air, and I felt a little bounce in my step as I crossed the motel parking lot to my car.

Tess was at the Java Hut when I arrived. She'd grabbed a small corner table and already had a tall latte. She wore a pink sweatsuit, and I was so glad to see her. I wanted to thank her for her advice about a second career and update her on my progress, and then I'd tell her how I'd misinterpreted her body language at the game, and surely we'd laugh it off. But as I approached the table, I saw a weighty look on her face. Maybe the notion of taking things to the next level with me was causing her some anxiety. I tried to be cheerful.

"Hey, there," I said. "What a beautiful day, huh?"

"Yeah," she said flatly. "I guess it is."

A waitress came by and I asked for an orange juice. I didn't want coffee on my breath this morning.

"Good game the other day," I said. "I saw Carter had a hit. Good for him."

"Yeah, well, Scottie Hoss seems to know a lot about baseball. He's not as encouraging as you, but he seems to know all the technical stuff."

"He's a Real Baseball Guy," I said.

"That's what I heard."

"So how are things with you?" I asked.

She slid her latte off to the side, perched her elbow on the table and grasped the tip of her chin. It was a serious pose. What could she have to say? Hopefully it was a sign the line of conversation was going to heat up right away.

"To be honest, I've been better, and that's what I wanted to talk to you about."

"How so?"

"I was talking to Scottie Hoss the other day, and Scott said he was happy to have Carter on his team, and was a little surprised he was able to draft him. He said *you* passed Carter up in the last round."

I was thrown for a loop. I didn't know what to say. I never would have imagined she'd find out how our draft went down, and never would have imagined she'd be offended by it. I still hadn't gotten the chance to thank her for the career advice, but so be it. Things were moving in unexpected directions.

"Really?" I said, playing for time.

"Yeah, really." She was direct, and wasn't giving me any time to think.

I stammered, "Well, um—"

"I know Carter's not a huge playmaker, but he loves

baseball, and he really needs the encouragement, and he always felt comfortable on your team."

Again, I stammered, "Sure, um—"

"You know," she said testily, "I'm sorry if I'm taking this personally, but maybe you noticed that Carter's dad is never around. I don't care about the technical baseball stuff. He's always being shuffled from one team to another. The same thing happens in soccer. It would have been nice if he could have had a little stability and encouragement somewhere, at least in this damned baseball league."

She pulled her coffee mug back in front of her as a satisfied look swept across her face.

I decided not to make any excuses. "I'm sorry."

She frowned and shook her head. My orange juice came, and I quickly took a drink; I needed to wet my mouth. I wondered if I should feel guilty for avoiding Carter, and I wasn't sure. I had a good reason—my marriage. But I'd already screwed that up, so what was the point?

I glanced around the crowded coffee shop, looking for anyone who might recognize us again and report back to Marcy. I didn't.

"It's hard to explain," I said. "Do you remember when I told you how Marcy reacted when she heard we went out for drinks? Well, I didn't want to complicate things any more with her. That's really the only reason I didn't draft Carter. I'm sorry if he got mixed up in that, but that's what I was thinking at the time, and that's what happened. Honestly."

"I thought you and Marcy had separated."

"We did—I mean, we are. But I guess you never really give up on a marriage. Not completely."

"I heard Marcy was seeing Reggie Knox," she said.

Did I hear that right? *Reggie Knox*? That bastard who used to crush my team and torment me? With *Marcy*?

"Say what?" I asked.

183

"Yeah," she said. "A friend of mine who works in Harrisburg saw them out together at a downtown restaurant. Reggie left his wife, you know."

"I know," I said, the words straggling out.

I was whip-sawed. My heart sank and my stomach hitched. Then a sick feeling—some dreadful combination of nausea and hopelessness—overcame me.

"Oh, boy," I muttered.

Tess gave a little shrug, hoisted her latte with both hands and took a sip. When she set the mug down, she had a distant yet thoughtful look on her face. We sat in silence for a few moments, and as she finished her latte, I peered into her eyes, the first time I looked at her that deeply. Her eyes were brown and lukewarm. I felt a coolness between us and didn't know what to do about it. My head spun with troubles.

I wondered if the local rumor mill had it right about Marcy and Reggie. But why not? Maybe Marcy had decided it was time for her to test the waters. I wanted to press Tess for more details, but also didn't want to further complicate things with her, not while she was ticked at me for spurning her son.

I wondered why Tess had used the word "date" to refer to this little meet-up. She was probably the type of woman who used the phrase all the time, and it dawned on me that we hardly knew each other. We'd been on the verge of a fling for some time, but flings aren't that serious, and she still hadn't given me any indication how far she'd be willing to go, and certainly hadn't signaled that she'd be willing to leave her husband.

It occurred to me that these two women mixed up in my life were different. I knew Marcy so well. And Marcy, I knew, would have handled this issue with her son differently. Marcy's eyes, so big and hazel, would fire up when the mood struck her just right, and this would have been one of those times. Like Tess, Marcy would have been an advocate for her kid, but instead of laying a guilt trip on me, Marcy would have given me a scolding, a no-bullshit, in-my-face assessment of exactly what I'd done wrong. And I think I would have appreciated it, at least after I'd had time to reflect on it. There's something more honest about a scolding.

I didn't bother finishing my juice. Tess and I said cordial but stiff goodbyes. She wished me luck with my team, and I wished Carter luck as well. As we parted in the parking lot, I held out hope that I might detect some hint that she'd forgive and forget, but she didn't say a word.

As she turned toward her big Lexus, I said, "Mind if I give you a ring soon? Next round is on me."

She stopped, one shoulder turned toward her SUV, the other shoulder toward me, and seemed to be searching for just the right words. "I'd have to check my schedule," she said, and clicked her car door open.

So I went back to my motel room, which Luciana had made up nicely, with just the right amount of cheap air freshener, and I changed into old clothes. I went to the baseball field and spent the rest of the morning mowing—one of my chief responsibilities as field maintenance director. Besides, I didn't know what else to do with myself. As the day warmed up, I broke into a heavy sweat while sitting atop the clunky riding mower and circling the field again and again.

I couldn't stop thinking about Marcy—could she be gone for good? Or just trying to exact some revenge, make me feel as lousy and jealous as I'd made her feel? Could Tess's friend, whoever it was, had mistaken Marcy or Reggie for someone else in that downtown restaurant? And what about Tess. Did I completely screw that up, too? Was there anything there to screw up in the first place? Even if there was, could it be salvaged? By the time I had half the field mowed, I was tired of trying to figure out both women. I was deflated, and couldn't help but feel very sorry for myself.

Game Two: the Rangers.

Reggie Knox's team.

I wanted to win.

Just looking at Reggie made me seethe—his tall and lean frame, red hat perched on his head like a drill sergeant, shiny black spikes and preppy khaki shorts. I hated the way he ran infield practice, with military precision, and I hated the way he organized his dugout, with bats and helmets lined up in perfect rows.

Still, I wanted to show Wesley that I had faith in him, so I tweaked the batting order and inserted him as leadoff hitter, with Johnny Joust hitting second. Other than that, I was throwing the best lineup I could muster at Reggie and his Rangers.

Marcy was late, which only added to my anxiety. I wanted to see which side of the field she'd sit on. Probably our side, I knew, because Wesley was, after all, her son. But even so, I wanted to see her make that choice. When the ump summoned Reggie and me to home plate to review the ground rules, I scanned the field looking for her, but I didn't see her anywhere.

So we started without her. When we reached the second inning, when the real baseball began, Reggie's pitcher threw wild, and Wesley drew a leadoff walk. I gave him the ear wiggle on the first pitch to Johnny, and off he went.

"He's stealing!" the Rangers yelled, almost in perfect unison.

Reggie's catcher heaved the ball to second base, and the shortstop, who'd anticipated the steal, was straddling the bag waiting for the throw. It was an accurate throw, only slightly high, and unusual at this level of baseball. The shortstop caught it cleanly and laid down the tag. Wesley slid hard into the base, but it didn't matter. He was out.

Wesley dropped his chin into his chest as he ambled

off the field, and as the cheers died down from the Rangers' dugout, I heard yelling from beyond the outfield fence. It was Johnny's Notoriously Obnoxious Dad, yelling something about "a decision like that." I tried to ignore him, and instead scanned the field for Marcy again, but I still didn't see her.

Marcy finally showed up in the bottom of the second, wearing an old Villanova sweatshirt over a pair of faded jeans, and holding a cup of coffee in a silver travel mug. It was an afternoon game, and I wondered why she needed coffee so late in the day. What had she been doing the night before? I shivered at the thought that she might be in one of those hot new relationships, the type where both parties are willing to abandon sleep to spend more time together. And, dare I even think it, have lots of sex.

She sat in her folding chair far down the first-base line. It was our side of the field. Yet I was afraid it didn't mean a thing.

Meanwhile, the game remained close. I pitched Gus Bloom, the stout eight-year-old who'd played solid catcher for us in the opener. While he struggled some with his control, Gus kept us in the game, and we were losing 5-3 when Wesley came up again in the third. I gave Wesley the bunt signal, a double elbow tap, and he laid down a decent bunt, just to the right of the pitcher's mound. The pitcher fielded it off-balance and whipped the ball to first, overthrowing the first baseman, and Wesley hustled down to second.

Reggie barked at his pitcher: "Plant your foot when you throw! You can't throw wild like that! Come on, get it together!" And I wondered, for the hundredth time in the past few days, what Marcy could see in this guy.

When Johnny came up, I didn't want to try any more steals, but I wanted to advance Wesley, at least to third. So I gave Johnny the double elbow tap. He bunted it hard, right back to the pitcher, who planted his left foot, wheeled to third and threw Wesley out. In the outfield,

Johnny's N.O.D. was leaning over the fence and yelling again.

"Another bunt? What kind of call was that? Come on, coach!"

Now I was fed up. I turned to the outfield and felt a Bad Coaching Moment coming on, which would have been my first of the new season. But I held it together. *Don't freak,* I thought. *Or you'll regret it.* So I simply folded my arms across my chest and stared him down. Almost as if on cue, Cindy Joust took him by the arm and led him back to their folding chairs. Even after they sat down together, I kept staring. It was time to make a point. As I glared at him, the N.O.D. sat restlessly in his folding chair. Cindy leaned forward in her chair and patted his knee. It was an exaggerated and patronizing type of pat, one that seemed to say, "Down, boy." I kept staring for just another moment, and figured I'd made my point. And because I'd also avoided a Bad Coaching Moment, I considered this a small victory.

In the top of the sixth, we were down 5-4 with Sean Keezel, the very bottom of our order, due to hit first. Sean struck out on three pitches, and Wesley followed and grounded out to first. That brought Johnny to the plate with two outs and the game on the line.

Johnny hit a slow grounder to the right of the first baseman, who fielded it cleanly then paused for an instant as he apparently realized that by moving to his right, he'd left first base abandoned. In real baseball, the pitcher hustles over to cover first in that situation for an easy flip-toss out, but expecting that in coach-pitch baseball is like expecting a toddler to know his multiplication tables. Reggie's pitcher was still on the mound, watching the play unfold with his hands on his hips. So the first baseman tried to race Johnny to the bag, and he lost by a step. Johnny was safe, with Moose coming to the plate.

Reggie flipped on his pitcher: "You have to be there! You can't stand there and watch the play like that. We're not playing golf!"

I was more concerned with my runner on first, the potential tying run. "Two outs," I yelled across the infield to Johnny. "You're running on contact."

I thought about giving Johnny the steal sign on the first pitch, a move that would have put him in scoring position, but decided against it. I remembered how easily the Rangers' catcher threw Wesley out earlier in the game, and I didn't want to take any chances with my best slugger at the plate. Reggie's pitcher, who was clearly tiring, threw two balls—one in the dirt and one above Moose's eyeballs—and then Moose jacked the third pitch to left-center.

Johnny didn't run on contact—not quite. He paused for just a moment to watch the ball sail into the outfield, and finally started tearing toward second as I screamed, "Go! Go!" The center fielder chased the ball down and hurled it to the shortstop, who fumbled the ball at the edge of the outfield grass just as Johnny was approaching third. In a flash, I processed my options and potential consequences. I had my fastest runner in position to score the tying run, and the shortstop had yet to secure the ball. But still, with a quick pick-up and a good throw home, Johnny's probably out. That is, assuming the catcher catches the ball. A bad throw or another fumble and Johnny's definitely safe. I sent him home. The shortstop scooped up the ball quickly. It was a good throw. The catcher caught the ball, and he made the tag. Johnny was out. Game over.

Once again, Reggie had bested me. And this time, it happened while he was apparently plucking my wife in the process. We lined the boys up at home plate for the usual post-game handshaking ritual, and I took my place at the back of the line, as always. When the boys finished shaking hands and dispersed to their dugouts, I met Reggie at home, shook his hand firmly and looked him square in the eye. Curtly, I said, "Good game." I wanted to say, *Good game, fuckface. Now keep your slimy hands off my fucking wife.* But I thought better of it, and instead turned my back on him and walked back toward my dugout.

I gave the Angels a brief post-game speech, something about this being only our second game and good things were sure to happen soon, because I was much more interested in tracking Marcy's moves after the game. From the corner of my eye, I watched her fold up her chair and stroll toward the outfield. She stopped beside the foul pole and shifted her weight onto one foot, as if she were about to wait for someone. Wesley, probably. But I couldn't be sure.

As Gene Murchie and I packed the gear, I kept one eye on her. When Wesley approached her, she didn't move. They exchanged a few words and she patted his hat as they turned toward the concession stand. Gene zipped the last of the gear into the big black equipment bag, and as he turned to leave the dugout said, "Good game, coach. We'll get them next time." I waved goodbye and thanked him, and he disappeared.

As I hoisted the equipment bag and began to leave, the Notoriously Obnoxious Dad appeared suddenly in the dugout. He was in the dugout aperture, blocking my path out.

"What's going on with this team?" he asked, his tone sharp and accusatory, and he was a fiery ball of energy.

I looked around for Cindy Joust, and over the N.O.D.'s shoulder I saw her, or at least I think it was her, with her back turned to us, chatting with two other moms beside the concession stand. Did she know she'd let her husband off his leash? At the same time, I wanted to track Marcy's moves. She was walking casually toward the concession stand as Wesley sprinted ahead of her. She was nowhere near Reggie Knox. I spotted him lugging his gear across the parking lot.

"Why do you ask?" I said, trying to remain calm.

"That was the worst coached game I've ever seen—

calling bunts in the wrong situation, sending a runner home with the game on the line and the clean-up hitter coming up. And why isn't my son hitting leadoff, where he belongs?"

This was the first time I'd ever seen him up close. His hair was a light shade of red, and he had pale skin, soft freckles and one crooked bottom tooth. He was in great shape—built like a fireplug, with toned biceps and thick forearms and calves. He wore penny loafers with no socks, and a long-sleeve pink shirt tucked tightly into pleated khaki shorts.

"Are you Dan Joust?" I asked.

"Damn right."

I looked over his shoulder again for his wife, who was still chatting with the other women and seemed oblivious to the fact that her husband had been let loose. His behavior was so over-the-top that I was no longer angry at him. I suddenly felt bemused.

"Pleased to meet you," I said, half-mockingly.

"Don't change the subject on me."

I couldn't help but chuckle.

"Where's your wife?" I asked. "It's Cindy, right?"

I leaned to my right, then to my left, straining to see past him each time and making it clear I was looking for his wife. And I hadn't forgotten about Marcy, who had just caught up to Wesley at the concession stand, and Reggie, who was loading his gear into the trunk of his black Volvo.

"Doesn't matter where she is," Dan said, shifting his shoulders as if trying to block my view. But he was too short.

"Good thing I'm working on a Little League novel," I said, feeling increasingly bemused. "I could use a scene like this for my book."

"What's that?"

"I'm just kidding."

"You're going to put me in a book?"

"No, no. Relax. I *said* I was kidding."

"I heard you're a writer."

"Old newspaper guy, to be exact. But I'm not working on a book. Maybe I should be."

His eyes turned to slits, a look of intense distrust. He balled his right hand into a fist and pumped it as he upbraided me: "I'm close friends with Sam DiNardo, you know. We go way back. We played in this league together as kids, and I don't think he'd want anyone in this league writing a book about it. This league has a great tradition— won a state championship in 1951, and my dad played on that team."

At last, Cindy Joust appeared behind her husband and grabbed him by both shoulders.

"Let's go, honey," she said. Her tone was light and condescending, as if she'd been through this a million times before.

"Wait a minute—" Dan said.

"I'm not waiting for anything, and you know the game's over and it's time to leave," Cindy said. With one hand on each of his shoulders, she tried to turn him around, and he reluctantly and slowly began to turn. I was impressed by how much control she exerted over him, especially in these blustery moments, and it reminded me of the story of her withholding sex from him for behaving poorly at the games, and I was confident that he'd listen to her, provided he wanted to make love to his wife anytime soon.

"Now say goodbye," Cindy said, as if talking to a six-year-old.

"I'll see you later," Dan said, his tone vaguely challenging, before walking away.

Cindy watched him leave, and I scanned the rest of the field once more for Marcy and Reggie. Marcy was on the trail that leads back toward our house, her folding chair strapped over her shoulder, while Reggie was still in the parking lot, standing behind the open trunk of his Volvo as he held an animated conversation with one of his assistants.

I wondered why the two of them hadn't met up afterward, and I wanted to believe that they weren't really an item, that the local rumor mill had run amuck. But I couldn't convince myself, and didn't want to be naïve. So I had to believe that, at least at this point in time, Marcy knew better than to be spotted with Reggie in front of me. Either that or she already knew Reggie well enough to avoid the son of a bitch at a game.

"I'm sorry about that," Cindy Joust said, and for an instant I thought she was referring to my battered love life, but then I realized she meant her husband's bad behavior. "I hope he wasn't too harsh. My husband takes this very seriously. He was an all-star as a boy, and that team almost made the Little League World Series, and now he has a very stressful job. He works for a very demanding state senator. So things tend to really get to him."

"I take it you're Cindy."

Up close, she wasn't quite as pretty as she appeared from a distance. While she had a lush voice and tight body, her face was hardening. Her lips were chapped, her skin creased and dry—the face of a once-beautiful woman who wasn't aging so well.

"Oh, yes," she said. "I'm Cindy. We've talked on the phone, but we haven't met, have we? What a horrible first impression you must have of us."

"Don't worry about it."

"Please," she said, her voice reassuring, "don't worry about anything my husband said to you."

20
THINGS REALLY GET
TWISTED AROUND
IN THIS TOWN

I woke up the next morning and, without even showering, drove to the field to mow. I'd started a pattern where I mowed at least once a week, twice if it rained heavy. The maintenance shed cried out for a cleaning—lime bags and rakes and shovels had been hurled in during the rush to prepare the field for the start of the season—but I didn't feel like it yet. I'd rather mow. There was always something calming about being outside and undisturbed on a tract of green grass, like listening to an Eagles tune on a rainy Sunday night. As I rode circles around the field, my stormy life seemed a little more serene, and I could think about everything in a healthier perspective. I thought about my teaching career, imagining various classroom scenes with spunky teenagers, and I thought about my team, imagining that we'd pull together after a hard-luck start and at least play .500 ball. On this day, I even caught myself wondering if I could somehow reconcile with Marcy, but I stopped myself before that vision went too far.

I was plowing through center field when Sam DiNardo appeared in the infield. A local insurance agent, Sam looked as if he'd come straight from work, dressed in dark slacks and a blue collared shirt and carrying his cell phone in one hand. When we made eye contact, he stopped at the edge of the infield grass and waved for me to come meet him. I rode over and shut the mower down. He looked perturbed.

"What's up?" I said.

"We have to talk."

"About?"

"I hear you're working on a book about our league."

"Are you kidding me?"

"Do I look like I'm kidding?" He stood erect, his broad shoulders stiff, his bushy eyebrows furrowed and thick as ever, eyes boring through me.

"Well, you heard wrong," I said plaintively. "Dan Joust told you that, didn't he? I can tell you exactly what happened, and believe me, I'm not working on a book."

"Let's hear it," he said in a weighty tone.

"My God," I said, "I can't believe you're taking this seriously. But okay, I can deal with that, and here's the truth: Dan flipped out on me after our game yesterday, as Dan often does, and I made a crack about writing a scene like that in a book. But it was a joke, and I immediately *told* Dan it was a joke, but he apparently only hears what he wants to hear."

"Dan's an old friend of mine," Sam said defensively. "So watch what you say."

"Okay, okay. That's fine, too. But it really was a joke. I'm not working on a book."

"But you're a writer, aren't you?"

"Old newspaper guy."

"And didn't you lose your job?" He sounded like a lawyer cross-examining a reluctant witness.

"Yeah, but I'm planning to start teaching. I'm going back to school for my teaching certificate."

"And aren't you one of those namby-pamby coaches who believe the weaker kids should play as much as the stronger kids? And who argues with the guys who just want to win?"

"That's not exactly how I would phrase it," I said, and now I felt like a badgered witness.

"Dan's not the only one who told me you're working on a book. Scottie Hoss told me the same thing. He said he heard it from Tess Sugarmeier, and everyone in town knows what's been going on between you and Tess."

My mind raced as I wondered why Tess would have said that, but then I remembered: I'd cracked the working-on-a-book joke at the Java Hut months ago. Did she take it the wrong way? Or was she out to get me now?

"Actually," I said, "that thing between Tess and me—that *alleged* thing—has been blown way out of proportion. Believe me. But—whatever. I can't control what people think or say."

"I think you're working on a book. About our league." Now he sounded like judge and jury.

"Have you been listening to what I've been saying?"

"You listen up," he said, rebuking me. "I can't remember where you're from, but this league is very special to the people in this town. It has a great, great tradition. This town has produced some of the greatest Little League teams in the whole state of Pennsylvania. Won the state championship back in 1951, and my father played on that team. Since then, we almost went to the Little League World Series three times. Three times! And *I* played on one of those teams. We may not be perfect, but the last thing I'm going to allow on *my* watch is someone in this league who writes some scandalous book about us."

"You haven't heard a word I said, have you?"

He locked his lips, folded his arms, his cell phone dangling underneath his elbow, and scanned the field.

"How often do you mow this field?" he asked tersely.

"Once a week, usually."

"Not enough. Has to be at least twice a week, especially when it rains."

"I do it twice a week when it rains."

"What's the shed look like?"

"It needs cleaning, but I was going to get to that."

"We have thousands of dollars worth of stuff in there. Lime and Quick Dry and equipment. It should have been cleaned up by now."

He stormed off the field and headed toward the shed. I climbed off the mower and followed him. I thought, *This is fucking unbelievable.* As he started picking through the shed, I tried to reassure myself that he'd cool down soon enough and this little misunderstanding would blow over. *Let him spout off*, I thought. *He'll come to his senses after he realizes I'm probably the only guy in town willing to do this shitty job.*

He climbed atop the stack of lime bags, tossed aside some rakes and shovels, and stood there eyeing the inside of the shed like a farmer surveying his crops. He came back out with a rake in one hand and pointed it at me. His thick shoulders were burning with energy, and his bushy eyebrows looked alive, like a pair of small animals that were about to jump off his face.

"I've made up my mind," he said. "We have a board meeting next week, and I'm making a motion that you be removed from all your duties in the league—as field director and manager. On two counts—neglecting your duties and acting in a way that embarrasses the league."

My jaw dropped. "You're out of your mind."

"I'll have the votes, believe me. You can show up if you want, but I wouldn't bother. If I were you, I'd go quietly."

He threw the rake back in the shed and marched off.

"Should I finish mowing?" I asked, but he didn't answer.

I finished mowing and cleaned out the shed, not completely convinced Sam would follow through on his threat. And even if he did, I thought, I should finish the job as best I could. Then, eager to learn more about Sam's power to remove me, I locked the shed and drove straight to the library, covered in grime and sweat, and still without a shower, and logged onto the computer to read the bylaws on the league Web site.

Sam knew what he was talking about. Buried deep inside the ninety-six-page bylaws was a clause spelling out the procedure for removing someone from the league. Upon motion by the league president, a majority of the five-member executive board could vote to remove someone for several listed reasons, including neglect of duty and acting in a way that publicly embarrasses the league. And it didn't take a politician to count the votes in this case: Sam had the votes to kick me out.

Besides his own vote, Sam could surely count on votes from Scottie Hoss, the new vice president and Sam's old friend and ally, and Reggie Knox, the treasurer. I might be able to muster two votes from Terry Hipple, the secretary, and Little Al, the friendly new player agent, but there was no way in hell I'd get Reggie or Scott. I might as well start packing.

I drove back to the motel and showered and went to a nearby pizza joint for lunch. I had two bad slices, with big dough bubbles where sauce and cheese should have been. As I forced the slices down between sips of Pepsi, I felt completely dejected. Somehow, my life appeared to be falling even deeper into freefall. Baseball, the only thing I'd had to sustain me during this prolonged period of unemployment and the breakup of my marriage, and one of my few remaining connections to my kid, was about to be snatched away from me. My only hope, given the league politics, was for Sam to change his mind. What were the odds he'd realize he was being irrational? Or realize how hard it would be to find a volunteer to take on the dirty field-maintenance job? After finishing off the pizza, I drove back to the library to check my email, holding out hope for some news from Sam.

Sure enough, there was an email from Sam. Bad news. He'd sent the agenda for the upcoming board meeting to the whole league, and the very last item made my chest tighten. "Vote to remove league officer, Nick Marhoffer," it read, "for neglect of duty and attempts to publicly embarrass the league."

I was finished.

The board meeting was scheduled for the following Wednesday, and my Angels had two games before then, one on Saturday and another on Tuesday. Before Saturday's game, I pulled Gene Murchie aside and told him the whole story so he'd be prepared to manage the team for the rest of the season.

"Un-fucking-believable," said Gene, who rarely cursed.

"I think it's a done deal," I said. "But let's not tell the kids yet, just in case things turn around somehow."

In Saturday's game, I pitched Moose against Terry Hipple's Padres, and Moose threw a gem. He held the Padres to five hits on fourteen strikeouts, and also hit two triples. I put Johnny back in the leadoff spot, with Wesley hitting second again, and it turned out to be a wise move. They each had one steal and scored two runs apiece, all on Moose's triples. We notched our first win, 6-1.

As we cleaned up our gear afterward, Terry Hipple came into my dugout and asked how I was holding up. He had a long, consoling look on his face, which confirmed that he was one vote for me.

"I've known Sam a long time," Terry said. "He was two years behind me in school. He's a good guy—he really is. But sometimes he takes things too seriously, and he doesn't always think straight."

"Case in point," I said.

"I'll give him a call, see if I can talk some sense into him," Terry said. "But I can't make any promises."

"I appreciate that," I said. "But I don't think he'll listen. He seems to be on a mission here."

"And if he doesn't listen? Is there any way we can outvote him?"

"No way," I said. "He needs only three votes, and he's got them. Even if I have you and Little Al, that's not enough."

"Have you thought about talking to Reggie and Scottie Hoss?"

"Not really," I said. "There's no point, and I'm not going to beg."

"In that case, I'm glad you guys beat us today. It'll help you go out on a high note."

———————

I went for a long run on Sunday morning, hoping it would relieve some stress and help me sort things out. I was dog-tired afterward but felt no sense of relief. I'd spent most of the run reflecting on my family's history in sports—Uncle Wes's football career, my marathons—and I felt like I was letting the whole family down as I faced certain eviction from my son's Little League.

When I got back to the motel there was a message on my cell phone from Terry Hipple. He'd bumped into Sam at church that morning.

"But it's bad news," Terry's message said. "There's no talking any sense into him. Whatever you did—or didn't do—really struck a nerve with him. He's already trying to recruit a new field maintenance guy. I heard him ask a guy outside of church."

I didn't bother calling Terry back. Instead, I called Little Al. Though I didn't know him that well, Al seemed like a reasonable guy, and there was no doubt he was the only other possible vote for me. He wasn't home, but his wife said he was at his law office and I should call him there. Al answered the phone in a hurried tone and said he could only talk for a couple minutes.

"I heard about your predicament," Al said. "I'm on my computer now. Let me look up the bylaws and see what they say."

He was silent for a minute; I heard only clicking from his keyboard.

"Yep," Al said. "I see the section he's citing. Looks like he has jurisdiction here. What the hell did you do to piss him off so much?"

"He thinks I'm writing a book about the league, and that I want to embarrass the league, but I'm not. I'm *really* not."

"I heard you were writing a book, too."

"Believe me, I'm not. Things really get twisted around in this town sometimes. I'm getting my teaching certificate, and I signed up to substitute at the high school next year. I'm planning to teach."

"Well, I'll take you at your word."

"I was hoping you'd vote for me, but it won't really matter, because there's no way I can get Reggie or Scott's vote."

"So you're toast."

"I'm toast."

"I'm sorry to hear that," Al said, though he didn't sound too bummed about it. "But listen, I have to go. A lot of work to catch up on. Big case this week. Good luck, buddy."

"Thanks."

For our next game on Tuesday, which appeared to be

my very last as manager, I did what any other dad in my situation would have done: I let my own son pitch.

We played Big Ed's Braves, who came into the game with a record of 3-0, and I wasn't expecting to win. I was only hoping we'd hold our own and they wouldn't hammer Wesley's pitching.

At first, Wesley looked nervous on the mound, and he struggled with his control. He walked the first two batters, and after the second he looked over at me and slumped his shoulders. I wondered if I should warm up someone else, but instead I clapped my hands and said, "Keep plugging. It's early. You'll settle down."

And sure enough, he did. He threw a little slower than most other pitchers, which, oddly enough, worked to his advantage. His pitches had a change-up effect and dove just as they reached the plate. The Braves' three hitter was a big eight-year-old named Adam Karpinsky, and he came up swinging. Wesley's medium-velocity fastball must have looked like easy bait to Adam, because he swung at the first two as if wielding a sledgehammer. But he missed them both. Wesley's third pitch came in at the shins and dropped just behind the plate, and Adam laid off it. The ump called strike three.

Wesley beamed and pumped his fist. Our side of the field erupted, and so did I.

"Yeah!" I shouted. "Keep bringing it, Marhoffer! Keep bringing it!"

For the next four innings, he threw accurately, giving up an occasional extra-base hit but only three runs. Our offense knocked in five, and in the fifth I called on Gus Bloom to close. Gus gave up one run in two innings, and we upset the Braves, 5-4.

The win left me with a bittersweet feeling: While it was Wesley's finest moment of the season, and the first time I'd ever beaten one of Big Ed's teams, I couldn't dodge the nagging feeling that it was also my swan song. I gathered the Angels on the bench for a post-game speech, choosing my words carefully because I'd decided not to tell them about my fate until it was sealed.

"I'm really proud of you guys," I said wistfully. "You have no idea how proud. That was a great team you beat tonight, and I hope you'll take this win and turn it into even better things to come. You're a great bunch of kids, and I want you to remember that. Keep making me proud, okay?"

"Okay!" they shouted, almost in unison.

As the boys filed out of the dugout, I grabbed Wesley from behind and gave him a bear hug. He wiggled out of it and looked around to see if anyone was watching, obviously concerned about the embarrassment that would follow if he were seen hugging his dad in public.

"Not here, dad," he said.

"What's the problem? You're too cool to get hugs from your dad?"

I scanned the backs of the Angles, all of whom were rushing toward the concession stand.

"Everybody's gone," I said. "Nobody's watching."

He rotated his head to confirm that nobody was watching. When he turned his head back toward me, he squinched his eyes, calculating. Finally, he leaned into me and gave me a quick half-hug.

Sometimes you take what you can get.

I hustled to pack the gear so I could track down Marcy. I had to tell her what was going on. She was waiting beside the concession stand, her fold-up chair hanging over her shoulder as usual. She was still dressed for work in a knee-length black skirt and white top with a big collar, but she seemed relaxed and content, the first time I'd seen her that way in a long time. Though my mind raced with jealous thoughts of Reggie Knox, and though I was tempted to try and confirm her new relationship with my old nemesis, I decided to stick to the one matter I had to discuss. Yet strangely, I also felt perfectly natural approaching her.

"Have you heard what's going on?" I asked.

"Are you talking about your book?"

"Oh, my God," I said. "There is no book. I can't believe you heard that, too."

"You're not working on a book?"

"No, believe me. I'm planning to teach, remember?"

"I kind of liked the idea of a book."

"No matter. Have you heard that Sam's going to try to evict me from the league tomorrow night, even strip me of my coaching duties?"

She set her folding chair on the ground by her feet and shifted her weight from one leg to the next. She put one hand on her hip and scratched the back of her head with the other. It was a sexy pose, though I knew it wasn't meant to be.

"Can they really do that?" she asked.

"Yes. I looked up the bylaws."

"All because of a book?"

"Alleged book."

"So there is no book."

"How many times do I have to say it? I'm going to teach."

She dropped her hand from her hip.

"Have you heard back from Penn State?"

"Any day now. I also signed up to sub at the high school next fall. I heard they need subs, and I'm excited about it. I really think it's going to work out."

"Okay," she said. "I believe you about the book."

"It's good to know you finally believe me about something."

"Don't go there," she said with a sudden edge her voice. She slapped both hands on her hips.

I took a half-step back. Suddenly the air between us thickened, and I knew I'd said something I shouldn't have, something that brought back bad memories that hadn't yet faded, and might never. I decided not to ask her about Reggie. There would come a time for that. I changed the subject back to my baseball woes.

"When should we tell Wesley? And how should we tell Wesley?"

She shifted her weight back and dropped both hands from her hips. She scratched her head again.

"Wait and see what happens," she said. "No use upsetting him if we don't have to."

"I'm afraid we're going to have to," I said. "Sam has the votes. I can count."

"Then come by the house on Thursday," she said, her tone firm yet sensible, and she bent down to pick up her folding chair. "Sit him down and deliver the bad news as best you can. That's what parents do."

21
EVENTUALLY YOU GET
USED TO THE PAIN

*T*he board meeting was in the school gym, with the heat set too high, as usual, and the immutable smell of sweat, spit and water-bottle swill seeping from the floorboards. Someone had arranged about thirty brown metal folding chairs on one half of the court, even though just a handful of people attended most meetings and six or eight chairs were the norm. In front of the rows of chairs, directly underneath the basketball hoop, was a long brown fold-up table with five chairs and five glasses of water. The water was another new touch.

As soon as I walked into the empty gym, I was reminded that this was where Wesley's baseball experience had begun just a few years ago. I remembered cramming in with all the Little Leaguers and their parents for League Orientation Night, and I remembered thinking that the guys who ran it took it way too seriously. I remembered exchanging glances with Marcy that said, *These guys are a little nuts.*

I'd become one of those guys. Was that such a bad thing? I didn't know. But I knew this much: In another hour or so, I wouldn't be one of those guys anymore.

I didn't have a speech prepared to save myself. Instead, I was prepared for the worst and felt a little numb; I was getting accustomed to bad news. If you get hit by enough trucks in life, or beaned by enough fastballs, eventually you get used to the pain.

I took a seat in the second row, and the executive board members filed in one by one, all carrying a notebook or clipboard. Sam walked in with his chest thrust out, still dressed in shirt and slacks from his insurance job. He shook hands with all the other board members and whispered something in their ears. He didn't even look my way, even though I was one of only three people in the seats. Also there was Terry Hipple's wife, Pamela. She was a quiet woman who looked like a librarian. She attended all the meetings and took notes religiously, apparently so that Terry, the secretary, didn't have to. And there was Big Ed, who wasn't on the board but seemed interested in seeing a good show.

Ed sat in front of me, turned sideways and crossed his long, thick legs.

"I thought you'd have a lawyer with you," Ed said to me.

"Be serious."

Sam set a pile of agendas on the front table and called the meeting to order. Pamela, Ed and I got up and grabbed an agenda and sat back down. The agenda was packed with relatively uncontroversial items—the equipment budget, concession stand staffing, the summer all-star calendar, and a couple of unpaid bills from team sponsors. And then me, the last item.

As I scanned the agenda and Sam addressed the equipment budget, I heard the gym doors open and close and someone walking toward the cluster of metal chairs. I didn't look up to see who it was because I didn't care—I'd resigned myself to the role of fall guy on this night. But then I noticed that Scottie Hoss, and then Reggie, and then Little Al, and even Sam, were all following this person with their eyes. So I turned to see who it was.

It was Tess, settling into the seat at the end of my row.

She wore jeans and a lavender scoop-neck top that showed a rung of cleavage. She set her purse on the hardwood floor beside her chair, held on to her Diet Coke, crossed her legs and tilted her head with an absorbed look on her face. Sam, whose monologue on the equipment budget had slowed as Tess strolled into the meeting, gave her a welcoming little nod and then picked up the pace. Seated three chairs away from her, I caught her eye and we exchanged the same congenial nod.

But why was she here? She'd never been to one of these meetings before. Usually, only the rabid Little League moms and dads attended these sessions, though occasionally a parent with a complaint would show up and air it. Could she be here to hammer the nail into my coffin? Tell the story of how I shunned her needy son? I checked the agenda, hoping to recognize another reason why she chose to show up, but nothing else seemed to make sense.

I thought about the previous moment, when she entered the gym to a good ogling from Reggie and the other guys at the head table. Would Marcy be interested to know? Know that Reggie really wasn't any better than me, at least when it came to gawking at other women? Maybe, maybe not. But she wouldn't want to hear it from me—she might not even believe me. So I ditched that idea.

The meeting moved along—the only item that sparked much discussion was concession stand staffing, because no one could offer a viable solution for making parents work their required shift when they'd offer excuses to avoid it, ranging from a late night at work to my dog is sick. Eventually, Sam tabled that item, saying he'd ask around the league for more ideas. Tess still hadn't said a word. The unpaid bills came next, but that didn't take long, because Sam simply instructed Reggie to contact the sponsors and lay a guilt trip on them about their promise to the kids.

Throughout the meeting, I sneaked some peeks at Tess, but I was more concerned with Reggie at the head table. Most of the time, he sat back in his metal chair, a detached look on his angular face. Every now and then, such as when Sam told him to contact the sponsors, he'd lean forward, drop his sharp elbows on the table and scratch his chin, as if suddenly interested. God, how I hated him. I hated him for looking disinterested, then I hated him for appearing interested. I recognized that there are different types of people in the world—the lucky and the unlucky. And he was the former while I was the latter. Never mind that months ago he'd offered to help with my job search. He was trying to steal my wife and was about to cast the deciding vote to kick me out of my son's baseball league. The son of a bitch.

Finally, Sam called the last agenda item. He cleared his throat and adopted a lawyerly tone. Everyone at the head table leaned forward. Big Ed sat up straight. Terry's wife scribbled furiously on her yellow notepad.

"It pains me to make this motion," Sam said. "But it's in the best interest of the league. Most of you probably know what it is by now, but I'll outline the details anyway. I recently learned that someone in the league has been working on a book about us, and that goes directly against our league bylaws, which prevent anyone involved in the league from publicly embarrassing us. After looking into it, I also learned that that same person has been neglecting his duties as field maintenance director, a very important job. The accused is Nick Marhoffer, and I see him here in the crowd tonight, and on the two counts that I just discussed, I'm making a motion that Nick be relieved from all his duties in the league."

"Let me ask a question," Terry Hipple said. "Do we

have anyone else lined up to be field maintenance director? It's a lot of work."

"Not yet," Sam said. "I have a few guys who are thinking about it, and until someone takes it, I have a Plan B in place, where every manager takes over responsibility for the field for one week. I think it will work."

"Plan B sounds a little complicated," Little Al said. "What week do I have it?"

"I'd have to check," Sam said.

"Make sure I don't have to be in court that week. That's why it could get complicated."

"What about Nick's team?" Terry asked. "Who will manage it?"

"We'll ask one of his assistants," Sam said, as if expecting the question. "We've relieved managers before, and it worked out fine."

"Even so," Terry said. "I want to speak up for Nick. I've gotten to know him pretty well over the past couple of years, and I think he's a good guy. The field looks fine to me, and Nick says he's not working on a book. So I take him at his word. I'm voting to keep him."

"I agree," Al said. "I'm supporting him, too."

"Can I say something?" Tess asked.

"Of course," Sam said.

She stood up and smoothed the front of her lavender top. She cleared her throat, and the sound of it carried across the quiet gym. She had the undivided attention of every male in the place. Pamela Hipple kept scribbling notes.

"I'm not exactly sure what's going on here," Tess began. "I heard about this vote to kick Nick out of the league, so I wanted to come and say something about him. I'm sure there are some behind-the-scene politics that I'm not privy to, but I still wanted to let you know how I feel. I get the impression that Nick's not the kind of guy who fits in very well in a baseball league like this—he doesn't know baseball inside and out, and he doesn't go all out to win every game. So I have a hard time believing this is just about his book."

I wanted desperately to interject: *There is no book!* But I held my tongue, partly because I wasn't sure where she was going with this.

"I've known Nick for the past couple of years," she continued. "He was an assistant on my son's T-ball team, and last year he was my son's head coach. While I've had some disagreements with him, he's probably the most caring coach in the league. He cares about the kids more than winning the games. In fact, I was disappointed when my son wasn't chosen for his team again this year. My son's no all-star—he just wants to have fun and be with his friends, and I just want him to have a good experience. He always felt like an equal member of Nick's team, and Nick gave him plenty of encouragement. We need more coaches like Nick in this league, not fewer."

I couldn't believe my ears. Her last-minute plea probably wouldn't matter much with the voters, but I was touched and grateful nonetheless. As she sat down, I mouthed the words *thank you* to her. She mouthed back *you're welcome.*

"Thank you for coming to express your opinion," Sam said coolly.

Sam scanned the mostly empty gym, as if waiting for someone else to speak up.

"What about you?" Sam said, looking directly at me for the first time all night. "Do you want to say anything in your own defense before we vote on this?"

I took my time answering. I thought about saying something vulgar, like *Fuck off and die, Sam.* Then I thought about complaining, something like *I'm getting railroaded here.* And finally, I decided to simply correct the record and say something dignified and short.

"First of all," I said, speaking slowly for emphasis, "I'm not working on a book, and I don't know how many times I have to say it. But I understand that people will believe what they want to believe, and I've come to realize that life is not always fair."

And with that, Sam asked for a second for his motion. Scottie Hoss gave the second.

"And now the vote," Sam said. "A yes vote is to remove Nick from his duties. A no vote is to keep him. Is that clear?"

He looked over at Terry's wife. "Are you getting all of this, Pamela?"

She shook her head yes without looking up from her notepad.

"All right then," Sam said. "Let's do this. Are we ready for the voting?"

There were sober nods all across the head table.

"Yes." Sam.

"Yes." Scott.

"No." Terry.

"No." Al.

I closed my eyes and braced myself for Reggie's yes vote.

"No," Reggie said.

Total silence in the gym. When I opened my eyes, I saw surprised looks all around. For a moment, everyone glanced around the room, eyeballing everyone else, as if we all needed time to process it. *Reggie voted for me?* It didn't make sense.

Big Ed broke the silence. "Whoa!" he roared.

Tess clapped.

"Wait a minute," Sam said, staring down Reggie. "Did you hear the instructions right? A yes vote is to remove Nick. A no vote is to keep him."

"I heard you right," Reggie said defensively. "I'm perfectly capable of understanding instructions."

"That settles it," Al said, "for good. We have a double jeopardy rule in the bylaws: No one can be brought up twice on the same charge. Nick stays in the league."

Sam fidgeted. He looked flustered. I still couldn't

believe it either. I didn't say a word, because I didn't know what to say. Big Ed got up and slapped me on the back with his meaty hand.

"Congratulations," Ed said, heading to the exit. "I'm glad I came to see it. Definitely better than *American Idol.*"

"Thanks," I muttered.

"I think it's time for a motion to adjourn," Al said.

"So moved," Terry said.

"Wait a minute," Sam said as he pored over a bunch of papers, his furry eyebrows tensed and scrunched together.

"I second the motion to adjourn," Reggie said.

"Forget it, Sam," Al said. "That's it. Believe me. The vote is final. I'm a lawyer, remember, and I know how to read bylaws. There's nothing else you can do."

"Fine," Sam said, exasperated. "We have a motion to adjourn."

"Yay," said almost everyone, except Sam. While people got up and started toward the exit, Sam leaned back in his chair and stared at the ceiling, a defeated look on his face.

Reggie bolted toward the exit. I met Terry and Al on their way out, shook their hands and thanked them for their vote, then raced to track down Reggie. He was halfway across the parking lot when I got out the door.

"Hey, Reggie!" I shouted. "Hang on a second."

He stopped suddenly but didn't turn around, as if contemplating whether he should. I jogged to catch up to him. It was past dusk, and the sky was almost completely dark, with just a thin, hazy band of sunlight still visible on the western horizon.

"I just want to say thanks," I said, a little out of breath. "I'm not sure why you did that, but I can tell you Sam was way off base."

"You're welcome," he said plainly.

"Honestly, I'm not working on a book, and I think I was taking care of the field pretty well."

"That's what Marcy told me," Reggie said.

"Marcy? Really?"

"She called me last night."

"What did she say?" I asked cautiously.

"She swore on her grandmother's grave that the book was a bad rumor. And she said you're a good dad, even though you weren't a great husband, and you don't deserve to be kicked out of your son's baseball league."

"She doesn't bullshit," I said.

"I know."

I wanted to ask about him and Marcy, wanted to confirm that he was indeed dating my wife, but it was too awkward. How do you ask that question? Considering that he had just done me a big favor that would at least help me maintain my relationship with my son, I decided not to push any other buttons. Let that one wait; figure out another way of confirming it. A moment of uncomfortable silence ensued, and then I said, "So I'll see you around."

"Yep," he said, climbing into his car. "See you around."

And then, Tess. I turned and saw her opening the door to her Lexus SUV. I waved her down and headed her way. She stopped and waited for me as she stood between the open door and driver's seat.

"That was very nice of you," I said. "I can't thank you enough."

"I'm not sure how much it helped, but I just felt like it was the right thing to do," she said. "I know I was pretty cold toward you the last time we had coffee."

"I really am sorry about not choosing Carter," I said. "Believe me, it had nothing to do with him, and I'm sorry if he got caught up in adult stuff. I promise you that the only reason I didn't pick him this year was because I wasn't ready to give up on my marriage."

"I understand," she said. "I still wish he were on your team, though."

"Maybe next year?" I cracked a smile, a we-can-get-along-again smile.

"Maybe next year," she concurred with her own little smile.

Maybe Tess was indeed the woman for me—she had class, in addition to her good looks and smarts, and she didn't deserve her bad marriage—but not yet. I was being completely honest when I said I wasn't ready to give up on my marriage that easily, and Reggie or no Reggie, I had at least a glimmer of hope with Marcy—the mother of my only son, the woman who, a decade earlier, agreed to build a life with me, and who had just helped fix my latest problem in life.

22
A SUPREME EFFORT TO CREATE A MOMENT

Good dad, not a great husband. As I drove away from the school, those words from Reggie's phone conversation with Marcy stuck in my head. Though I could have used a beer, I decided to drive straight to my motel room, where I still had a copy of *Win Your Ex Back in Ten Easy Steps* sitting in a pile of overdue library books. If I was going to compete with Reggie to win *my* ex back, I needed expert help.

I turned to Step Three: Reopen Pleasant Lines of Communication.

"Often," author Franny Lake wrote, "we value the simplest courtesies, even if we don't realize it, and those simple little moments when we interact with each other offer us a chance to remind someone that we not only value them as a person, but love them deeply." And so Lake preached the value of "courteous moments," and recommended "making a supreme effort to create those moments, no matter how brief or small those moments may seem."

I decided to create a moment. I'd go to the house after she got home from work the next day. I'd be contrite—and, of course, pleasant. And perhaps I'd acknowledge that any role she played in my defense was much appreciated, regardless of her relationship with Reggie.

I dropped by at 6:30 p.m., because I knew dinner would be over then and she and Wesley would be settling in for the evening. It was a warm night—a perfect night for baseball. The parking lot and bleachers at the field were packed when I drove by. I thought briefly about stopping to see who was playing and check the score, but decided against it. I had more important things to do.

Wesley was skateboarding on the sidewalk, and Marcy was sitting on the stoop. She wore cut-off shorts and flip-flops, a half-full glass of white wine beside her. She looked perfectly content, and she didn't seem at all bothered to see me.

"They voted to keep me," I said. "And if you did anything on my behalf—"

"What did I do?"

I didn't say anything.

"Oh," she said, with a satisfying tip of her head. "So he listened to me, huh? Good, I'm glad. Does that mean you're still Wesley's coach?"

"Yes, and Sam has to drop the whole issue. There's a double jeopardy rule in the bylaws."

"I didn't want to see you get railroaded for something you didn't really do."

"That happens to me sometimes," I said, and immediately recognized I was heading into dangerous territory. I changed my tone to heavy sarcasm and added, "Must come from being an old newspaper guy. People don't like to believe what they hear from us."

She rolled her eyes and seemed to appreciate my tone.

"You're referring to our marriage, of course."

"I didn't say that," I said playfully.

"I know how to read you."

We were having a give-and-take, which came as a huge relief. It was just like the old days. But I didn't want to take it too far.

"Seriously," I said. "I'm trying to accept what happened between us. I'll be okay with it, even though I wish it hadn't turned out this way."

She nodded slowly, as if she wanted more time to process what I'd said. I felt emboldened and decided to push my luck.

"What about you and Reggie?" I asked.

"We didn't go *out*," she said, a lovely flush rising to her cheeks and coloring her neck. "We had lunch. We just talked. But I don't think it's any of your business anyway."

"No, no ... You're right. Like I said, I'm coming to terms with everything, I think."

She nodded again—slower this time, more thoughtfully.

"Your team looks great," she said, an obvious attempt to change the subject. "I'll bet you're proud."

"It's early, but I'm glad we're playing .500 ball so far."

"It's more than that. They've just *looked* great these past couple of games. Organized, together. Wesley's having fun, too. Finally. He was so psyched about pitching the other day."

I nodded along, but most importantly, I felt a connection to her for the first time in a long time. Did she feel it, too? Encouraged by the whole tenor of our talk, I decided to change the subject back to us.

"So what's going to happen with us?" I asked. "You and me."

She tilted her head and raised her eyebrows slightly. I could tell she was in no hurry to answer. I sat down on the stoop beside her, but was careful to keep a little distance.

"I don't know," she finally said. "I think about it a lot, though."

"And?"

"I just think—a lot."

I didn't reply, and she must have sensed I longed for a more detailed response.

"I'm not like you," she said. "I'm not that impulsive. I like to think things through, and I'm still thinking."

After waiting another moment, I decided I should leave. It had been a good talk, the nicest talk we'd had in a while, and I thought it best not to push.

"Thanks again for putting in a good word for me," I said as I stood up. I gave her a soft pat on the back, which suddenly felt appropriate, or at least friendly. It was the first time I'd touched her in months. She took it as if it were the most natural gesture in the world, and then the corner of her lip curled into a tiny smile.

"You're welcome," she said.

———

Giving Wesley a chance to pitch turned out to be a stroke of genius. Not only did it give me a chance to see that he had some aptitude for hurling, even though he didn't have the arm strength yet to throw a hard fastball, it gave him a nice boost of self-confidence.

At our next practice, Wesley showed up first, wide-eyed and perky.

"When am I going to pitch again?" he asked.

"I'm not sure," I said. "But you'll get another chance."

"I can't wait. I have a curve ball now. Moose taught it to me at recess today."

A curve ball? One pitching outing and this eight-year-old kid thought he had a curve ball? Hell, half the pitchers in the minor leagues couldn't throw a decent curve ball.

"Just keep throwing regular pitches," I said. "Don't try anything fancy. You've only pitched once, and you have a long way to go before you try throwing anything different."

"Want to see my change-up?"

"No. Regular pitches only. No curve balls, no change-ups. Got it?"

He shrugged, the kind of shrug a teenager gives when he doesn't like his new curfew. But his experience convinced me that I should give more kids a chance to pitch, and I resolved to let every kid on my team pitch at least one inning that season. It was a bold idea, one that shattered an old notion about how to manage a Little League team. How, after all, can the weaker kids get the job done? Didn't matter to me. These boys were still so young, and every single one of them wanted to pitch, just like they each wanted to be the next American Idol. I wasn't looking to win every single game—my goal for the season was a respectable .500 record. Besides, I'd survived the wrath of the league president and his notoriously obnoxious friend; I could surely survive some bad pitching.

I started out with an olive branch—I let Johnny Joust pitch in our next game against Little Al's Indians.

Just before the game, Michael Musenridge Sr., aka Moose Sr., leaned over the fence at the end of the dugout and waved to get my attention. At first I wondered if he was waving for someone else, because Moose Sr. and I had never conversed. Though he lived on my street and our sons now were pals, he showed up at Moose Jr.'s games only occasionally and rarely mingled with his neighbors. Not only did he have two boys playing in older divisions, but he was coach of the high school wrestling team, and his day job as a UPS bigwig required him to be out of the house by 6 a.m., which allowed him to be at the high school gym after school. So whenever I was on his end of the street I often saw the oldest Musenridge boy handling the mowing or the trash takeout.

I sauntered over to the fence, though I couldn't imagine what this burly guy wanted to talk about.

"I hear Dan Joust has been giving you a hard time," he

said, as if we were old buds.

"You haven't heard the half of it," I said.

"I think I did. Dan went whining to Sam, who tried to give you the boot."

"That's it in a nutshell."

"Listen," he said, as his tone segued to calm and sensible, a voice he must have used a thousand times before for teary-eyed teenagers who'd just had their shoulders pinned to the mat. "I'll talk to them. I wrestled with them both in junior high school, and I know they can be knuckleheads sometimes."

"Where were you a week ago?"

"I just heard about it yesterday. Don't worry. I think you're doing a great job with this team. Coaching is a lot tougher than people think, and it's easy for people to criticize. Keep at it."

"I will."

It was a nice vote of confidence from someone with real coaching credentials. It also left me with a trace of guilt because I'd once judged his youngest son a goon. More than anything else, it was comforting to know that I now had the strapping high school wrestling coach watching my back.

"One other question," he said with a wink. "When is my son going to pitch again?"

"Soon," I said, winking back at him.

"Not soon enough."

"I'm pitching Johnny today."

"Ooh," he said. "Interesting choice. So you're reaching out to your harshest critics."

"You might say that. But I've also decided I'm giving every kid a chance to pitch."

"Whoa. Really?"

"Yes, really. Which means I might need Moose Jr. to come in and save some of them."

"Starting with Johnny today."

"Maybe."

"That'll work," he said with another wink, and turned toward the bleachers.

Johnny threw hard but lacked control, bouncing balls in the dirt, whipping them way outside, or sailing them up above the eyeballs. Every time he surrendered a walk he became increasingly upset. He clenched his teeth after walking the first batter, and pounded his glove on his thigh after walking the second. He struck out the third hitter, but after walking the fourth, he clenched his teeth, pounded his glove and kicked the dirt. All the while, his dad was leaning on the edge of the outfield fence shouting instructions at him.

"Get your arm all the way back! You're short-arming the ball!"

"Settle down, Johnny," I said. "Focus on this next batter."

"Get your balance in your wind-up!" yelled his dad.

"Just settle down now," I said again.

Throughout the inning, Johnny never acknowledged his dad. After his fourth walk, which sent in a run, he clenched his teeth, pounded his thigh, kicked the dirt and spit in the grass.

"Step straight with your lead leg!" his dad yelled. "You're stepping off to the side!"

Johnny struck out another batter but then walked in a second run. I called timeout and went out to talk to him.

"Bend your back when you release it!" his dad yelled. "Bend your back!"

When I saw Johnny up close, this tough little redhead looked as if he was about to cry. His freckled face was smudged with dirt and sweat, and I wondered if a stray tear or two had already trickled down his cheek. I felt sorry for him.

"Pitching is hard, isn't it?" I said gently.

He nodded, his lips locked, as he fought back the tears.

"Listen," I said. "Try to block out everything around you. Focus on that catcher's glove, nothing else. It's just like playing catch with the catcher. Relax, and throw straight into his glove. This is the bottom of their order, so if you throw strikes good things will happen. I know you're a tough kid, so I know you'll settle down and get out of this."

He gave another lip-locked nod.

"And try to remember," I added as I started off the mound. "We're having fun out here."

The next pitch was a strike at the chest. Then a ball high, then another strike at the chest. The fourth pitch came in a little high, at the batter's chin, but he swung and missed. Johnny had gotten out of the inning and had given up only two runs. It could have been worse.

I thought about replacing Johnny in the second but decided to give him another shot. It wasn't much better. He walked the bases loaded again, notched two strikeouts, then walked in another run. He ended the inning with another strikeout, but all the walks had run up his pitch count, so I was comfortable replacing him in the third with Moose Jr.

"And by the way," I said to Moose as I sent him out for the third, "no curve balls."

Though he stuck with his fastball, Moose couldn't control his pitches either, allowing ten walks and five runs in three innings. It was his first bad outing of the season, and we lost 8-5. Because Moose surrendered more runs than Johnny, I braced myself for another confrontation with the N.O.D. after the game. Could he argue that I blew the game by replacing his son? I kept one eye on him as I collected the gear, but his wife stayed on him as he folded their chairs and strapped them across his shoulders. Then Moose Sr. approached the Jousts beyond the foul pole. They appeared to have a friendly chat—I could see them swaying and laughing together. Even so, I decided not to take any chances. Though I wanted to initiate a meet-up with Marcy at the concession stand—to make a supreme effort whenever I had a chance—I wanted to get out of there before any baseball shit hit the fan, so I hustled my gear into my car and drove away.

23
ARE YOU CALLING ME A HOMEWRECKER?

Marcy called me the next day while I was bellied up at the bar at Sudzies. It was just after dinner and the bar had drawn a decent happy hour crowd. When I saw her number on my cell phone, I answered immediately, without even thinking about why she might be calling. A letter from Penn State had arrived at the house, she said. Then she asked me something—I thought she asked to open it.

"A little louder," I said. "I'm having trouble hearing you."

"Where are you?" she asked, raising her voice over the mix of music and voices in the background.

"Sudzies."

"Who are you with?"

"Nobody."

She didn't reply.

"Trust me," I said. "I'll put you on with the bartender if

225

you don't believe me."

"No need," she said. "Can I open the letter?"

"Yes, please."

After a moment, she said, "You got into the teaching program. Congratulations."

"Thank God," I said. "I could use some good news."

"I'll leave it here on the kitchen counter," she said. "You know the spot—right beside the toaster, where everything piles up. Come get it when you're in the neighborhood."

I thought about driving over right away, but also wondered if that would make me seem too eager to see her. This was tricky business, this whole matter of creating pleasant moments. But I'd regretted my decision to leave the field after yesterday's game without trying to talk to her. Hadn't Franny Lake advised a supreme effort for even the smallest of moments? I realized once I'd left that I shouldn't have been so wary of the Notoriously Obnoxious Dad. Not only was his wife sticking by his side, but Moose Sr., my new ally, would have been there to protect me as well. I'd blown an opportunity.

"I'll be over right now," I said to Marcy.

"I have to run an errand," she said. "So it will be on the counter."

"Then again," I said, recalculating, because I wanted to see her as much as the letter, "probably tomorrow. We have a game, so I'll come by afterward."

"That's fine by me."

We played Scottie Hoss's White Sox the next day, and I was hardly interested in the game. I was bound and determined to flirt with a good-looking woman afterward—Marcy. Plan A was to track her down at the concession stand, strike up a conversation about the teaching program, a subject that clearly interested her, and then walk together to the house, where I'd pick up my acceptance letter. And if that plan failed, I'd make a supreme effort toward another opportunity: Plan B was to seek out Tess, whose son played on the White Sox, and gauge whether I should be turning my attention toward her.

I threw Gus Bloom at the Sox, and he gave up only one run over three innings, striking out eight. Next I brought in Trevor Murchie for his first pitching opportunity, and he had a respectable outing, allowing three runs, due largely to eight walks across two innings.

As for Marcy and Tess, they spent the entire game in their usual spots and routines—Marcy alone in her fold-up chair in a grassy spot down the outfield line, eyes hidden behind her sunglasses; Tess with a Diet Coke in the middle of the White Sox bleachers, chatting pleasantly with other parents. I saw no reason why Plan A, or at least Plan B, wouldn't come together.

We had a 6-4 lead entering the sixth when I called on Moose Jr. to close. Moose found his mojo again, striking out the side, and we were back to .500 with a record of 3-3.

It was a perfect May evening, warm and breezy, and by the time I loaded the gear in my trunk the concession stand was crowded. More crowded than usual. The tables were packed with Angels and White Sox slopping up pizza and nachos and small groups of parents hovering and chatting happily. It was like a little town picnic. As I crossed the parking lot I saw Marcy standing off to the side as usual, waiting alone for Wesley with her folding chair slung over her shoulder, sunglasses angled above her forehead. She wore a sleeveless peach shirt, tight jean shorts and flip-flops. In those tight shorts, her legs looked creamy and sexy.

Tess and Scottie Hoss formed their own little two-person group, posted on the edge of the crowd at the opposite end of the stand. Waving her half-full Diet Coke,

Tess wore velvet brown lipstick and a short-sleeve avocado V-neck over three-quarter length jeans and expensive-looking sandals. Scott stood erect with his hands in his back pockets, his black White Sox T-shirt untucked and hanging down over his gray gym shorts. They were giggling together like school kids.

I headed straight for Marcy, but as I got closer to the stand she started walking toward the crowd. I was disappointed, so I picked up my pace, hoping to catch her before she engaged someone else. She scudded through the crowd, past the players at the picnic tables, one hand fastened to the strap of her folding chair, and I picked up my pace a little more. She blew past clusters of parents, and I wondered where she was going. I started into a little jog. As she zipped by another group of parents, I realized with dread that there was only one group left for her to see: She was headed straight for Tess and Scottie Hoss! I shifted into a full jog. I caught up to Marcy just as she confronted them.

Tess and Scott suddenly stopped talking. They looked at Marcy and me as if we'd just arrived from Venus.

"Oh, hi," Tess said awkwardly.

Marcy tightened her grip on the strap of her chair.

"I'm just curious," Marcy said pointedly, "what's wrong with your husband?"

"Excuse me?" Tess said.

Scottie Hoss took a step back and said, "Meow."

I took a step forward and said, "Listen—"

"No," Marcy said, waving me off while staring down Tess. "I want to know what's wrong with this woman's husband."

"Nothing," Tess said defensively. "I'm not sure what you're implying."

"Don't give me that," Marcy said. "You know damn well what I'm talking about. I'm not exactly sure what happened between you and my husband, but I don't like it. And I can tell you that Scott's wife won't like it either, and you should think about the consequences of your actions."

"Are you calling me a homewrecker?" Tess said, as if she wanted to throw gasoline on the fire.

Marcy didn't bite. She paused, and I could tell she was choosing her next words carefully.

"That's one word for it," Marcy said, turning away from us. Then she spun back around, waving a finger at Tess. "But mostly I want you to know that your actions impact other people, too."

"The nerve," Tess said, spitting out the words.

Marcy turned again and stormed off. Tess looked at me as if I should say something.

"I'm sorry," I said. Then I went after Marcy.

She tore past the picnic tables and clusters of parents and stopped on the opposite side of the concession stand. I caught up to her there. She looked past me toward the picnic tables, checking on Wesley. He was perched happily in the middle of a table of Angels licking nacho sauce from his fingers. Then she shielded her face from me and wiped her eyes with the back of her hand. She'd started tearing up.

"Don't," she said. "Just don't. That was really hard for me."

"I just wanted to say—"

"Don't." She ran her fingertips under her eyes, wiping away more tears.

"But—"

"I'd like to be alone right now."

I wanted to ask this: *But what about you and Reggie? Why are you so upset about me and Tess if you've been going on lunch dates with other guys?* I was confused, but at the same time I felt a terrible urge to lean forward and kiss her cheek, or give her a little hug. But I didn't. I took a step back, reminding myself that we'd agreed that her dating life wasn't any of my business, and telling myself to respect how she felt.

"I'm going to say goodbye to Wesley," I said. "Then

I'm going to walk over to the house to get that paper from Penn State."

"I'll wait here," she said. She clenched her eyes shut, then slowly opened them and blinked, as if trying to blink out the tears and the sadness.

24
THE KIND OF FATHER
I'D BECOME

I knew the scene at the concession stand would quickly spread through the local rumor mill. If Tess didn't spread the word, Scott would surely tell someone, who would in turn tell someone else. And even if Tess and Scott clammed up, which I figured was unlikely, there were enough parents standing within earshot at the time. Because I was unsure who would spread the word, I was also unsure how everyone would be portrayed when word hit the street. Would Marcy somehow be the villain, or would Tess? Would Scott and I be handed a role, even though we each did little more than stand back and watch?

Despite my concern for how the scene would play out in local lore, I admired Marcy for her grit and her willingness to stand up and do what she thought was right, no matter the consequences. But still, it was an indication of Marcy's complicated feelings toward me and Tess and how our lives had played out, and I wasn't sure what it meant for me.

As I nursed a lager at the bar at Sudzies, I tried to figure it all out. I'd told the story to Chuck the bartender as soon as I sat down, and he responded with the obligatory barman's chuckle before he got busy with drink orders from the waitresses. So as Chuck poured one pint after another and handed them off to the waitresses, I tilted my head toward the television screens above the bar, which showed a Yankees-Red Sox duel, and I soon concluded that the Marcy-Tess confrontation didn't bode well for me.

It meant this: Marcy was the type of woman who would choose to do whatever she felt was best for her and her son, and she would tackle the consequences head-on, and no amount of pushing or prodding with suggestions gleaned from relationship gurus, even a best-selling one, would impact her whatsoever. I had to wait for her to figure things out on her own, and that left me feeling helpless. It also left me wondering if my relationship with Tess—or my near-relationship, or whatever you wanted to call it—was in jeopardy. Tess had clearly turned her attention to Scottie Hoss, and now she had reason to steer clear of me.

I regretted that I hadn't said something to Marcy in that moment she cut me off while she was wiping away her tears. I was confident that not asking about her and Reggie was wise, but I should have said something. I'm sorry, at least. Really, really sorry. Or don't forget I love you, perhaps. Would it have been the wrong time to say I wish I had you back?

But I didn't have her back, and I was beginning to think I never would. For all the little signs she'd given me recently—her excitement over my teaching plans, her claim to be thinking long and hard about us, and then her big confrontation with Tess—she still went on lunch dates with guys like Reggie and she still seemed distant with me. Especially in that moment when she said *I'd like to be alone right now.*

———————

The next day was a complete washout—sheets of rain fell on Misty Hill for half the morning, and The Weather Channel's radar showed a second green blob headed our way for the afternoon. Our practice that day would be rained out, so I drove to the library to email the parents about it. With little else to do, I spent the remainder of the afternoon poking around the library. I listened to CDs, read newspapers, and browsed through the book aisles. In the biography section, I spotted a book by Rick Tannabaugh, son of the great running philosopher Angelo Tannabaugh, and yanked it from the shelf.

It was titled *What You Set Your Heart Upon,* coined from this poignant James Baldwin quote, one of old Angelo's favorites: "Be careful what you set your heart upon, for it will surely be yours." The title alone told me it was a cautionary tale, told by the son of a man with an impetuous heart, a man who'd inspired millions by urging them to follow their heart. I immediately began skimming through it. It was published in 2003, ten years after Angelo died from a surprise heart attack at a small marathon in Massachusetts. Rick, one of Tannabaugh's eight children, had detailed his father's life and revealed his flaws. While revered by runners across the world for his poignant and inspirational prose, Angelo Tannabaugh, the wise old English professor, had been a bad dad. Once a heavy smoker, twice divorced, he'd often neglected his kids, four from each marriage, and run around with other women, usually one of his admiring young students, while he pounded the pavement and wrote so eloquently about the sport he loved. The black-and-white cover photo on his son's book was haunting. It showed a lanky Angelo in his flimsy running gear, before a Boston Marathon, circa 1965, his young son Rick at his side, head turned, looking longingly away from his dad. In the prologue, I found a

Salvador Dali quote that was another of Tannabaugh's favorites, one that seemed to describe the old runner himself: "Have no fear of perfection—you'll never reach it."

That image of Angelo contrasted sharply with the man whose book I'd stuffed into my gym bag when I raced in high school. I'd dig out the book before meets and page through it in the locker room. I'd find comfort and inspiration as soon as I'd see the cover, with Tannabaugh's broad face and pug-like nose, and I'd search for passages such as this: *Any athlete who's ever won anything will swear that they weren't content in the least with anything they'd done previously, nor worried about what they'd someday become. The here and now is all that matters—this game, this title, this moment in time that offers the chance to do the very best they can at the thing they love. Prologues and epilogues don't matter.* Then I'd go out on the dusty cinder track in Johnstown and run like hell.

Now I stood alone in the whisper-quiet Misty Hill library, squeezed between two stacks of books, books about men great and evil, men such as Lincoln and Churchill and Hitler, and I stared at the book by Tannabaugh's son, and I wondered, shamefully, what kind of father I'd become, what the epilogue to this turbulent period of my life would say. Would my son someday see me as hard proof that you'll never reach perfection?

———————

Next up was our second game against Big Ed's Braves, who we'd upset in Wesley's pitching debut. Because we'd already beaten Ed's team once, I felt no need to win our second matchup. I decided it was a good time to pitch my weakest kid, chubby Sean Keezel. My plan was to start Moose Jr., bring Sean in to pitch one inning in the fourth, then see if Wesley could close it out.

It was hot and buggy—the heavy rains had bred legions of gnats that swarmed all over the field. When the ump, a portly old guy named Ted, called the managers to home plate for the ritual pre-game meeting, all three of us were besieged by the tiny bugs. We tried waving them away from our faces but had little success. For that and other reasons, baseball was not the first order of business.

"What happened with your wife and Tess Sugarmeier?" Big Ed asked as he waved a beefy hand at the gnats. "I heard they got in a big catfight over at the concession stand."

"It was just a little argument," I said.

"I heard Marcy slapped Tess in the face," Ed said.

"You heard wrong."

"I heard about it, too," Ted said. "I heard one girl grabbed the other by the hair and wrestled her to the ground."

"Neither," I said testily. "I was there, and nobody touched anybody. They exchanged words, and that was it."

"I'm sorry I missed it," Ed said, flashing a greedy smile as he waved at another pool of gnats. "Which one are you hooked up with these days?"

"Neither," I said. "Can we move on here? Aren't we here to play baseball?"

"Oh, yeah," Ted said. "You guys know the ground rules, right?"

"Right," Ed and I said together.

"What about these gnats?" I asked, waving across my face with both hands. "What if they don't let up?"

"What are we supposed to do?" Ted said dryly. "I've never heard of a game postponed due to gnats. Let's play ball."

The game moved along slowly, with batters and pitchers taking regular breaks to swat at a cloud of gnats in their faces. Outfielders ripped off their hats to use as swatters, and the game was riddled with errors. Twice a ball was hit toward a kid who was swatting instead of paying attention to the batter, and that kid had no chance to make the play. Moose Jr. pitched fairly well for us—

accurately, but without his usual zing, and the Braves batters regularly put the ball in play. But because Moose received little help from his defense, the score was 6-6 after three innings.

As planned, I brought in Sean Keezel to pitch in the fourth, and as expected, he struggled. He lacked arm strength and threw lob pitches that often bounced in front of home plate, and he walked his first two batters on just eight pitches. Now the pace of the game seemed downright miserable.

Though I'd originally hoped to pitch Sean for a full inning, I decided then that I'd pull him if he walked one more batter, because this was proving excruciating. He threw three bouncers to the next hitter, and then came his best pitch of the day—another lob, but stronger than the rest. It came in high and dropped at the plate, right at the batter's shins. It was close, so very close, and I thought it was a strike. But nope. Sean didn't get the call. Ball four.

I called timeout and jogged out to the mound. "Good effort," I told Sean, patting him on the back. He didn't seem too bummed about being replaced. He just shrugged and bobbed his head, and about half the parents in our bleachers gave him a polite round of applause. Next pitcher: Wesley.

"Not to put too much pressure on you," I said after handing him the ball on the mound, "but here's the situation: Tie game, bases loaded, nobody out, and their clean-up hitter's up."

He looked at me like I was crazy.

"Have fun," I said, trying to relieve the pressure.

After Sean's lazy lobs, Wesley's medium-velocity fastball must have looked like fresh meat to a hungry animal, because the Braves' clean-up hitter ripped the first pitch down the left field foul line. It sailed deep into the outfield—but just foul. Whew, I thought. From the Braves' dugout, I heard Big Ed yell, "Be patient." I countered by telling Wesley, "Keep it down." Didn't matter. He kept it down, but on the next pitch, the batter showed the required patience and jacked the ball deep into left again. This time it was fair. All four Braves runners raced home before our left fielder tracked it down and chucked it into the infield. Grand slam.

On the mound, Wesley slooped his shoulders and dropped his chin to his chest, then pulled his cap off and swatted away a pack of gnats. I was sure the heat and the bugs made it harder for him to perk up after serving up a homer, but I wanted him to learn how to act when a play doesn't go his way.

"Come on, Wes," I said. "Positive body language. Forget about it and focus on the next play."

But his body language remained anything but positive. He tilted his head sideways, a sulky look on his face, without lifting his shoulders even a smidgen. I hated it when he acted this way. For some reason, I thought back to that day two years earlier when we sat in the warm sun along the third-base line in Baltimore and watched ten innings of baseball, the first time Wesley had sat through a full baseball game without constantly pleading for snacks or souvenirs. That's what I really wanted out of baseball, I thought as Wesley stood on the mound waiting for the next batter. After the days of Little League were behind us, I wanted to kick back on summer nights and watch games together, the distinct and homey voices of announcers like Bob Prince and Lanny Frattare, the Pirates announcers I'd listened to as a boy, serenading us. I wanted to wake up the next morning and comb through the morning paper for box scores and stats, and debate who has the best glove or the most power or the best curveball and the best shot at making the playoffs. I wanted to know that we'd always be able to drive to the ballpark, buy a couple seats along the third-base line, stretch out with a hot dog and a beer, and simply watch a ballgame together, no matter how old we were, father and son.

As Wesley delivered the next pitch to the number-five

batter, a kid named Josh who was just as big as the clean-up hitter, my head was hardly in the game. So I was startled when the ball shot straight toward Wesley's head. Wesley snatched his glove up to protect himself, barely deflecting the liner with the tip of his glove. From there the ball pounded Wesley square in the forehead before dribbling toward the second baseman. Wesley staggered off the mound and twirled, looking aimlessly for the ball. Our second baseman picked it up as the runner crossed first, and I immediately called timeout and darted out to the mound. A hush came over the entire field.

"Are you okay?" I demanded to know, as Wesley began collecting himself.

"I'm fine."

I lifted the brim of his hat but saw no sign of any trauma on his forehead. I felt for a bump, but there was none. I held up two fingers.

"How many fingers?"

"Two."

I added two more.

"Four."

I dropped one.

"Three. I get it, Dad. I'm fine."

Ted the ump met us on the mound, and Big Ed joined us with a pair of ice packs in his hand.

"How is he?" Ted asked.

"Not sure," I said.

"I'm fine," Wesley insisted.

"Tell me the truth about how you feel, son," Ted said. "Any headache, or dizziness? Do you feel sick in the stomach at all?"

"No."

Ted held up two fingers. Wesley rolled his eyes and said, "Two."

"You might want to sit him down, just to be on the safe side," Big Ed said. "Good thing he got a piece of it, but it still looked like it hit him pretty hard. How about some ice?"

Wesley shook his head no, then glanced around the field. Behind him, all of his fielders stood motionless, gloves hanging at their sides, and off to his side, all of the Braves were leaning face-first into their dugout fence, everyone leering at him.

"Are you sure you're not dizzy?" Ted asked.

"Maybe a little," Wesley admitted, turning his eyes away from the base runners.

"Could be wounded pride," Ed said. "But I'd give him a break anyway. Keep an eye on him."

"Definitely," I said, taking Wesley by the shoulder. "Let's go."

I took the ice packs from Ed and we walked off the field together. Wesley didn't seem to mind that my arm was around his shoulders the whole time. Parents on both sides gave him a round of applause, and Marcy met us in the dugout, looking frazzled.

"My God," she said, examining Wesley's forehead before kissing it.

"I'm fine, Mom."

"He said he feels a little dizzy," I said, passing off the ice packs to her. "I'm not sure if that's because of the heat or the homer, but we should keep an eye on him."

"I sure will," Marcy said, rubbing Wesley's back. "That was so scary."

Wesley spent the rest of the game on the bench, sulking and sipping Gatorade and chewing on sunflower seeds. Marcy sat with him for an inning and then went back to her folding chair, apparently convinced he was fine. I'd called on Trevor Murchie to pitch after Wesley, and he did an admirable job under the conditions, but the game had already gotten away from us. We lost 13-6, but I wasn't too bothered; I felt a measure of relief over the fact that Wesley had dodged a serious head injury.

I met Marcy by the concession stand afterward, and the only topic worth discussing was Wesley. Of course we'd both been scared to death, and I reminded her to keep an eye on him for the next day or two. That's what they told us at the coaching clinics we attended before every season. I had one beer at Sudzies then had my growler jug refilled to take back to my room. As nerve-wracking as the day had been, it had also left me exhausted. I was half asleep with a half-finished beer on the nightstand when Marcy called me at 10:30, panicked.

"It's Wesley," she bawled. "He's throwing up."

"Get him to the hospital. Now! I'll meet you there."

25
WHAT WERE WE THINKING?

As soon as I slapped my cell phone shut, the moment that Wesley was blasted with the ball became one of those moments that live forever, that we replay in our mind again and again. The details may change over time, but the moment, in some form, never ends. I replayed it as I hopped in the car, and as I drove through the sparse late-night traffic, past each little shopping center, the Sunoco, Dairy Queen, Applebee's, Dunkin' Donuts, CVS and Rite Aid, all with their empty parking lots.

I hadn't seen the ball leave the bat. Instead I picked it up in midair, just before it nicked Wesley's glove. My mind had been wandering, but something in the *ping* of the bat grabbed my attention and I sought out the ball while it whizzed toward Wesley. As I replayed the scene, I picked up the ball about five yards from him. He was still bent forward, feet staggered with his right in front of his left, a natural position after delivering a pitch. His glove came up automatically, defensively. Did I have the details right, or were they changing already? His head rocked back, just a bit, when the ball hit him. Yes, I was sure I had it right, all the details, at least so far. He looked lost as he staggered off the mound. Was he really looking for the ball? Or looking to regain his senses?

Now, in the car, I felt a titanic dose of guilt for not taking him to the hospital right away. Gene Murchie could have managed the rest of the game for me. Why didn't I? Why didn't Marcy insist on it? What were we thinking? *Keep an eye on him.* Those were my words to Marcy after our son took a laser shot to the head. Jesus Christ, what was I thinking? What kind of dad just says *keep an eye on him?*

Another reminder that I had no reason to fear perfection.

Of course I'd never reach it.

Suburban Hospital sat atop a well-manicured bluff about a mile outside of Misty Hill. The long and winding driveway that led to the four-story complex was lined with red and white tulips, gold daffodils and low-cut box hedges. The grass on the rolling hillside was thick and trimmed, and every ten yards or so was a small redbud tree with a mound of fresh pine mulch packed around its base. Under any other circumstances, the setting might have put me at ease, but as it was, I had a hard time slowing down to obey the knee-high wood signs that read "10 mph."

As I sped toward the emergency room, I resented the perfect little signs and the meticulous landscaping. It had been just a few years since Suburban Hospital's reputation was marred by a state report revealing its mortality rates were among the highest in Pennsylvania. My newspaper had tracked the story diligently, as administrators embarked on a major effort to improve care and their public relations. Subsequent annual reports showed progress, but folks in nearby Misty Hill remained wary. Even so, because Suburban had the only emergency room within a five-minute drive, we kept coming. After all sorts of emergencies. Bike crashes. Falls from trees. Line drives to the head. We had little choice.

Marcy's red Mazda was parked in the carport, and I pulled in behind her. The emergency room was mostly empty. Only two people were waiting in the hard-blue plastic chairs—a teenage girl with her leg propped up and a woman with a disgusted look on her face who appeared to be her mother. In a huff, I said to the desk nurse, "I'm Wesley Marhoffer's dad."

"We just sent him back," the nurse said, then directed me through a set of wide swinging doors and down a hallway toward a small room where the door was half open. I checked the hallway floor for vomit, but it was clean. The entire hallway smelled like disinfectant, and I wondered if it had recently been cleaned, but it was hard to know because it was also a typical hospital smell. Just before I got to the door I saw Marcy's feet through the half-open door. She was sitting in a blue plastic hospital chair, wearing flip-flops.

There are times when you don't have to ask any questions; it's clear to those around you exactly what's on your mind. This was one of those times. As soon as I burst into the room, Marcy looked up at me and answered, "The doctor's on his way. He vomited once more in the car ride over here, but not since."

I nodded carefully and considered what other questions I should ask. Wesley sat atop the padded hospital table, his shirt off and his feet dangling off the edge. He looked worn-out and spooked. Marcy sat in a plastic chair to his left. She looked tired and frightened.

"Do you feel dizzy, Wes?"

"Kind of."

"What about a headache. Do you have a headache?"

He winced. "Yeah."

I leaned over and kissed him on the top of the head. "They'll take good care of you here, pal. Don't worry."

I gaped at Marcy. She looked back at me, square in the eye. We didn't say anything, but I could tell from the look in her eyes, her big hazel eyes, that she was just as sorry as

I was that we hadn't brought him here right away. I let out a soft sigh, pursed my lips and gave a little nod. It was my way of saying I was sorry, too.

The doctor was a small, thirty-something woman with a pockmarked face and wire glasses. But she had a confident demeanor, as if she'd already stared down the worst possible circumstances and knew how to handle them. She's a spitfire, I thought as she blew into the room. She'd make a good lead-off hitter.

She carried a clipboard and wore a long white coat over a purple blouse, and she didn't bother looking at Marcy or me. Her eyes remained locked on the clipboard, and her right eye twitched just before she finished reading.

"I see," she said in a straight, rhetorical tone. "Baseball to the head. About four hours ago. Vomiting tonight. Reporting a headache. Hasn't lost consciousness."

Her eye twitched again as she pulled out a scope and peered into Wesley's eyes. She glanced into his ears then back to his eyes. She worked quickly.

"What's your name, slugger?"

"Wesley."

"How old are you?"

"Eight."

She turned and looked at Marcy and me, as if seeking confirmation. We both nodded yes.

"Good," she said. "I see a little bruising on your forehead, slugger. Is that the spot where the ball hit you?"

Wesley nodded, and she pocketed her scope and examined the spot more closely, tracing it with her fingers. Then she looked back at Marcy and me, a businesslike expression on her face. I trust this woman, I thought.

"I want to do a CAT scan," she said. "I want to check for intracranial bleeding. It's likely he has a concussion, but the important thing to look for is intracranial bleeding."

"What does intracranial bleeding mean?" Marcy asked, a quiver in her voice.

"It's bleeding inside the skull. Head trauma can cause it.

Don't be alarmed, but it can be serious, which is why I want to do the CAT scan right away."

Marcy let out a deep sigh. I nodded yes and said, "Let's go."

A nurse came in and helped Wesley onto a gurney, and we followed them down the vanilla-colored, disinfectant-scented hallway. Then around a corner, and down another hallway, through a big set of doors, and around another corner, and down another hallway. When we got to the imaging center, I realized that I wouldn't be able to find my way back on my own. The nurse told Marcy and me that one of us could accompany him inside. Marcy volunteered immediately, and I sat in one of the blue plastic chairs in the hallway as mother and son went behind closed doors for the scan. I'd already seen enough of those chairs for one night, and I hated them already. Besides, they were a loathsome color of blue, Post Office blue.

I realized, oddly, that my heel hurt. In the rush to leave the motel room, I pulled on my Nikes but no socks, and the back of the right sneaker was rubbing hard against bare skin. I loosened the shoestrings in an attempt to relieve the soreness, but it didn't do much. The chair was uncomfortable, and I was tired. The hallway was empty. I rested my elbows on my knees and dropped my head in my hands. I thought, *God, cut us a break here, will you? Just one break.*

I remembered what I'd been thinking four hours earlier when the bat hit the ball and the ball zoomed toward my son's head. My *only* son's head. How I longed for the perfect father-son relationship, sunny afternoons along the third-base line followed by mornings with the newspaper and the box scores. How dreamy, how naïve. Now we were facing something horrible. Intracranial bleeding? What the hell was that? It sounded awful. Would it kill him? Brain damage? My son, a vegetable? I felt helpless and alone there in the hallway on that cheesy plastic chair.

The soreness in my heel wouldn't go away, so I took off my right sneaker. I felt absolutely no sense of self-consciousness about sitting there in a public hallway with one shoe on and one shoe off—what the hell did it matter at a time like this?

They were in there almost an hour when the doctor with the pockmarked face appeared in the hallway. Her footsteps made almost no sound on the hard hospital floors, and she'd sneaked up and startled me. She said it would be just a few more minutes and then went inside. A few minutes later, the door opened and out came Marcy with her arm around Wesley, who looked dogged and disoriented. The doctor followed, a black-and-gray image of Wesley's brain in her hand.

"No sign of intracranial bleeding," she said. "We'll have a neurosurgeon here in a few hours, and I want to consult with him, just to get some confirmation. In the meantime, I want to keep your son here overnight for observation. But other than a concussion, I think it looks good. The concussion likely explains the vomiting and headaches."

I breathed a huge sigh of relief, and Marcy blurted, "Oh, thank God." She wrapped both arms around Wesley and squeezed him hard. He hardly reacted—he just stood there and tipped his head lazily. Without thinking, I bent over, with my one shoe on and one off, and wrapped my arms around them both. As soon as I did it, I wondered if Marcy would mind, but she didn't seem to. She just kissed Wesley's neck again and again. For that one brief moment, we were a family again. I wished someone would take a picture of us, because I knew it probably wouldn't last.

"Let's go see the nursing staff," the doctor said. "They'll get him set up with a room. It's time to get this little guy some sleep."

I let go of them and sat down to put on my right sneaker, as a tear welled in the corner of my eye.

We were told the maternity floor was half empty but fully staffed overnight, and so Wesley was assigned a room there. It was a spacious, single-bed room with an orange leather couch and plenty of room for a cot. Marcy had told the staff she'd spend the night, and so did I, and she didn't object. A skinny young orderly brought the cot, and a thick-bodied nurse brought us little overnight bags with travel-size toothbrushes and toothpaste. The lights were dimmed. I asked Marcy if she wanted the couch or the cot. She asked the nurse if we could push the cot beside the bed, and the nurse said yes, and Marcy chose the cot and the three of us wheeled it over. The nurse said she had instructions to check on Wesley every two hours. As we settled in, and Wesley curled up in the bed, his eyes closed halfway as soon as Marcy pulled the sheet over him. I heard a baby cry down the hall.

I flashed back to eight years ago, the night Wesley was born. My baby son in a rocking hospital crib, beside the couch where I was spending the night. Marcy asleep in the bed. I remembered the flood of fear and uncertainty that had washed over me. As it turned out, I had good reason to be apprehensive, but things didn't turn out so badly, did they? God knows, they could have been better. But they also could have been worse. At least Wesley was healthy, apparently. At least we'd dodged that bullet. At least the three of us were together for the night.

Marcy turned the lights all the way down and checked on Wesley again. She rubbed his back softly as she checked his eyes. She looked at me and pinched her fingers together—the sign we'd used when he was a baby to indicate his eyes were closed. She propped the pillow on her cot and crawled on top. I stretched out on the couch. The curtains were half open, and a swath of moonlight cut across half the room. Marcy lay facing me, and I could barely see her face, which looked pale and weary in the soft moonlight.

"I feel so guilty," she said, as another baby cried down the hall.

"Why?" I asked, though I knew exactly what she was talking about.

"I should have brought him here earlier."

"I feel the same way. When we go to those coaching clinics at the beginning of the season, they tell us to be really careful with head and chest and eye injuries. But it's hard to remember what they tell us about everything. The only thing that sticks in my mind is to watch them closely. And that doesn't mean shit."

"I don't know why I felt so comfortable at the time," she said. "What kind of mother watches her son get hit in the head and doesn't rush him to the hospital?"

I felt a surge of relief: She wasn't blaming me. Then I felt a ton of respect for her, because she was big enough to take responsibility. Maybe I'd known that about her before, but now she reminded me of it.

"Don't beat yourself up," I said. "We're both responsible. Either one of us should have had the good sense to bring him here sooner."

"God," she said, huffing and shaking her head. "I feel like we got very lucky tonight."

"I know."

"And what if that ball hadn't nicked his glove? What if it had hit him straight-on? What then? My God, it's too horrible to think about."

"It is."

I tried not to think about that scenario—it *was* too horrible to contemplate.

"I'm still not convinced everything's all right," Marcy said. "Why is she consulting with an expert in the morning? But I feel better—I think. Do you know what I mean?"

"I know exactly what you mean, but I think he's going to be all right. A concussion is serious, but if it were really serious, like bleeding inside his skull, I think the doctor would have seen it on the CAT scan tonight. I really do."

"I hope you're right." Another huff. She tossed and then turned on the cot, then turned back.

"Close your eyes," I said. "Try to relax. Try to get some sleep."

"I'm not going to be able to sleep. No way. Especially when they come in to check on him. I'm going to want to know exactly what they see."

I stretched my legs out and extended my arms above my head, but I couldn't get comfortable, either.

"Going to be a long night," I said.

"Nick," she said, and I could tell by her tone she was changing the subject. "Can I ask you something?"

I thought, *Ask me if I still love you. Please. Because I do. I really do. I love your big, beautiful eyes and every little freckle on your lovely face. I love that you're honest, spunky, and real. I love that we had a family together and we'd already been through some of life's fires together. And ask me if I miss you. Because I do. And ask me to be Wesley's full-time dad again. Please. Because I really want to. Ask me to come home. Please, please. I'm dying to.*

"Ask me anything," I said coolly.

She propped herself up on her elbow, and I saw her face at a new angle in the moonlight. She still looked exhausted, but there was also a touch of curiosity in her face.

"When I asked you to get out of the house," she said, then paused, as if reviewing each word in her mind. "When I asked you to leave, why did you stay around town?"

I turned on my side to face her, propping my left elbow on the couch and my head on my left hand. "What do you mean?"

"I mean ... Well, what I mean is, I would have thought you'd go back to Johnstown or something. Go stay with your mom. You had no job, no prospects, no income. Or I thought maybe you'd look for a job somewhere else, another newspaper town, maybe another state capitol. Albany or somewhere."

"You should see my credit card bill," I said, a hint of deadpan in my tone. It drew a little chuckle from her.

"I'm not sure I want to, but I'll worry about that later," she said.

"Smart move."

"But seriously," she persisted. "Why did you stay here?"

"I didn't stay for Tess Sugarmeier, if that's what you're wondering."

"Not entirely."

I tossed the question around in my mind. Indeed, it was going to be a long night, so I felt no hurry to answer. It dawned on me that I was, basically, a fatherless child, and I didn't want to be a childless father, too. The thought of leaving town, with her and Wesley behind, starting over somewhere and staying in touch with my son only through awkward phone conversations, then showing up on Christmas Day with an expensive present that Wesley wouldn't really appreciate, had never crossed my mind. At least not seriously. Deep down, I was the type of guy who stuck things out, who didn't stop at the twenty-mile mark just because my legs felt like Jell-O. But how do you explain all that to your estranged wife in a dark hospital room at 1 o'clock in the morning with your son nursing a head injury across the room.

"I was just taking it one day at a time," I said. "So I never really thought about going anywhere else."

She tossed my answer around in her head. I could tell that she also felt that time was slowing as we waited for the 2 a.m. check on Wesley.

"I have to admit," she said. "I kind of admire you for staying around."

Life delivers lessons at unexpected moments, and this one suddenly took hold of me: Sometimes all you can do is be there.

"Does that mean you forgive me?" I asked.

"Oh, God," she said breathlessly. She yanked her elbow out from under her head, dropped back on the cot and stared up at the ceiling.

"Forgive?" she said, as if talking to herself. "It's a serious word."

I didn't respond. She paused for another moment, then blew a puff of air up toward the ceiling.

"Right now," she said, "I'm not sure I forgive myself for not bringing my son to the hospital sooner. That's still weighing on my mind—big time. I still can't get the words *intracranial bleeding* out of my head."

"I understand," I said. But this was the most open conversation we'd had in a while, and I wasn't about to let the moment go that easily. I wanted to pry further. "Can I ask you another question?"

"Depends," she said, "on what it is."

"It's about you and Reggie. What's going on between you two?"

"Oh, that," she said. "I told you we just had lunch."

"And you refused to tell me anything more."

"That was all—just lunch. Maybe it was a feeler for a date, but I didn't feel like he was the type of guy for me. I told him afterward that it was a nice lunch, but I didn't think it should lead to anything. He seemed a little upset, but he let it go."

Whew. Reggie was out of the picture. Under any other circumstances, I might have let out a mighty cheer. But not on this night. I was too exhausted, emotionally and physically. Besides, another thought shook me: If she wasn't seeing Reggie, why hadn't she repaired things with me? Was she done with both of us? Ready to move on to someone else?

"And now," she said in a tone that suggested she expected tit for tat, "are you ready to tell me exactly what happened with you and Tess."

She propped herself up on her elbow again. Even in the dim light, I could tell she raised her eyebrows.

"Nothing," I said. "Maybe something almost happened, but nothing did. I'm not sure what else to tell you."

"That's not what I mean," she said. "You've told me that a dozen times before. What I mean is: Why were you interested in her? Obviously, you were."

"Oh, boy," I said, and rolled onto my side. Then I remembered how well my little crack about the credit card bill had worked earlier, and I felt the urge to try the same tact.

"Bad Husband Moment?"

"Sometimes I hate it when you're glib," she said flatly. "Forget it."

She dropped onto her back again.

I regretted trying to dodge that question. I knew I should explain myself.

"I'm no saint," I admitted. "And I know I've made my share of mistakes over the years. But in this case, I was so obsessed with being a good dad, and then a good coach, that I lost sight of what it takes to be a good husband, too. And then when things got tough, when I lost my job and tensions flared in our marriage, she was there, and she paid attention to me. And yes, she's very attractive, and attractive women bring out the worst in men, so there you have it."

She sat up slowly. "I see."

It might have been the poor light, or her equanimity, but I couldn't read her. "That's your only reaction?"

"We covered a lot of ground tonight," she said, lying back on the cot. "Maybe more than we should have. Let's try to get some sleep."

"Maybe you're right."

I rolled onto my back and closed my eyes. From down the hall, I heard another baby cry.

26
YOU CAN GO HOME NOW

$\mathcal{A}$t 2 a.m., the husky nurse came in and turned on the lights and woke Wesley. She examined his eyes and asked how he felt. "Tired," he moaned, and she concluded that he seemed fine. Same drill at 4 a.m., and the nurse once again concluded that he was doing well. I dipped in and out of sleep between each check, and I suspect Marcy did, too, but I was certain that neither one of us got much sleep. After the 6 a.m. check with a new nurse, a young blonde with frizzy hair, who also concluded that Wesley seemed well, I volunteered to get up and find us coffee, and I came back with two Styrofoam cups full of bad vending-machine java.

As we finished our coffee just after 7 a.m., both of us moving about the room slowly in a wired haze, the doctor with the pockmarked face came in, showing no signs that she'd been up all night on the graveyard shift. She told us she'd just reviewed Wesley's CAT scan with the neurosurgeon, who saw no signs of danger. No intracranial bleeding. It was a concussion. Keep him home resting for a few days. No athletic activity. Rest is very important. Give him Tylenol if his headache persists. Visit your family doctor in a week for a follow-up, and if he suffers another head injury, get him to a doctor ASAP.

"You can go home now," she said.

Marcy, sitting at the edge of the cot, slumped forward as she heaved a sigh of relief. I was standing on the opposite side of Wesley's bed, the near-empty Styrofoam cup in one hand, and my initial reaction was similar, but then I stopped in mid-sigh. As the doctor's last words rung in my head—*go home now*—I realized that I couldn't.

The frizzy-haired nurse pushed Wesley outside in a wheelchair, and he seemed to enjoy the ride, as Marcy and I followed a couple steps behind. It was a crisp, sunny morning—blue skies and puffy clouds. On the hill that sloped away from the parking lot, the tulips and daffodils and redbud trees dazzled in the sun. Our cars were parked side-by-side—I'd moved them while Wesley was being admitted to his room—and we said goodbye to the nurse and walked slowly across the parking lot together. All three of us looked frumpy—Wesley and me in our wrinkled T-shirts, Marcy in her baggy summer shirt and blue-jean shorts, the same clothes we'd worn to the hospital the previous night. We stopped beside Marcy's Mazda, and I dipped down and hugged Wesley and then kissed the top of his mussy head. I gave Marcy a peck on the cheek.

"I love you, Wes," I said. "And you too, Marcy."

I hadn't planned on saying it—it just came out. Immediately, I wondered if she'd say it, too.

She hardly missed a beat.

"Thanks, Nick," she said, patting me on the shoulder. "Thanks for being here."

She clicked her car doors open with her remote key chain, and Wesley crawled in the backseat.

"I'm going to take a couple days off from work to stay home with him," she said.

"I'll stop by to visit," I said.

"That's fine," she said as she eased into the driver's seat.

She closed the door. The closing sound, a *clong*, reverberated in my head. We waved goodbye.

It seemed like the kind of morning, so bright and vivid, that lends itself to a moment of clarity. Yet I felt more confused than ever. Standing there alone in the parking lot, waving goodbye to my son and estranged wife, after spending a long night with them in the hospital, I had no idea where I stood with them, no good idea of where my life was headed. Of course I was operating on little sleep, but I don't know if that would have helped.

Quite possibly, Marcy and I were now friends. Though Reggie was out of the picture, I'd received no sign whatsoever that I was back in it. *Thanks for being here.* That was all I got after our ball-to-the-head scare, middle-of-the-night confessionals, and my admission to my wife that I still loved her. *Thanks for being here*—it's the kind of thing friends say to each other. No matter how much she may have admired me for sticking around, forgiveness was a whole different ballgame. Maybe we'd reached a point of mutual respect, where we could communicate freely about our lives, and especially Wesley's, without hard feelings, and maybe that would be as far as I'd get. But I'd earned the right to remain a father. I'd always be there for Wesley, and that realization made me feel a little better. Maybe not in the same household, but close enough.

As I drove back to my motel, I thought about Tess for the first time that morning. I knew more about her than I'd been willing to tell Marcy, and while Marcy preferred to think of her as a bimbo, I knew Marcy was wrong. Tess was, in addition to being stunningly good looking, smart and social. And perceptive. She knew how to read people and situations. She harbored no misperceptions about her own bad marriage, or about her son's shortcomings, and she knew when other men could use a pat on the back. If she and I were destined for each other, was that such a bad thing?

I wondered if it was time for me to accept where my life was heading and deal with it like a grown-up. Time to look for an apartment? Maybe even a divorce lawyer? Time to move on. But first I needed to get some sleep. I told Luciana that I didn't need maid service for the day, and I hung the do-not-disturb sign on my doorknob to sleep half the day away.

I knew the field needed to be mowed, but when I woke up in mid-afternoon I decided to put it off for a day and go see Wesley. I knew Marcy wouldn't mind; in fact she'd probably be expecting me. I wasn't making a supreme effort for pleasant moments or anything like that—I just wanted to see my ailing kid. He was sprawled out on the couch when I got there, playing Xbox football. Marcy was in the basement, and I heard the door to the dryer bang shut. Wesley told me he still had a little headache but felt better overall.

"Mom gave me Sylenold," he said.

"Do you mean Tylenol?"

"Yeah, maybe. Mom also said I get to stay home from school again tomorrow."

"Fine with me," I said, squeezing into a spot at the end of the couch.

"I'm not allowed to play baseball yet," he said glumly.

"I know. We'll talk about that later. But you can come sit in the dugout with your team if you want."

He nodded yes, eyes fixed on a computerized likeness of Peyton Manning calling signals for the Colts offense, while Marcy blew into the room with a basket of unfolded whites. She dropped it on the living room floor and casually said, "Hey, Nick." She was in her bare feet, hair in a ponytail, wearing a baby-blue tank top over dark-blue gym shorts. She plunked down in the leather chair across from the couch and started folding. Two pairs of her panties, white with pink trim, sat atop the basket, and she folded them without flinching. She set them on the armrest beside her before moving on to a heap of Wesley's socks.

"So he feels better," I said, trying to pretend her panties weren't staring right at me.

"Yeah, I'm thinking he should still take one more day off from school."

"If you want to go back to work tomorrow," I offered, "I'll come over and stay with him."

"No," she said. "I've already called off, and I'll feel better if I'm here with him."

"Okay."

"And remember," she said firmly. "No baseball."

"I know, I know. I told him he could come sit in the dugout with his team."

"Good idea."

I turned my attention to Wesley's Xbox game, where Manning was moving his squad into the red zone, as she focused on finishing up the whites. I watched from the corner of my eye as she folded three more pairs of her panties and put them in the same spot on the armrest, no apparent qualms. I wasn't sure if I should be reading into it or not, but I decided to do my best to ignore it. Considering how she'd responded that morning with her loveless *thanks for being here*, and considering she'd probably had less sleep than me, I doubted she was sending any signals. Yet when she finally packed all the folded whites into the basket and hauled it upstairs, I felt a dash of disappointment that her panties had left me.

I stuck around and we decided to order pizza for dinner. I kept the conversation light, deliberately avoiding any talk of forgiveness and the like. And I sensed that Marcy wanted to keep it that way—she spent the rest of the afternoon on more household chores, rarely engaging me in conversation—which reinforced my suspicion that the time had come for me to face the heartache of a broken marriage and fractured family.

"I'll pick up the pizza," I said after Marcy phoned in the order.

"Do you need money?" she asked.

"Um, actually...Yeah, I do."

After downing three slices and a Coke, I said my goodbyes to Marcy and Wesley and decided it was time to get drunk.

Really drunk.

My-world-is-crashing, hide-my-car-keys drunk.

I started with a lager at Sudzies, but I wanted company, so I flipped open my cell phone, called Rocco and asked him to join me. "I think my marriage is over," I told him.

"Give me a few minutes, and I'll be over," he said.

I was on my second beer when he arrived. He bellied up on the stool beside me and ordered a lager. I told him the story of Wesley's blow to the head, our night in the hospital, and Marcy's cool response to me in the parking lot afterward.

"So do you know a good divorce lawyer?" I asked.

"Are you serious?"

"I don't want to do it," I said. "But I think it's time to talk to one. See what my options are, things like that. I'm still living in that shitty motel room."

"Ouch."

"So do you know one?"

"Curtis Graverson," he said. "He's in the book. Tell him I referred you."

"I will."

I drained my second lager and waved down Chuck the bartender. "Another one, please. And a shot of tequila."

"Make it two of each," Rocco said, finishing his beer.

"Salt and lemon?" Chuck asked.

"Hell, no," I said. "Give it to us straight. And if there's a worm in that bottle, I'll take that, too."

"Whoa," Rocco said, then grudgingly nodded his approval.

We slammed our straight tequila shots, growled at the burn in our chests, and chased them with a gulp of beer. I scanned the bar and saw that the Thursday happy-hour crowd had thinned out.

"Let's go downtown," I said. "This bar's dead, and those bars get more crowded."

"What the hell," Rocco said. "I can go in late on a Friday."

"Attaboy," I said.

We finished our beers, and, thankfully, Rocco picked up the tab. He also volunteered to drive. In the car, I bummed twenty bucks off of him, just to be certain that I had enough cash to buy drinks for the rest of the night.

Our first stop was Lumpy's, near the Capitol, but it was pretty dead, too. Halfway through our first beers there, I suggested we head down Second Street to a new party bar called The Barbershop, which had opened in a converted barbershop and drew a lot of rowdy young-professional types. It featured an old barber's chair beside the bar, where patrons could lean back while a bartender poured a big shot down their throat for ten bucks.

"I could use a barber-chair shot," I told Rocco.

"Oh, man," he said. "I hear those make for rough hangovers."

"So what?" I said, draining my beer. "When you're ready to call a divorce lawyer, a rough hangover doesn't sound so bad."

"Okay," he agreed. "I'll buy you one barber's shot, but just one."

Yes, it seemed odd that Rocco was serving as the voice of reason, but hey.

Even on a Thursday night, The Barbershop was filling up with drinkers who were eager to start the weekend early: guys in dark denims and untucked going-out shirts, girls in low-cut jeans and tight shirts showing ample cleavage. Most were twenty-somethings, but some thirty-somethings mixed in without looking out of place. Amy Winehouse blared through the sound system—*You know I'm no good.*

Rocco squeezed into an empty spot at the bar, ordered us two bottles of beer and paid for my barber's shot. Nodding affirmatively, he pointed me toward the end of the bar and the vintage red-leather barber's chair with padded headrest. There I met one of the bartenders, a blonde girl wearing shorty shorts and a halter top and toting a full bottle of Jose Cuervo. "We don't get many requests for tequila," she said. "How do you want the salt and lemon?"

"Fuck it," I said. "Pour it straight."

"As you wish."

I settled into the leather seat as a small crowd of drinkers gathered to watch. I tilted my head back and opened my mouth wide. She dumped the Cuervo down my throat, and the crowd around me let out a cheer.

It was like swallowing a quart of kerosene. I choked it down, staggered out of the chair, pounded my chest and coughed a few times. Some dude offered me a high five, and I obliged him. Rocco clapped me on the back.

"How are you feeling?" Rocco asked.

"Like a million bucks."

"Good," he said. "Let's mingle."

We weaved through the crowd along the back wall, knocking shoulders with people and brushing the backs of others. Rocco knew one guy along the wall; he gave him a friendly shoulder squeeze, exchanged a few words and we moved on to the side wall. Rocco spotted another guy he knew, gave him the same shoulder squeeze and exchanged a few words again, and we moved on again. When we stopped in the front corner to sip our beers and scan the crowd, I saw a group of five attractive thirty-something women enter the bar. Though I didn't know all of their names, I recognized them all—Misty Hill moms. Tess included.

"Awesome," Rocco beamed. "Looks like it's Girls' Night Out."

I locked eyes with Tess, then flashed a smile. She smiled right back. It was a glossy smile that suggested this wasn't their first stop on Girls' Night Out. Her lips were glazed with crimson lipstick, and she wore tight jeans and a tight black V-neck that revealed slivers of belly and cleavage. Two of her friends wiggled into a spot at the bar and ordered drinks.

Rocco and I sauntered over. Rocco struck up a conversation with one of Tess's friends, a busty blonde, while I went straight up to Tess.

"I'm sorry about that scene at the concession stand with Marcy," I said. "I tried to stop her, but she was on a mission, I guess."

"It wasn't your fault," Tess said.

"I'm glad you feel that way," I said.

Tess's friends at the bar passed glasses of red wine back to the rest of their group, and Tess reached for her glass and took a sip.

"We're all dealing with a lot," Tess said. "Sometimes our emotions get the best of us."

I thought yet again about Marcy and what she'd said to me that morning—*Thanks for being here*. I deserved better. Of course our marriage had been complicated, and of course she'd been operating on little sleep after an emotional night at the hospital, but I still deserved more than a loveless response. And I was suddenly aggravated by it. That struck me as a healthy sign, though, because I remembered that anger was supposed to be down the list on the stages of grief. So maybe I'd finally snapped out of the denial stage, and now I was moving on.

And who was here now? Tess. Right here in front of me, looking fabulous.

"I think my marriage is over," I blurted.

"Join the club," Tess said, holding her wine glass up as if for a toast.

Though I wasn't sure why she wanted to toast that, I clinked her glass with my beer bottle anyway. "What do you mean?" I asked.

"I got a call yesterday from a reporter at the *Telegraph*," Tess explained, "asking me what I knew about Joe's relationship with a female lawmaker. She's a lawmaker that Joe lobbies, and they do more than legislative business together, if you know what I mean."

"Wow. I'm sorry."

"I didn't tell Joe about the call," she said. "I'm waiting for the right time, which would be after I consult a divorce lawyer."

"Curtis Graverson," I suggested. "I hear good things about him."

"Yes," she said, holding her glass up for another toast. "I have an appointment to see him tomorrow afternoon."

We toasted Curtis Graverson.

"I've been meaning to tell you something else," I said "Remember when we had coffee back in February, and we talked about second careers? The advice you gave me that morning about pursuing a teaching career was the best advice I'd gotten in a long time."

"I'm so glad," she said.

"I followed up on that idea, and I've been accepted into the teaching program at Penn State-Harrisburg. I'm going to make it happen."

"That's fantastic."

We toasted my new teaching career.

"You deserve it," she said, and she gave my arm a gentle squeeze. "You're a good guy."

"And you're a good gal."

We toasted good guys and gals. A drop of wine slid down her chin and she wiped it away with the back of her hand. "Oops," she said with a tipsy smile.

I just wanted to look at her, all of her. So I tilted my neck back and took her in—her silky brown hair and full lips, her tight V-neck and perky breasts, her saucy low-cut jeans and smooth belly.

Her lips glistened. Her eyes beckoned. She was *here*.

"Wanna blow out of this popsicle stand?" I asked.

"I do," she said.

We told our friends we were leaving, and the response was a mix of knowing winks and nods. I overheard one of Tess's friends say, "Ooh."

I took Tess by the hand and led her outside. It was one of the first balmy nights of spring, so even on a Thursday people were strolling the city sidewalks, though most of them appeared headed to one of the bars, and Second Street was packed with cars.

"Did you drive?" I asked.

"Nope."

"Me neither. We'll hail a cab," I said, edging up to the curb to look for a taxi in the oncoming traffic.

"Where do you want to go?" she asked.

"I know a great four-star hotel across the river," I deadpanned. "Unfortunately, that's not where I'm staying, but we can still go back to my two-star room."

She giggled and said, "Lovely."

I squeezed her hand while we waited for a cab. She squeezed back, affectionately.

"I feel single already," Tess said, as a gaggle of twenty-something girls passed behind us. "And it feels great."

"I'm not sure how I feel about that yet," I said. "But I feel great right now."

"I think it helps that it wasn't my fault," she said. "Everything that happened in my marriage was Joe's fault, and that makes it easier for me to deal with."

"I get that," I said, waving down a taxi.

The cab pulled to the curb and I opened the door for Tess. "Scoot in," I said, much the same way I'd say it to Wesley.

And then I froze. Four words Tess had just spoken, plus the thought of Wesley, combined to hit me like a wrecking ball: It wasn't my fault.

I took a half step back from the door as Tess slid into the back seat. I felt the booze swimming around my brain, but through it I saw a flash of clarity. What was I about to do?

So far, nothing that had gone wrong in my marriage could clearly be construed as my fault, even though I certainly shared a good deal of the blame. My marriage to a wonderful woman had dissolved largely because of a mix of bad luck and bad impulses on my part, and there were gray areas at almost every turn. But this?

How to explain this to Wesley someday, when he's old enough to understand and brave enough to ask why his mom and dad split up? Would I be able to look him in the eye and say with absolute certainty that it wasn't my fault? Would I be able to tell my only son that I did everything I could to steer his life away from the banes of loneliness and emptiness? That when it mattered most, I did my part to ensure his life wasn't made to break his heart?

This would be worse than anything I'd done so far. This would be destructive. A bad decision, black and white. A point of no return.

This would be my fault.

"Wait a minute," I said.

She leaned into the open door and looked up at me wide-eyed, trepidation seeping into her face. "What's wrong?" she asked.

"I can't do this." I took another step back from the cab.

Her face sunk. Then she looked wounded. She slid into the open door and swung her feet onto the pavement. "But I thought—"

"Look," I explained, "if this were another time and another place, I'd love to be with you. You really are a great girl, and you deserve much better than what you have. But this is more complicated than that, and I'm going to have a hard time living with myself if we do this now. Please believe me when I say this has nothing to do with you, but I just can't do it."

"I don't know what to think," she said sadly.

"Remember, we're all dealing with a lot right now," I said. "You said as much when we started talking in the bar."

She pulled her legs back inside the cab. "Please take me home," she said to the driver. "Hilltop Circle in Misty Hill."

"You'll feel better about this in the morning," I said.

"Have a good night, Nick," she said coolly, then reached for the cab door and slammed it shut.

I shuffled back into the bar, no longer feeling like a million bucks. Now I felt depressed—a boozy night full of emotional ups and downs had caught up to me. I told Tess's friends that she'd taken a cab home, and a couple of them shot me surprised, what-did-you-do looks. I shrugged at them and asked Rocco to drive me back to Misty Hill. He said he would, after he exchanged phone numbers with the blonde he'd been flirting with. They plugged each other's numbers into their phone, and Rocco gave her a friendly pat on the butt.

On the way home, a cop pulled us over as we entered Misty Hill. The cop told Rocco he'd been swerving and asked if he'd been drinking. But Rocco talked his way out of it. Turns out, Rocco knew the cop's dad, the local fire chief, and had secured big state grants for the fire company.

As Rocco pulled back onto the road, I told him, "I can never figure out how you cruise through life so easily." He seemed flattered.

27
UP AND DOWN
AND SIDEWAYS

*F*ighting a crushing hangover, I went to the field the next afternoon to mow, and was greeted by Sam DiNardo. He had the doors to the maintenance shed pulled wide open and was standing in the entranceway, his bushy eyebrows shifting back and forth as he looked over the inside of the shed.

"There you are," he said gruffly after I snuck up from behind. "I was wondering when this field was going to get mowed. There's a game here today."

His demeanor gave me the impression he hadn't heard about Wesley, which surprised me, given the light-speed at which news and rumors usually traveled around Misty Hill. I decided not to tell him. I didn't feel like talking to him about anything at all.

"I'm on it," I said curtly as I cleared a path for the mower. "Right now."

After I shoved aside a half-used bag of mound clay, a

couple of rakes and a rubber mound cover that had been dropped in a heap, I felt the urge to make Sam work a little, especially considering he was still dressed in his khakis and collared shirt. "Want to help me push this thing out?" I asked.

It was a hot and humid day, a searing reminder that summer was right around the corner, and he was in no hurry to help.

"How do you usually get it out?"

"Push."

He finally squeezed behind the mower with me, and though we both pushed, he didn't seem to be much help. When we got it outside, he dusted off his hands and looked back suspiciously at the mound cover that was crumpled inside the shed.

"Why isn't that thing on the mound right now?"

"I don't know. I guess the coaches of last night's game forgot."

"It has to be out there every night. What if it rains?"

"Easy, Sam."

"Don't tell me to take it easy."

I hopped on the mower and started it, hoping the roar of the engine would drown out anything else he might say. I threw the mower into gear, gave him a patronizing little wave, and sputtered toward the field. I was amused by the sight of him standing there, slightly agitated, as I motored away.

Still, it was a miserable day to be mowing. Just sitting atop this broiling machine in the thick humid air was enough to drain me, but my hangover made it even worse. Halfway through the job I was slumped in my seat and sweating bullets. I kept glancing over to the shed and to the parking lot, hoping Sam would disappear, but he didn't. I really didn't feel like dealing with him anymore. I saw him go in and out of the shed and concession stand a couple times and poke around the bullpen. The second time he emerged from the shed he had a clipboard in hand, but I didn't think much of it; he was a clipboard kind of guy.

When I finished I stopped the mower in front of the shed, climbed off and wiped my sweaty forehead with my T-shirt. At the water fountain beside the field, I took a long drink, then wiped my forehead again before putting the mower away. Sam tromped out of the concession stand, heading my way, clipboard in hand, and I wasn't amused.

He ripped a page from the clipboard and handed it to me.

"Here," he said. "I'd like all of these items addressed by the end of the weekend."

It was a to-do list. A ten-point to-do list. Boy, was I pissed.

He wanted a sign made and posted instructing managers to cover the mound after each game. He wanted the bullpen mounds rebuilt and new rubber covers purchased for those mounds and the weeds around the bullpen fences pulled. He also wanted weeds pulled on the outfield warning track, and he wanted new grass seed planted in a dead spot in front of the pitcher's mound. He wanted the bases painted, the mower oiled, and a new inventory tallied of lime, mound clay and drying agent. Finally, he wanted the shed cleaned out.

Behind him, kids began arriving for that day's game. Two SUVs pulled into the parking lot, and a kid in a red uniform with a bat bag strapped over his shoulder jumped out of each and bowled toward the field. I didn't want to make a scene then and there, so I didn't say a word to Sam. I simply folded his list, jammed it into the pocket of my grimy gym shorts and turned into the shed.

"Thanks," Sam said in a condescending tone that sent one last jolt down my spine. "And before I go, I'll take one more look around the field to see if I forgot anything."

I scanned inside the shed—it really was a mess. Bags of lime and clay piled here and there. Little piles of light-brown drying agent on the floor. Extra bases and old brown work gloves thrown about. Rakes leaning every which way. But it was the middle of the season—what the hell did he expect? I thought about cleaning up some, but then felt a bit overwhelmed, and I wanted a break, and when I turned around Marcy was standing there.

"I figured you'd be here," she said.

"What do you want?" I asked, and immediately realized how terse I must have sounded. So I quickly changed tones: "Is everything all right with Wesley?"

"Yes, he's fine. Are you in a bad mood?"

I huffed and turned back toward the mess in the shed.

"Yes, I'm in a bad mood," I said, picking up a rake and tossing it in the corner. "Sam's here breaking my chops about the field and everything, and it's hot as hell, and I drank too much last night, and I'm tired and sweaty, and my life's a mess, and I don't have a job, or a real place to stay, and my son just escaped a serious head injury, which scared the living shit out of me, and on top of it all I think my wife wants a divorce. So yes, bad mood."

"I see," she said quietly.

"So what do you want?"

"I came over to tell you that I'm done thinking."

I was afraid to hear what she was going to say next, afraid she was ready to declare our marriage dead, ready to tell me that I'd screwed up too badly, that there was no going back, and that I wouldn't get even one more shot at making things right again. Go get a fucking divorce lawyer, buddy. I didn't look at her. I diverted my eyes toward the inside of the shed, as if something in there still demanded my attention, while I asked the inevitable follow-up question: "About?"

"About us."

Oh, God. Here it comes.

"I want you to come home."

I froze. Didn't know what to say. Did I hear her right? So I turned toward her, slowly, cautiously, and studied her while I left those words—*come home*—suspended in the few feet of space that separated us. I wanted to be sure that what I'd just heard was real, that it matched up with what I was seeing, that I wasn't drunk or dreaming, that my feet were square on the ground and I knew the difference between up and down and sideways, and that Marcy was really and truly and finally standing straight in front of me asking me to come home.

She looked bad, as if she'd been up all night again. Circles under her eyes and a pale hue in her cheeks. Yet I also thought she looked beautiful. She wore her usual around-the-neighborhood casual attire—flip-flops and gym shorts and a gray T-shirt—and her hair was pulled back in a ponytail, this time with strawberry-blonde wisps sticking out at all sorts of angles. She was gazing at me with those big hazel eyes. She looked so sincere, so real, so perfect.

"You're serious?" I asked.

"Yes."

"Home for good?"

"I'm serious. Home for good."

Life sure brings its surprises.

"Why? What happened to change your mind?"

"Nothing happened. Nothing specific. Like I said, I've thought this through. I've thought it through completely, and I've come to terms with everything that happened. It's just not the same without you, and I miss you, and Wesley misses you."

I thought back to the previous night, the moment at the cab. I felt a sudden mix of guilt and gratefulness—I'd come this-close to jumping into bed with another woman, but somehow, amid a bender driven by self-pity, I'd managed to save myself. It's okay, I assured myself. These things happen. In the end I did the right thing. I hadn't been thinking, just reacting—reacting to Marcy's cautious thought process. And that was understandable, after all. I'd underestimated her, but it was okay, because she'd been underestimating me, too.

"I never cheated with Tess," I said.

"Let's not talk about that now."

"But I didn't, and I want you to know that. I want you to believe me."

She gave an exaggerated but genuine nod as she said, "I believe you. But that's not really the point, is it?"

"No, it's not. I guess I kind of felt ... unloved."

Another heavy nod. Then she looked me square in the eye and said, "I love you."

I locked the shed and there we were, face to face. A black convertible pulled up, a father dropping his son off for his game, and the radio was blasting a classic rock station. Paul McCartney's voice rolled across the parking lot: *Maybe I'm amazed at the way you pulled me out of time.* We kissed. A soft, slow kiss. I drew back and glimpsed her face, then we kissed again. Just as slow and deep as the first one. *Maybe I'm amazed at the way I really need you.* I pulled back again said, "I love you, too."

I took her by the hand and we walked toward home. Fuck the to-do list, I thought. And fuck Sam. I'm going home with my wife.

Finally.

"Did you tell Wesley you were coming over here to get me?"

"No. I sent him to Felicia Spinelli's for a little while. It will be a surprise when he comes home."

"So we have the house to ourselves right now?"

"We have the house to ourselves."

She closed the door behind us and we kissed again in the foyer, and I remembered how sweaty and dirty I was from mowing in the hot sun.

"I need a shower first," I said.

"I'll come with you."

The song was stuck in my head: *Maybe I'm amazed.*

We hustled up the stairs and dropped our clothes on the bathroom floor. Last on the pile were her panties, the white ones with pink trim, which settled on top of our T-shirts and gym shorts. I smiled and she returned a cute, knowing smile.

"I noticed your mouth hanging open as I folded them yesterday," she said.

"I wondered if you were sending me some sort of message."

"No," she said bluntly, as she pulled back the shower curtain. "I was just too damn tired to get up and fold them somewhere else, but I quite enjoyed your reaction."

She held the curtain open while I leaned into the shower and cranked on the water. I stepped in first, and she followed. Her light skin, dabbed all over with those tiny freckles, glistened as the water covered her body. She shook out her strawberry-blonde hair, wildly, as if she wanted to shake out all the strands and the accompanying stress from the past several months, and then with both hands she pulled it back behind her ears, where she let it hang. I grabbed the soap—the expensive cocoa butter soap that she'd always splurged on—but she took it from my hands. I was already aroused. She lathered me up, then I took the soap from her and lathered her up. After we each rinsed off, we kissed again as the water splashed off our shoulders. Another long kiss. She stopped and put both hands on my chest, then pushed me into the stoop at the back of the shower. I sat down, she straddled me, and we made love.

Afterward, we lay on top of our bed, wrapped only in towels with the air conditioning blasting, and wondered how we should tell Wesley that I was moving back home.

"I think we should sit him down," Marcy said. "Or maybe *I* should sit him down and explain it to him."

"Why?"

"I think little boys need to have certain things explained

to them, in a certain way."

"How much have you told him so far?" I asked.

"Not much."

"How much do you want to tell him?"

"I'm not sure."

"I'm glad you're on top of it."

"Stop it," she said, elbowing me in the side. "I'm serious. I want to handle this the right way."

"All right," I conceded. "You go get him from Felicia Spinelli's and sit down with him when you get back. I'll get my car—it's still parked at the field—and I'll go check out of the motel."

"Oh, yes, I almost forgot: *Please* check out of that motel. I don't want to be paying for that any more than I have to."

At the motel, I packed up quickly and checked out with the evening clerk, a skinny twenty-something guy I didn't know well. He didn't seem to realize that a long-time guest was leaving—he just printed out my bill, without making eye contact, as if I was yet another philandering husband who'd checked in for a couple hours with his mistress. Only my bill was much steeper: Ninety-eight nights multiplied by thirty-four dollars, plus seven-percent tax, a total of $3,565.24.

Whew, I thought. For some reason, I was glad I hadn't stayed one hundred nights. It wasn't a completely logical thought, because there were many more charges elsewhere—restaurant bills, bar tabs and cash advances—and I figured the whole shebang came to almost ten thousand dollars. But that was a problem for later. I signed the slip and was on my way.

Wesley was parked on the couch when I got home, leading the virtual version of the Colts offense downfield against the Steelers.

"Hey, bud," I said, dropping my bag on the living room floor.

Ten-yard completion for a first down.

"Hey, Dad."

"How are you feeling today?"

"Good."

"Did Mom talk to you when you got home?"

"Huh?"

"Did Mom talk to you?"

Incomplete pass down the middle.

"About what?"

I heard Marcy closing cabinets in the kitchen.

"Marcy," I said, raising my voice just enough to travel into the kitchen. "Did you talk to him?"

"I did."

"And what did you tell him?"

She came into the living room, drying a glass with a dishrag.

"Wesley!" she scolded. "Turn that thing off. Pay attention to your father."

"One minute," he said.

"No. Now!"

Troy Polamalu intercepted a Manning pass at the goal line, and Wesley let out a groan: "Ahhh."

"I told him," Marcy said, "that Mom and Dad have come to terms with everything that happened, and we love each other very much, and we love him very much, and Dad is coming back to live with us."

Wesley, still smarting from either the interception or Marcy's order to turn off the Xbox, or perhaps both, lumbered off the couch and turned the game off.

"Isn't that cool?" I asked him.

"Yeah, cool."

"That's it?" I said. "Just cool—that's all you have to

say?"

He turned away from the television and, for the first time since I'd walked back in the house, looked me straight in the eye.

"Really cool," he said.

Marcy rolled her eyes disapprovingly.

"I think you can show a little more enthusiasm," she told him.

"But I always knew he'd come back," Wesley said.

Marcy and I cocked our heads and shot each other the same stunned look, the look parents give each other the first time they realize that their kid actually knows more about something than they do.

"That's strange," I said, "because I didn't know."

I met Wesley in the middle of the room and rubbed my hand through his hair. He nodded and cracked a smile, his way of showing that it was indeed really cool.

Of course, you take what you can get.

———————

We spent a lazy night at home, the three of us lounging around, flicking through the television channels, occasionally arguing over who should control the remote. Wesley won most of those battles, then started to doze off while we watched the second of back-to-back episodes of *Dirty Jobs*, and we coaxed him into heading upstairs to bed. Marcy and I then crawled under the sheets in our room and made love again. Quietly and gently. Unlike the wild session in the shower, there was already a familiarity about our lovemaking which I found comforting. Afterward, we lay in the dark, naked under the sheets, with the air conditioning humming, and said little to each other. I thought she might have fallen asleep when she turned toward me suddenly and propped her head on her elbow. Conversation time.

"Do you remember," she said earnestly, "when you told

me earlier today that you didn't cheat, and I said I believe you?"

"Yes," I said warily.

"Well, I do believe you. And I know I wasn't a great wife after you lost your job, and I understand what was going on in your head at the time, or at least I think I do."

"Okay—"

"But I want you to know this," she continued. "If you ever turn your attention toward another woman like that again, I'm not going to put up with it."

"Okay—"

"Do we understand each other?"

"Yes," I said obediently, fully aware that I had no other choice. "We understand each other."

"Good," she said in a tone that changed abruptly to one of pleasant satisfaction, and she dropped her head back on her pillow. "Now let's get some sleep."

28
HERE WE ARE

So I atoned for my mistakes and repaired my marriage and reunited my family, largely by sticking it out, by staying around and enduring the rumor-mill chatter, a cheap motel room, the lonely nights, and a drunken spree that brought me to the precipice of another thoughtless and unscrupulous roll in the hay. How appropriate. Because I wasn't a Real Baseball Guy, I wasn't the type to swing for the fences or bring the heat, or any of those other baseball clichés so often applied to real life. I was, instead, an old runner, a plugger. If nothing else, I knew how to persevere, personal anxieties and family history be damned, and sometimes that's as good as anything. These journeys are never perfect, not even close. Just as importantly, I'd accomplished something that my own dad probably wouldn't have. I'm not sure what he was trying to escape by drinking himself to an early death—maybe it was that worn-out steel town, or maybe a tedious career of crunching numbers—but I never even entertained the thought of escaping my own little family and the troubles

I'd tossed into our lives.

Wesley missed our last few games while recovering from his concussion, but he spent each game with us in the dugout, always wearing his red Angels cap. Our last game was an 8-6 loss to Little Al's Indians, and it was largely uneventful—no injuries, bathroom incidents, meltdowns, or smackdowns. Afterward, as we lined up at home plate for the ritual post-game handshakes, Wesley mixed in comfortably with his teammates in the middle of our line and I felt a trifle of relief that our season had ended with a whimper, not a bang.

When the school year ended the following week, Marcy and I hastily arranged a week-long vacation at the Jersey Shore, where there were rental deals to be had due to the slumping economy. We found a two-bedroom condo for seven hundred dollars just two blocks from the beach in North Wildwood, and we left the Saturday after school let out. Never mind that we had a credit card bill of nearly ten thousand dollars to settle from my motel room, bar bills, and cash advances; we'd decided to start chipping away at that in the fall, when hopefully, I'd be bringing in some extra income as a substitute teacher.

Our vacation was like a second honeymoon, only with a boy in tow. The weather was perfect, warmer than usual for early June, and the crowds were thin. Of course we'd brought our baseball gloves, and Wesley would take occasional breaks from riding waves so that we could play catch on the beach. In the late afternoon, we usually returned to our condo, where Marcy and I had a couple drinks, and in the evenings we strolled the boardwalk, where Wesley pumped one quarter after another into arcade games. By 11 p.m., Wesley was usually in bed, wiped out from a day of beaching and boardwalking, allowing the adults some time for late-night lovemaking.

Just days after we returned to Pennsylvania, I walked into the Misty Hill Mini-Mart to pay for two dollars in gas for the red container for my lawn mower, and the headline from that morning's *Telegraph* jumped out at me from the stand beside the counter: "Lawmaker and Lobbyist Connected in Tryst." It was the story Tess had been contacted about, and it sketched Joe's complicated and apparently sordid relationship with Jacqueline Madden, an attractive, blonde, two-term (and married) Democratic legislator from suburban Philadelphia.

The *Telegraph* had begun piecing the story together when a reporter had spotted Jacqueline and Joe together at the bar at the Harrisburg Hilton late on a Friday night, and they appeared "excessively friendly," according to the paper. The reporter then requested the records for Jacqueline's state-issued cell phone and saw a whole series of late-night and weekend calls to Joe, who, along with Jacqueline, declined to comment for the story. On one particular Saturday night, Jacqueline had placed eleven calls to Joe between 10 p.m. and midnight. There were policy issues at stake as well, which made the whole situation even seedier—Jacqueline was the prime sponsor of a bill to repeal a new tax on natural gas drillers in Pennsylvania, and one of Joe's main clients was the natural gas industry.

Over the next several weeks, the *Telegraph* did a fine job of following up on the story, forcing an ethics investigation in the House. And then the paper followed up with a story about the divorce paperwork filed in county court by Tess Sugarmeier.

On the day the divorce story ran, Marcy came home after work and asked me if I'd seen it. Her tone was matter-of-fact, and I couldn't tell how she felt about it, or where she was going with the question.

"Yes," I said cautiously. "I saw it."

"It explains something about that woman," she said, a touch of satisfaction entering her voice.

She left it at that, and so did I. It was the only time Marcy mentioned it. It was enough to let me know she was following the story, and it also left me suspecting that the scandal had given her a strange sense of closure over what had rocked our marriage.

At twilight one day in late autumn, Marcy and I went to the grade school for Wesley's parent-teacher conference. Temperatures were dropping, and we bundled up in heavy jackets for the first time since the previous winter. We were expecting a smooth conference with Mr. Ford, Wesley's first male teacher. Mr. Ford was a popular thirty-something guy who liked to play the guitar and work on cars, and he impressed many of his fourth-grade boys with stories about both the cars and guitars.

So Wesley was enjoying a solid fourth-grade year, and while I knew real life could bring surprises and hazards at any moment, I felt prepared for them. I felt strapped in for the ride through middle school and teener baseball, when my son would be in the grips of puberty, probably turning his attention from baseball cards to porn sites, and perhaps even turning his parents into near-strangers who saw him only in passing on the way from his bedroom to the bathroom in the morning. Then high school, and if all went well and he survived puberty well enough, he'd avoid shooting heroin and phoning bomb threats into school, and maybe he'd find a nice girlfriend, maybe even play high school baseball. Then off to college, hopefully as a strong and confident young man ready to make his mark, while I'd fight the urge to smother him with reminders that he was still the only boy in the world with my blood running through his veins. And Marcy's, too.

Just as Marcy and I passed through the school's heavy front doors, with the first winds of winter at our backs, we bumped into Tess. She rounded the front hallway corner with a man in a dark power suit—her soon-to-be ex-husband, Joe? As far as I knew, I'd never seen Joe Sugarmeier, but the man with Tess looked vaguely familiar. He was six-feet tall with a cleft chin and a shock of black hair with light traces of gray around the ears. He wore a solid burgundy tie and black shoes that shined, even in the poorly lit school hallway. He looked the part of either a lobbyist or senator—it was hard to tell them apart sometimes—and the only sign of strain on his entire body was under his eyes, where dark circles stood out against an otherwise fresh, fortyish face.

I'd seen him somewhere before, but I couldn't determine when or where. Could he have been to the Little League field, and watched quietly from the bleachers without me knowing whose dad he was? Could I have simply pumped gas across from him one day at the mini-mart? After all, it *was* a small town, and the odds that you could live there for years without crossing paths with someone at least once were pretty slim.

He and Tess appeared to be arguing. Tess, in a puffy North Face jacket, had a determined look on her face and was waving her right hand in a chopping motion, as if to drive home a point. The man in a suit had a bewildered look on his face, and his shoulders slumped in a defeated way. I don't think Tess saw us at first, because she and this man headed straight for the exit and the doors that Marcy and I had just entered.

When Tess and I finally made eye contact, she stopped talking and let the man in the suit finish saying something as her eyes darted between me and the floor. It was as if she wasn't even listening to the man in the suit anymore. I can't say if it was conscious or not, but for some reason I put my hand on Marcy's back. I placed my hand there gently and left it there. I knew that Marcy had seen Tess by now, too, but I didn't turn my head to see where Marcy was looking. By leaving my hand on Marcy's back I knew the unspoken signal I was sending: I was with her, so let's just keep moving along.

Another couple came through the doors behind us, and a blast of cold air passed between the Marhoffers and Sugarmeiers as we passed in the hallway. None of us said anything, except the man in the suit, who was still finishing his sentence to Tess. I overheard this much: "...and keep in mind that a lot of parents have to deal with this sort of thing." Naturally, I became concerned about Carter, a nice kid who was now stuck in the middle of an ugly public divorce, and I could only conclude that now he was having problems of some sort in school. I was reminded of Wesley's separation anxiety in third grade after Marcy had kicked me out—the frequent trips to the nurse's office, and the allegedly bad stomach ache for which I was summoned into school—and I was relieved that he was back on the right track. But I didn't feel any better than the Sugarmeiers—only luckier. Maybe I cared about my own marriage more, and maybe I'd worked harder to preserve it, but I also knew how easily things could spin out of control. How could I ever forget?

It was a silent march toward Wesley's classroom, thanks to our brief encounter with Tess Sugarmeier. Marcy didn't say a word. Maybe she didn't know exactly what to say, or maybe she let the silence speak for her. Consequently, I didn't say a word either. As we walked through the chilly hallway together, I heard only the sound of her heels striking the hard-tile floor, then some muffled voices and a door closing in some other corner of the school. I finally broke the silence when we got to Mr. Ford's room. "Here we are," I said plainly, holding the door open for Marcy.

She raised a finger in the air, stepped back from the door, and reached into her purse. She pulled out a tube of lipstick. It was a new shade for her—a dark shade of cherry, and I just noticed that it was similar to the smoky crimson that Tess was so fond of, but better suited to Marcy's pale, freckled skin. She touched up her lips. And slowly, deliberately, she capped the lipstick and placed the tube back inside her purse. She still hadn't said a word, but raised her eyebrows at me as she nodded yes, a look that was hard to read. I wasn't sure if she was signaling that she was ready to go inside, or shooting me a warning: *I'm watching you. Don't ever forget it.*

ACKNOWLEDGEMENTS

Many friends and fellow writers played a role in making this book what it is, either by brainstorming or offering feedback during the long and winding writing process. That list may be too long to include everyone, but I certainly want to say thanks to Willard Cook, Lynne Davies, Donna Talarico-Beerman, Ally Bishop, Jonathan Rocks, Cory Brin, Joseph Giomboni, Lauren Stine, Tom Borthwick, Barbara Taylor, and Rachel Lee.

A special thanks to Nancy McKinley, Gale Martin, and Mary Beth Matteo. Your feedback in workshops was crucial. Also, to Kaylie Jones for all of your input on the manuscript from start to finish.

Most of all, thanks to my lovely wife Wendy—my main brainstormer, first proofreader, and biggest supporter.